Rise

Rise

Book 4 in the Fielding Series

by Kimberley Ash

TEA ROSE
PUBLISHING

Dedication

For my wonderful siblings and siblings-in-law.

This isn't about you.

Except the bits that are.

Contents

Author's Note

This book contains brief discussions of past assault and toxic parenting.

Chapter 1

Megan Fielding was *fine.*

"Hey, hey, hey!" she said to the early-morning concierge in her building.

"Morning, Ms. Fielding!" He smiled back. "Happy New Year! How was the wedding?"

"Beautiful. You wouldn't believe the mountains. And my sister's clients gave her a handmade animal-hide wedding dress. I've never seen anything like it."

"You've always told me she was unique."

Megan nodded. "Made sense she'd have a wedding like no one else."

Made sense her favorite sister would find a husband in Massachusetts but somehow, they'd both end up settling two thousand miles away from her family. From Megan.

But Megan was fine with it. *Fine.*

"You're up early," the concierge said.

"Yeah. Gotta get back to real life."

"Well, we missed your smiling face around here."

Good. That was what Megan did. Made other people's days better. She adjusted her scarf, ready to face the January air. "Have a great day!"

"You too."

One human interaction down. A few dozen to go.

Not that she didn't *like* people. They just needed... *handling.*

At least she was up so early, there wouldn't be many of them at her favorite coffee shop. Oh Beans! had been a staple of her day since she'd first started at Fielding Paper ten years ago.

As she moved through the departments of the family business, learning so she'd take over one day, the grumpy owner and crew of baristas at Oh Beans! was the one group she didn't have to impress. She'd won their affection through sheer longevity.

Her sturdy boots, new ones bought in Taos, were thick and warm and complemented her calf-length shearling coat perfectly. She was ready for her world. Everything was as it should be.

Megan put her hand on the horizontal bar that opened the door as though greeting an old friend.

But the moment she entered, she could tell the atmosphere was off.

It still smelled heavenly, with freshly ground coffee and Roman's Danishes sweetening the air. The morning baristas who'd worked there when she left for New Mexico were still behind the counter—well, two of them. One was sitting at a table at the back of the otherwise deserted room with a man Megan could hardly make out. This was unusual. Sophia was usually full-stretch into the morning routine. Was the stranger a relative? But then why was the atmosphere so charged?

A dark scruff of stubble all but hid half the man's face. He wore a baseball cap and hoodie parka pulled up, despite being in the warmth. He wore heavy-rimmed glasses and didn't look up like the others did when Megan came in.

"Hey, stranger!" Grace called to her from the espresso machine.

"There she is," Roman, the owner, said in a growl that somehow still carried over the noise of the steamer.

"Hey, guys." Since they were trying to be normal, Megan would as well. It was none of her business who the other guy was. She loosened her collar and scarf and walked up to the counter. "How've you been?"

"You're in early," Roman said. It sounded like an accusation.

"I just couldn't wait to see your sunny self again, Roman." She smiled. Okay, maybe she had to work a little to get these guys to like her. Not having people like her was anathema to Megan. And since no one ever walked up to her and said, "I like you; you can relax," Megan kept on working.

"How was New Mexico?" Sophia asked, standing. The stranger was hidden from view behind her back.

"Incredible," Megan enthused, while Grace went straight into making her drink. A large café au lait with a caramel shot, extra froth. Roman's pick of the Danishes. "You should've seen the mountains in the snow."

"Your Instagram has been hopping," Grace said. "Your family is disgustingly beautiful."

Megan usually saved her account for photos of events that supported her brother's foundation, but she hadn't been able to resist posting photos of Sam and Ty's wedding. "Thanks. I think."

"Pecan," a voice said suddenly from behind Sophia as Roman reached for the bakery shelf. "Don't give her the cherry, Roman. She likes the pecan better."

Megan's thoughts screeched from Taos back to the room in front of her. She recognized that voice. For the last five years, the whole world had recognized that voice. Smooth, Italian. Consonants hidden behind his teeth. Pronounced "Roman" with a rolled R.

"Hello, Megan," the voice said, then, "It's okay, Sophia," and Sophia stood to one side so Megan could get a good look at the stranger.

He rose from his shadowy corner and tipped up the baseball cap, letting the hood fall behind him. His hair was shaggy and unkempt, and not in a styled way. The effect was heightened by his stubble. Megan had always seen him clean-shaven.

His piercing gray eyes held hers. No mistaking the man with those eyes.

"Alessandro!" she exclaimed. The anonymity, the quiet early morning store, the hoodie and the ballcap all clicked into place. "Well," she went on more quietly. "This is a surprise. You guys must be thrilled to see him again."

Sophia grimaced, Roman rolled his eyes, and Grace said, "You're kidding, right?"

"What?" How could anyone not be happy to see Alessandro Rosselli, former barista of this corner of Boston, now the hottest actor in Hollywood? Not to mention the most beautiful man Megan had ever seen. Which was beside the point, but she couldn't help it. He was taller than her, unless she wore her heels, which she almost always did. Even those thick glasses couldn't hide his silver-gray eyes.

She hadn't been this close to him in so many years, she wanted to turn away to compose herself. When he'd been her barista, there had been a counter between them, which had been a good thing. His charisma radiated off him, even now when he wasn't smiling.

With five years of morning small talk, she'd learned about the highs and lows of his auditions and his introductions to the American movie industry. She'd known he'd be discovered one day and whisked away from them to the bright lights of LA. She'd been so very right. Five years ago, she'd walked into the shop and Grace had told her he'd gotten his big break. He was off to Hollywood and would never come back.

Which had been *fine*.

"Don't you ever go on the internet?" Sophia said.

"I was traveling all day yesterday," she said. "I've only been posting photos from the trip. What's going on?"

"Our sweet little Alessandro," Grace said, barely containing her obvious relish, "got himself arrested the other day."

"Sweet?" Alessandro asked the air. "Little?"

"Um," Megan said. Those were the words he chose to focus

on? He was supposed to be living his best life over there on the West Coast. "Arrested?"

Alessandro grimaced but didn't say anything else, so Grace helped him out. "He and Nicola Kulik partied hard over New Year's. Got into a leeeetle scuffle with a photographer. Right, 'Sandro?"

"Something like that."

"And now his manager has told him to lie low until it blows over. So of course he comes to the safest place in the world, with his best pals."

"Who he's ignored for five years," Roman growled even lower than Alessandro had.

"That's not true," Sophia said. "Remember all that traffic we got after his first big interview? When he mentioned us?"

Megan remembered that, too. The place had been mobbed for weeks. People's memories were short, though, and they'd soon gone back to more convenient coffee shops, leaving Oh Beans! to the Waterfront regulars.

"So you're back in town for a while?" she asked Alessandro.

"For a while, yes," he said. He'd looked at her throughout this exchange, and now he took off his glasses. Those pewter eyes pinned her in place.

"Well," she said, trying to lighten the atmosphere and clear her deer-in-headlights feeling. "You might want to take a box of Roman's coffee to go, because you won't be able to set foot in here after seven a.m. You remember."

"I do."

She didn't know why this thought made her want to touch her throat. Of course he remembered the crowds. It was just... with the way he was looking at her... and the way he'd told Roman what her favorite Danish was... he seemed to be remembering more than just a bunch of customers.

"So how are you, Megan?" he asked.

"Oh! I'm fine! You know me," she said like a complete fool through her skipping heartbeat. Now she wanted to reach for the ends of her hair. "Running my brother's PR takes up all my time right now."

"Are there any departments left for you to move to?"

He remembered that she'd been moving from department to department, learning everything she could about the company before getting an office on the executive floor.

"Yep. Just manufacturing. Then it's the C-suite all the way, baby! I can't wait to steal my brother's coffee mug every day."

"You won't be sad?" Grace said. "Seems like PR is a good fit for you."

"Oh, well." She smiled big. Her personal feelings didn't matter on this one. She was moving in a month, and that was that. "Let's get back to you, Alessandro! Are you really in trouble? And where's Nicola?"

According to the fashion blogs Megan followed, Nicola was his girlfriend. As blond and bubbly as Alessandro was dark and brooding, they made a great couple on the red carpet.

"She went home, too. Back to Poland."

"That's a shame." Why hadn't they holed up in some random city together? Why hadn't he gone to his native Italy? Why wasn't he with his family if he couldn't be with Nicola?

Why had he come back to Boston?

"It's not a big deal," he said. "It will blow over."

Megan frowned for a second but cleared her expression. It was none of her business, no matter how hard he was staring at her. That was just his movie-star quality shining through his no-good, very bad day. Making her feel like she was the only person in the room. He'd always been like that. No one could say "mocha latte extra foam" like he could. Like it was a love language. A promise. Three-quarters of the people who came into the shop had to have been in love with him.

"Here's your coffee, Megan," Grace said.

What? What was coffee? "Oh, yes." She came back to herself, gave Alessandro the big smile she used to disarm any hint of confusion, and turned away to pick up the cup and the bag containing her Danish. The mixed scents of coffee and caramel made her mouth water. "Life-giving elixir," she said, bringing the cup to her nose and taking a deep sniff. "Well, guess I'd better get to work."

"And I should go," Alessandro said, looking at the huge clock installation on the wall beside him. "Before the crowds descend."

"You were very well camouflaged, by the way," she said. She kept the cup by her face, as though it could stop him from noticing that she had trouble looking away from him. "I would never have known it was you until you spoke."

"Noted," he said. "It was good to see you."

"Um," she said. "Yep! You too!"

And she walked out without saying goodbye to any of the others.

♦

"Hi!" she sang at the security guards at the front desk of Fielding Paper. "How were your holidays?"

They beamed at her. "Great. And yours?"

"It was beautiful. Annoyingly beautiful. I could never match it."

"You're getting married too?" one asked, eyes wide.

"Ha. No, thank you. Men are too much trouble." She grinned to show she was joking. Men weren't too much trouble. Making sure someone was happy twenty-four hours a day? Never being able to close the door and relax her iron grip on her smile? That was too much trouble.

She had the elevator to herself at this early hour. Getting back to her floor—what had been her floor for two years—was nice.

No, *Megan*. Nice wasn't good enough. *Be better than nice.* She threaded her way through the open-plan area to the coffee room and coat closet. Once she'd put away her coat, scarf, and gloves, she checked the coffeepot and the refrigerator for milk and cream, took out a few more teabags from the storage closet for those who wanted them, and then took her purse and coffee to her desk, which sat in its unexciting spot, just like the others. Leo, the SVP of communications and her father's best friend, had told her she could take an empty windowed office, but she'd smiled big and shaken her head. No one liked someone who jumped the line. Within a few weeks, she'd convinced him to set it up as a pumping room for a new mother who'd just returned to work. Leo was pretty easy to convince. He just hadn't thought of it because he was her father's generation and thoughts like that didn't come organically to him. It was Megan's pleasure to see the gaps in what the company offered and fill them. Now they had pumping rooms on every floor.

As the rest of her team arrived, everyone stopped by her desk to ask about the wedding and her trip. Incredible, she said over and over. Beautiful. Stunning. *Isolating. Painful. Final.*

"Must have sucked flying back into freezing cold Boston," a saleswoman said.

"You forget we were skiing in Taos!" Megan laughed. "And I always love coming home, no matter how much fun I had." No matter how empty Boston might suddenly feel.

"Hey, Meg," Leo said, coming over and scattering the small crowd that had gathered. Megan liked him—genuinely, not just because she had to. She'd seen the support he'd given her brother, Kane, and while that support had finally turned Leo's hair white and he hadn't retired when he should have, he never complained and always came to work with a positive attitude. Megan appreciated that and learned from it.

"Good morning!" she sang. "Good Christmas?"

"Great, thanks," he replied. "I don't have to ask if your holidays were good."

"Kane told you?"

"He told me about his spill down the black slope and how you laughed as you went by."

Megan covered her mouth. "It's the sibling code. His pride was hurt more than his butt. Besides, I brought him a brandy the size of a Big Gulp that night. He was fine." There was that word again.

"Well, I can't say I'm not glad to see you back," Leo went on. "I've only got you for another month before they steal you over at manufacturing."

Megan's job was to learn, to observe, to listen, to help, to smile, to encourage. She was damn good at all these things. One more department to go, and she'd become a vice president with an office on the top floor. Observing, listening, helping, et cetera, et cetera. A few unspecified years after that and she'd be a senior vice president. One day, she'd take over for Kane, and then all the skills she'd learned would be needed. The last ten years had been one long internship. One looooong job interview. A test.

"Don't worry. We're ready for Kane's tour of the mills next week." In fact, Megan was so ready, her inbox was beginning to look worryingly empty. They couldn't give her the juicy new projects she wanted. So she was left doing busy work while she waited to move.

Kane sauntered into the department at that moment. "You ready?" he asked Leo. "Hey, Meg."

Megan kissed his cheek, then appraised him from a PR point of view. Flawless, of course. Custom suit, a subtle tie, his hair its trademark messy. The years had added silver to his temples, which enhanced his credibility in interviews.

"Do I pass?" he asked with an indulgent smile.

"Just about." She sniffed. But she couldn't pretend to be distant from her loving and annoying big brother.

She wasn't just useful for Kane's sartorial choices. During her years in PR, Leo had taught her how to write speeches that told the truth about the recycling industry while providing poetry and cadence, and Kane had taught her how to move and inspire an audience so they'd be eating out of her hand. Megan could talk for Kane in her sleep. She would have *loved* to be doing the PBS interview this morning.

But she couldn't. Because her brother had put a strict embargo on Megan getting anywhere near the cameras.

"I don't know how I'm gonna learn how to speak for the company if I can't speak for the company," she'd said mildly when he'd first told her.

"Meg," he'd said, rubbing his hand through his hair. "You know why I don't want you out there."

Kane had negotiated an uneasy peace with the press ever since he'd almost gotten himself killed saving the company while they were hounding his soon-to-be wife. That had been right before Megan started working at Fielding Paper. Even if she didn't owe everything to her family, she loved business, and Kane would eventually retire and they'd need a new leader. Their eldest sister, Cat, was busy with her teenage boys' basketball lives; Thea had started a career as a teacher while she raised her boys with her new husband, and Sam, of course, had gone. That just left Megan. She had to do this.

"Listen," Kane had said. "Just–do this for me, okay? I don't want to be worrying about the media going after you the way they went after Ellen. Sam and T and Cat have been able to stay out of the spotlight, but you're working here and they know about you. I want you to have a whole lot more media training before they get a hold of you. And I want to be on Xanax before I have to watch you make a speech."

Megan was on social media plenty and no one had come after her yet. She'd taken all the media training—hell, she'd taught some of it in the last few months. She'd observed how her brother dealt with his minor fame since she was a kid. She'd given speeches in college that had gotten her a summa cum laude degree. And if Kane wanted her to take over the company one day, she was going to have to start sometime.

But this was her brother, and she could see the pain in his eyes. "Okay," she'd agreed. "Whatever works for you." And she'd hugged him to show she knew where he was coming from.

So now she straightened his tie, said, "Enjoy PBS," and went back to her seat.

And that was *fine.*

♦

Chapter 2

Despite telling the others that he had to leave, Alessandro instead folded into the nearest chair. *Merda.*

She'd come into the coffee shop so fast, her quick, determined step a sound he'd listened for years ago. And he'd had no defense against her—except for dear Sophia, who'd been a hell of a bodyguard.

Megan Fielding remained the most beautiful woman Alessandro had ever seen, and he'd just come from LA. Dark brown hair that cascaded over her shoulders. Dark eyes that caught all the light in the room and reflected it back to him. And that smile. She used it on everyone, but each time the smile told people that she was happy to see them, happy to talk to them. That she was sharing a joke he hadn't even heard yet. He'd dropped cups and pots for weeks before he'd learned to steel himself against that smile.

He'd stood up and revealed himself this morning without even realizing he'd done it. His manager would have murdered him if she'd known.

"Lie low," she'd said after he'd gotten out of jail.

"I have the Studio fundraiser in two weeks," he'd reminded her.

"Okay, okay." Yasmin had tapped her chin with a short, manicured nail. "That's good, actually. Do the fundraiser—it shows you can be serious."

Such an eye-rolling remark. His whole thing was being serious. With his background, having people take his acting work *seriously* was all he ever strove for.

He didn't have to pretend to care about the Studio, a program offered at the community center near where he'd lived when he first came to Boston. They'd held acting classes at a price he could afford back then, so once he'd made it big, he donated to them every year. He wasn't even their only celebrity alum, but this was the first time he'd been able to get back for their fundraising event.

"Do the fundraiser—"

"I was going to—"

"But until then, stay in your hotel room until this all blows over. Don't contact Nikki except through me. No clubs. No restaurants. I'll talk to Donna and Nikki's publicist, and we'll figure out a schedule to bring you both back."

Most of those words made no sense. He wasn't about to go to his adopted hometown and sit in a hotel. His relationship with Nikki might be only for the cameras, but if she wanted to talk to him, neither Yasmin nor anyone else was going to stop her. And "bringing them both back"? She had to be overreacting. One party where things had gotten a little out of hand—thanks to Nikki, though Alessandro hadn't said that to Yasmin—wasn't about to kill his career.

But over the years, he'd learned that arguing with Yasmin made his life more difficult. And she did—usually—handle his affairs with professionalism and expertise. Most importantly, she was always on his side. Which he appreciated after years of struggling to break into the business with no support from his own family.

So he'd just nursed his bruises and his ego, told her he'd do what she said, then gotten on a plane. Coming home—what he called home, anyway, because Rome certainly wasn't it—had soothed his soul from the moment he'd heard the first missed R from his driver. And he knew where he'd go, whatever Yasmin said.

He'd gotten the hotel room like she said, because the security would stop people from showing up at his door. The Rosette was used to hosting famous guests, and he only had to give his alias for them to arrange everything. But he couldn't stay up there any more than he could throw himself in the Charles River and disappear. And if he used the driver Yasmin had arranged, she would know his every move.

So he'd gotten up at a ridiculous hour and walked in the dark and in the best disguise he could think of to Oh Beans! before anyone else would be there. He wanted Roman's coffee, sure, but he also wanted to soak in a group of *normal* people, people who weren't connected to the insane world he'd just–temporarily–left behind.

Roman, Grace, and Sophia had treated him just as he'd hoped. Which was to say, they'd hugged him and told him off and complimented him and insulted him all in the first ten minutes. And that was all the equanimity he'd been given, because then Megan Fielding had walked in and turned him into that stumbling, pitcher-dropping fool she'd met ten years ago.

The door to the coffee shop opened, and instinctively Alessandro pulled the peak of his baseball cap down low. He really did have to go. If people found him here, he wouldn't be the only one inconvenienced. He tended to draw crowds, and time was marching.

He stood again, scraping the chair along the ground as Grace greeted the newcomer. The jarring sound made him duck his head, which was good, as the stranger had turned to look at him.

"What can I get you today?" Grace asked loudly. "Roman's just put out the pecan Danishes. You won't believe the caramel drizzle."

Alessandro slipped out behind the customer, sending an apologetic grimace to Sophia and Roman for not saying goodbye. He had to go to the Studio today anyway, and his disguise wouldn't protect him forever. Eventually, someone was going to know he was in town.

With nothing else to do for two hours before the Studio opened, he went back to The Rosette and showered and changed before checking his social media mentions. In the low thousands—not too bad. Not the one point four million hits the blurry footage of him trying to get Nicola out of that club had gotten three days ago.

Nikki's social media, however, showed shots of herself on the plane, in the Warsaw airport, and in the countryside on the way to her parents' home. She might as well have hung a sign on herself and stood on Rodeo Drive. So why had he just hidden himself behind his reading glasses and a thick hoodie?

Alessandro ordered room service breakfast and paced while he waited. Nothing to do but sit in his own thoughts. Ugh. He walked to the floor-to-ceiling windows in the suite's sitting room and looked out over the mixture of old and new that made up his adopted hometown. His heart rate slowed.

Then he remembered the situation he was in and the phone call Yasmin had relayed from the producers of his next movie. He had a no-controversy clause, "standard stuff," Yasmin had said, that did not take kindly to handcuffs and a night in jail. His biggest budget movie yet was on the line if he didn't turn his reputation around. Years of work, destroyed by one misplaced joke from Nikki.

Maybe.

He started pacing again.

He knew he should take the car to the Studio, but he had too much nervous energy to burn up, so after he'd eaten, he walked across town—and yes, despite Nikki's showmanship, he stayed in his cap and hoodie, though his reading glasses had made him queasy on the walk to Oh Beans!—to the community center where the Studio held its classes. However, the people he passed were too intent on their phones or their conversations or in hiding their faces in their scarves from the cold to look at him. He should remember to only come back in the winter from now on.

The center was a stocky, contemporary building that filled a block between an empty lot and a strip of stores with their shutters half-closed. Alessandro had never seen them all open at the same time. The letters on the side of the community center, though, were clean and bright, and a window in the side was cheerfully painted with Bruins players in a picturesque snowfall. The art classes were still going strong. *Buono.*

He pulled open the heavy doors and breathed in the smell of cleaning fluid and perfume that somehow welcomed him every time he came. He'd always had such mixed emotions when arriving here. Sometimes hope from a callback. Sometimes despair when a casting director had glanced at him and said "no" before he'd even gotten a word out. Full-on celebration when he'd gotten his first play.

Once he had a couple of those under his belt, he was able to give back to the group and squash some of those feelings. Now, he wondered how much of his next paycheck he could afford to give the center. Five years of big checks was great, but LA and all the expenses his fame entailed were not cheap. But this neighborhood didn't have much, which made community centers like this worth their weight in gold.

First, he went to the main office. Charlene, the source of most of the perfume, squealed and came around her desk to hug him.

"Tell me," she said, holding on to his elbows—about as high as she could touch him without stretching—"is it true? Did you knock a guy out with one punch?"

"It was a lucky punch," he said. Well, what did people expect? He'd been in three action movies, one of which had busted his rib. He knew how to throw a fake punch. The photographer had unfortunately moved in the wrong direction.

"I bet! Well, it's good to see you, Alessandro," Charlene said. Her head came to his chest, though her hair went a lot higher. "You here to see Etta?"

"To see all of them if I can."

"Well, you can go on into the gym."

Alessandro hugged her once more and walked down the artwork-lined corridor to the gymnasium slash theater slash dance hall slash event space. He'd acted in front of his first real audience here. And he wouldn't be worth the insurance his new production had taken out on him without it.

Four women sitting at a table in front of the black-draped stage jumped up to hug him as Charlene had. Etta, the director of the center, was a black woman as petite as Charlene but with a buzz cut. Susie, who ran the Studio, had given Alessandro some of his harshest critiques and some of his highest praise. She was in her usual uniform of jeans and a yellow tee that rocked against her green shoulder-length curls. Jaelyn was a successful actress whose career had spurred on everyone in Alessandro's class. She now had a regular gig on a police procedural show on cable TV.

And finally there was Melanie, a trans woman who was building her career in the Boston theater world. "Don't hug Melanie," Susie grumbled. "She's quitting us. Traitor."

"What?" Alessandro said, of course ignoring his old teacher.

"I got *Wicked!*" Melanie cried.

"*Fantastica!*" Alessandro hugged her again. "That is the best news I've heard all year!"

"Alessandro," Etta said. "You. Are. A. Movie. Star. Good news probably falls in your inbox twice a day."

"That isn't real. Melanie in New York is real. It's the mother ship calling you home."

He loved to see her face like this: confident, fulfilled, illuminated from the inside. Melanie had dreamed of Broadway for as long as he'd known her. He, on the other hand, kept waiting for someone to pop out and tell him the whole Hollywood thing was a joke, and every photo of him seemed to reflect that, at least in his eyes.

"Don't congratulate her," Susie complained. "She's taking all her social media knowledge with her. Now how are we going to handle the publicity for the fundraiser?"

"Schedulers," Melanie said. "I told you. I'll set it up before I leave."

"But we were going to do videos during the kids' classes this week, and I need the person with the camera here to, yuh know, *film* them."

"I know." Melanie sat down on one of the chairs. "I'm sorry about that. But rehearsals start Monday." She grabbed her hair with two hands, her elbows on the table. "You can do it, you know," she told Susie. "You only need a cell phone."

"And editing software and music and a few extra *hours* to put it together. And I'm swamped with collecting everything for the auction."

Alessandro pulled himself up a chair and sat, amused and pleased that after their brief greetings, he was getting no more attention than any other alum. Their focus was always on the next student, the next kid who needed help.

"And I've got a budget meeting with the board like two days after the fundraiser," Etta reminded them, "and I need to bury myself in spreadsheets."

"I'll film them," Jaelyn said. "I don't know a ton about editing software, but if my phone camera can do it, I'll figure it out."

"Can you?" Melanie all but fell on her neck. "That would make me feel so much better."

"Actually, what days are we talking?" Jaelyn said, her face twisting. "I forget I have a day job these days. Is it after school?"

"Yeah," Susie said.

"Hmm... I might be filming."

Susie threw up her hands. "Don't *do* that to us!"

"I'll do it," Alessandro said. "I don't have anything better to do right now."

They looked at him as though they'd forgotten he was there. Which made him smile. Being the one in the room everyone stared at had gotten too comfortable.

Showing up to classes and taking video of a hundred kids didn't exactly count as hiding in his hotel room. But he wasn't going to tell these ladies that. Their selflessness when it came to the Studio had always made him feel inadequate. If he could help, he'd help, and Yasmin would just have to deal with it.

Wouldn't it be good for his image? To help? Like she'd said? Would he be considered a *serious* actor again?

He shook the thoughts out of his head. This wasn't about how he looked to the world. It was about how he looked to these women, who he respected perhaps more than anyone.

"Don't you have a movie coming up?" Susie said, almost accusing him.

"And why are you here so early anyway?" Jaelyn added. "We weren't expecting you till next week."

He chose to answer Susie rather than Jaelyn. "I do not have to start training for the movie until March."

Jaelyn narrowed her eyes at him but didn't speak. Alessandro glanced at her, and they exchanged an understanding nod. She was thinking about his arrest, something Melanie's "betrayal" seemed to have thrown out of the others' heads. Jaelyn understood that he was here to get away.

"Okay, great, but can you edit them and upload them? And

who's going to monitor the accounts and reply to the comments?" Susie wailed.

"I'm sorry!" Melanie said, clutching her hair again.

"I can do the filming," Alessandro confirmed. "The social media part, not so much."

He'd had an assistant, but she'd gone back to school last fall, and he hadn't replaced her. Between Yasmin, Donna, and the rest of his team, and the fact that mostly he reposted Nikki's exclamation-mark-filled essays, he didn't need one.

But representing a whole organization? Taking over from Melanie, who'd been running that side of things since he was an unknown? Nope.

"We can't help it, Melanie," Etta said, patting Melanie's arm. "You *are* the PR in this place."

PR... "I know someone in PR," he said before his brain had caught up with his mouth.

"Of course you do," Jaelyn said. "But I don't think your publicist has time for our little fundraiser."

"I didn't mean Donna," he said, though his brain was screaming at him to *shut up, shut up now!*

He had no earthly idea what exactly Megan Fielding did for her company. It barely made the news anymore, and if he did happen to catch the name, Megan's older brother was always the Fielding they focused on. When Alessandro had left for Hollywood, Megan had been in the accounting department and had made jokes about the wonder that was a quarterly report. The department didn't seem to be where she belonged. With her looks and her style, being the face of Fielding Paper seemed a much better fit. That or sales. Alessandro knew all about selling product. He wouldn't wish it on anyone. But maybe Megan had flourished there.

"'Sandro," Susie said, "who do you mean?"

"I... I don't know. Forget I said anything. She might not be able to help. She has a full-time job."

Though she'd sounded regretful that she was leaving the department. Maybe helping the Studio would be a way to continue doing something she liked.

Ugh. He had no idea what Megan liked. He was just an ex-barista to her. She would no more help him and these ladies than she would turn down one of Roman's pecan Danishes.

"Worth asking, though, don't you think?" Etta asked.

And when Etta asked, you didn't prevaricate. You didn't pretend you had something better to do. You told her you'd give her your best shot.

"Okay," he said. "I will ask her."

♦

Chapter 3

No way Megan was going to see him again. No way. The only reason she'd go back to Oh Beans! early the next day was so she could get into the office and continue catching up after her vacation.

"Good," Sophia said as soon as she walked into the rich-smelling coffee shop. "You're early again."

"Glad I can oblige," Megan answered, unzipping her dark-green faux fur-trimmed coat. "And just out of interest, why is that good?"

"Come on back," Grace said, opening the counter flap.

Megan paused mid-zip. "What?" Go behind the counter? Enter Roman's sanctum sanctorum? She couldn't have been more stunned if Meghan and Harry had invited her in for tea.

"Come on, come on, before another customer shows up." Grace beckoned her impatiently, so Megan had no choice but to follow her behind the counter, down toward the kitchen, and then to a corridor with doors leading off either side.

Alessandro was there.

Megan swallowed audibly. "Oh."

"Hello, Megan," he said. In all the years she'd known him, he'd never learned to say her name as Americans did. His pronunciation was more like "May-gan." Megan loved it. It made her sound more exotic than she was. As though she came from anything other than generations of WASPs who'd been in Boston since the Mayflower.

"What—what's going on?"

Her nervousness wasn't helped by the googling she'd done

the day before, which had told her all she'd missed over New Year's. Alessandro and Nicola Kulik had been at a party on New Year's night at one of the largest clubs in LA. A club big enough for any photographer or journalist to get in, right alongside the celebrities. Opinion pieces asserted that celebrities knew this and went to Perfection to be seen. But something had happened in there, something that had led to either Nicola or Alessandro or both of them punching a guy. And the club owner, presumably knowing that a) his club would get even more notorious, b) no publicity was bad publicity, and c) he needed to keep those paps coming, had called the police.

Alessandro and Nicola had been photographed outside the club, Nicola still fighting, Alessandro possibly trying to calm her down before the police put cuffs on them both, until they disappeared into the cruiser. The next day, the gossip sites had been full of shots of Alessandro and Nicola leaving the precinct building separately and looking a lot less like their glammed-up selves.

Alessandro's image usually didn't make him out to be a bad boy. Those who swooned over his Getty images got the idea that he was too bored with reality to give it his attention. He usually glowered at photographers, and candid shots of him revealed little else. People who asked for his autograph reported that he was quiet and polite, but not overly friendly.

From Nicola's pictures of her trip back to Poland, Megan could tell she was an altogether different kind of celebrity. One who didn't seem to be able to stay off her Instagram. Alessandro, on the other hand, had gone black-ops silent on social media since his arrest.

When Megan had seen him yesterday, Alessandro had looked little better than the shots of him outside the police station, but today, his hair was combed back and the dark stubble was already growing into a short beard. That only drew her attention to those beautiful gray eyes of his, so surprising against his dark-olive skin and black hair.

"I did not want the others to have to deal with my presence in the store," he said, twisting his mouth. "I might have made Sophia pull a muscle, jumping in front of me like that yesterday."

"She was happy to. They all were," she said, because that was obvious. "You're part of the family here."

"I did not want to assume that. Thank you for letting them be... cloak-and-dagger with you."

Megan smiled at that, though she tried to cover it. She'd sometimes joined in the crew's attempts to teach Alessandro American idioms. He'd clearly been keeping up with his homework.

"Very good," she said. "So why *are* we being so cloak-and-dagger?"

Seriously. Why the *hell* would this man ask to see her somewhere no one else would see? Megan's early-morning brain, coupled with the unreality of seeing Alessandro in the flesh, couldn't come to a conclusion. Sure, his mere glance could flay the clothes right off her skin. But only she felt that, surely?

"I wanted to ask for your help," he said. "Roman said we can use his office. Would you?"

The other thing he did was to be extra polite. Far too polite for Boston. Maybe Mary Poppins had taught him English back in Italy.

"Sure."

They went into a room that looked like a hurricane had taken up residence there just a few minutes before. Roman's inability to corral paperwork stood in stark contrast to the clean and shiny store beyond the corridor. Somehow, two chairs had been spared the tornado, though she and Alessandro had to sit almost knee to knee to fit in the unoccupied space.

He immediately leaned forward. Now Megan caught his scent, and she had to hold herself still not to sigh. Of *course* he smelled as good as he looked. Tom Ford's Tobacco Vanille, she'd bet. She knew these things. The same way she knew that his black leather jacket was an Armani from three seasons ago. Nothing wrong with three seasons ago. If her clothes fit her the way that jacket fit him, she'd never stop wearing it.

Actually, her clothes *did* fit her well. Controlling her image was very important to Megan. She stopped gazing at the jacket and straightened up, arranging her maxi skirt over her knee.

"I'm involved with an acting school called the Studio, in Allston," he said. "Do you know it?"

She shook her head. "I'm afraid not." Where was this going?

"Here's your coffee, Megan," Grace said. Megan hadn't even heard the woman walk into the room. So much for not obsessing over Alessandro.

"Thanks." Yeah. Coffee. That would help clear her mind.

"You two look cozy," Grace commented.

Maybe the coffee was hot, but Megan felt her cheeks flame.

"Anyway!" Grace said breezily. "'Sandro, you sure I can't give you a refill?"

"Not right now, thank you," he said, somehow sounding polite while obviously saying, *Go away.* Grace waved at them and disappeared.

"Does she know what you're doing here?" Megan said.

"Yes." Alessandro blew gently into his coffee cup. Megan did *not* watch his lips purse. "And they think it is a good idea. But you do not have to do it if you are not—"

In his last movie, *The Drummer*, Alessandro had had to relay a gamut of emotions from fury to despair. But Megan didn't think she'd ever seen him play anyone this uncomfortable with the task at hand.

"Do you want a kidney or something?" she joked. "Because

that's a hard no, but whatever else you need, I'll help if I can. Actually, even if it *is* a kidney, if you'll die without it, we could probably negotiate."

She got a smile out of him—*okay, heart, stop fluttering like a teenage fangirl*—and he shook his head. "I—I would like to do this myself, but I cannot. And you said yesterday that you are working in public relations."

"Yes." She tried to put the two pieces of information together—this acting school and her time in PR, but he finally spit it out.

"I am here for a fundraiser they are having next week, and they just lost their publicity person. We need someone to upload videos, monitor the social media accounts, and reply to any questions."

Megan sat back, dislodging a pile of papers behind her, which slid to the ground with an aggrieved *shhing* sound. "Oh, shoot."

"Roman's office has always looked like this. He will not notice."

"Maybe I could help him out with that one day." She tried to straighten one single pile, but her attempts merely threatened to push over another stack. "I like organizing. Anyway. You used to go to this school?"

"Yes. When I first came to America. I would not have my career without them."

Wouldn't be in that four-thousand-dollar jacket. "It's nice that you remember that." Five years away from Boston was a long time. Two of her sisters had gotten married in that time.

He flicked off the idea with a grimace. "It is the bare minimum. They're good—the kind of good you do not meet in my job. They think only of the next child they can help. If I could give them all my money, I would." He glanced at her. "So while I am here, I am giving them my time. But I don't know how to... I don't use social media much. Melanie—she is our previous publicity person—had to leave, and she says she has put together some pre-scheduled posts or something. It is over my head. And I could hire an outside PR firm, but it's a small job and the fundraiser is next week. So I thought of you."

Megan took a sip of her coffee to stall. How did a man with Alessandro's visibility not know how to schedule posts? Surely, before all the fame had come to him, he'd kept up his own accounts? She'd certainly followed him once she'd learned he was an aspiring actor, but now that she thought of it, his feed hadn't exactly been curated. When he'd had a play, he posted behind-the-scenes shots. He'd thanked all his costars. Then he'd be silent for months, apart from the odd shot of a friend's successful movie debut. Now that he was famous, his social media consisted of official trailers, links to interviews, and reposted pictures of him with Nicola Kulik.

So okay, this sounded like something the technologically taciturn man in front of her would do. "Can I see the school's Facebook account?" she asked.

He got his phone out of an inside pocket and pulled up the page. The logo for the studio was bright and eye-catching, but their about section was empty, with only the address listed. They had no pinned post, and the photos the mysterious Melanie had posted often appeared in the middle of the night.

Megan pursed her lips. "Does Melanie do this kind of thing as a job?"

"No. She's an actress. She was fitting it into her schedule. All the volunteers do."

He was beginning to look broody and pissed off again. She hadn't seen that expression on his face since his last movie poster. Megan held up the hand that wasn't holding the coffee. "No shade to Melanie!" she said quickly. "I'm just trying to get an idea of what you need."

They needed an overhaul of their Facebook page, for a start. She imagined their Instagram and other accounts were just as spotty. And how was their website? How were they getting sign-ups for the fundraiser?

Megan's heart quickened, just a little, at the thought. She liked making people look good. Maybe she could help this organization that was so important to Alessandro. And maybe Kane would see that she was good at this and that speaking out wouldn't put a target on her forehead.

"What kind of fundraiser is it?" she asked. Too bad it wasn't pinned to the top of their account.

"A silent auction."

"How are you involved? Are you giving away a date with you?"

She smiled, but he didn't. In fact, he was staring at her with a heat so penetrating, she fidgeted in her seat. "I was joking," she murmured.

Then he smiled, wider than she'd yet seen. And it didn't help her attraction to him at *all*, because it just turned his dark good looks boyish and irresistible. "I am the MC of the event. And I have some props from my movies to include in the auction. The tickets are for sale through the website," he said. "Sales are not where they were this time last year." He shrugged. "The economy has not been good."

"Do they know you're going to be there?" she said before she could stop herself.

He smiled again, this time bashfully. "I am on the flyer. And so is Jaelyn Jones. Do you know her?"

"Yes!" Jaelyn was a fantastic actress. "Is she connected to the school as well?"

"She got her first lead role just after I got there."

"Wow. This is a good school, huh."

"The best."

Megan looked away from his intensity, back to the Facebook page on the phone he was still holding out to her. She perched her coffee on the tiny corner she'd cleared from the desk. "May I?"

Her fingers touched his as she took the phone from him. No big deal—just a tingle in Megan's fingertips, just a feeling that made her want to snatch her hand back and smooth out her hair. Just a buzz like the one he'd given her when he'd joked about her paying to take him to dinner.

She risked a glance at him. He was looking at the phone and seemed completely unaffected. So she pulled herself together. "You're nowhere on this page," she said. "And neither is Jaelyn."

"I am sure we are somewhere in there."

Now that the phone was safely in her hand, Megan's professional world kicked in. "Alessandro," she said. "You're *the* pull at this event. You and Jaelyn, but let's be honest, it's you. TV still doesn't have the cachet film does. They should have you guys on the banner, on a pinned post, and on their profile pic." She leaned over his phone, scrolling. "Daily posts, possibly twice a day. And definitely on Insta. Tagging you, tagging Jaelyn. You should get whatever other celebs you know to repost. This thing should be sold out in a day. Is Jaelyn in town? You should take promo shots together."

The ideas filled her mind and she didn't realize she'd stopped talking until she glanced up from the screen to see Alessandro smiling warmly at her. "You know what you are talking about," he said.

"Well, yeah. But this isn't rocket science. They should—"

But there was no "should." Megan knew a dozen people who could use basic social media skills to improve the Studio's profile. But that didn't mean the people who ran the Studio did. "Sorry," she went on. "Marketing your business kind of runs in my family."

"This is not a business," he said. "It's a nonprofit."

"I get that." She tapped the screen. "But social media won't know the difference. You don't have to pay for ads to get more clicks." Then she laughed and gave him back his phone—keeping her fingers well away from his this time. "You're worth four ads and a repost all by yourself."

Alessandro's eyes flicked up to hers, then dropped to his phone. "So you will help us?" he asked.

Who was ever going to say no to him? "Sure," she said. "I'd be happy to."

"That is great. Thank you, Megan."

"My pleasure." And it was. Not just because she enjoyed hearing her name on his lips, but because she remembered the jolt of excitement she'd gotten *before* his fingers had touched hers. It was the same feeling she got when Leo trusted her to write Kane's speeches. When a friend had a black-tie event and asked for her advice on what to wear. When she'd organized the baby shower for Kane and Ellen's last daughter.

Thrilled. She was *thrilled* to do this.

"May I ask you a question?" he said.

"Of course!"

"I... Before I asked you, I looked online for you. For you in your business world, I mean."

"I'd be surprised if you didn't," she said.

"But you weren't there." He swept his hand to the side, as if erasing a presence. "You do not take part in the events your brother is the star of."

"I do. Just not in front of the cameras."

"Forgive me, Megan," he said, and she did. Immediately. Whatever he said next. "But why does your brother not use you as well as other employees? You"—he waved an expressive hand at her coat, which was gratifying—"you dress like people I knew when—when I lived in Italy. And you are good with people. So I wondered if you prefer not to be involved with the public."

She picked up her coffee cup and another cascade of papers

fell, like quarters in an arcade game. "Dang it. I really have to help Roman with this office." She took a sip of coffee so she had time to measure her words.

"My family doesn't do publicity unless we have to," she said. "Being in front of the cameras nearly got my brother killed."

His eyes widened. "That is terrible. I did not know."

"It was before I started coming to the coffee shop. This guy was setting fires in Fielding paper mills, and because Kane had let the cameras into his life before, they went crazy, saying he was too busy having fun while people lost their jobs. It was right around when he met Ellen—his wife—and she got pulled into the madness too. Now he only does events for the company. He doesn't want the rest of us anywhere near the press."

"Us?"

"My sisters and me."

"He has other sisters? No brothers?"

"No. Just four sisters. Enough to drive any man crazy."

"Four sisters?" Alessandro's lips tightened, and he looked away. "And you all... you sound close."

"Yes, absolutely. We have to be. Well, we're kind of stuck with each other, you know? Our parents died when I was very young. Kane and my oldest sister basically raised me."

"I am sorry. I should not have asked."

"You wouldn't know." She nodded at his phone. "Unless your research went back about twenty years."

He shook his head. "I am sorry I asked something so personal. Will you still help with the Studio? I promise you will not have to deal with me too much."

Megan laughed out loud. "If your team likes what I suggest, you're going to be the one person I see most often. I'll just have to suffer through."

He smiled and bowed to her. "I will be at your command."

Okay, of course she liked the sound of that. The man didn't

even do it on purpose. He just said "at your command," and a nation swooned.

"Would you like to visit the Studio?" he asked. "Get to know the directors?"

"I'd love to! In fact, I should. Before I start changing anything. Why don't I go after work today?" She nodded at his phone, the lackluster Facebook page now hidden. "Better not to waste any time."

"Are you sure? That is very short notice," he said slowly. "You just came home."

"I'm not that busy. Since I'm moving to manufacturing in a couple weeks, they're not putting me on any big projects."

The thrill was replaced by a lump of rock in her stomach. Why did the word *manufacturing* have to toll with such a heavy sound?

Pressing down the impending doom in her gut, she smiled big at Alessandro. "I can be finished by five thirty tonight. If you send me the address, I can meet you there."

He shook his head. "The neighborhood is not great. I'd rather pick you up from work."

"Oh, okay." Then she remembered who she was talking to. "Wait. Aren't you here incognito?"

"Well, yes. My manager wants me to keep a low profile until the arrest becomes last week's news. But this is different. It is more important than an unflattering photo and some rumors about my love life."

She nodded, though rumors about her brother's love life had led to physical attacks on his wife. "Okay then," she said. "So I'll see you tonight? Are you coming in a car?"

"Yes."

"Then stay in the car. I'll come out to you. What's your cell phone number?"

For a second she'd forgotten who he was. But Alessandro gave it to her as easily as if he gave it out every day. Now mindful of his privacy, she put his number in her phone under the letter A. Just in case.

She texted him a brief *It's me* and checked that he received it and her number.

"Thank you," he said again. "I will see you tonight."

Megan stood. Unfortunately, he did, too, so they were very, very close in that tiny space. With her heels on, Megan could look Alessandro right in the eyes. And if she didn't know better, she'd say his pupils in those gorgeous Ian Somerhalder grays were dilated.

"I'm sorry," he said and extricated himself first, moving into the hallway. Megan told all the parts of her that had touched him—honestly, just her clothes... and her knees and almost her forehead—to calm down, then allowed him to back up so she could leave.

"All good?" Sophia asked breezily when Megan came back through. A half dozen people were in line already. Megan hadn't realized how much time had passed in Roman's office. She had to dodge around Grace, who was making four drinks at once.

"All good!" she sang in a voice that sounded loud and strident. "See you tomorrow!"

And this time she left without her coffee cup.

♦

Chapter 4

Megan was updating the department handbook with all the events she'd worked on in her tenure when her cell phone rang with the Darth Vader march.

It was her oldest sister, Cat. Sam had changed the ringtone when she was here last summer, and Megan hadn't had the heart to change it back.

"Hey," she said into the phone.

"And to you," Cat said. "Need you for something."

Megan glanced at her computer clock. She had twenty minutes to finish up her work and get outside to Alessandro. And much as she would do anything for her sisters and brother, much as she owed them, right now she could do without Cat asking a favor.

"What do you need?" she said.

"When you come over Sunday, can you bring a few dozen of those mini-brownies you make? The boys' b-ball team is coming over for the afternoon, and there isn't a sheet cake in the world…"

Typical Cat. *Her* birthday was this weekend, but *she* was the one planning the party—two parties, it sounded like. This was why Megan couldn't make fun of her, at least not to her face.

Cat's twin boys, seniors in high school, took up everyone's lives with basketball most months. A little thing like turning forty-six wasn't going to stop that schedule.

"I wish you'd just let us take you out to dinner," Megan said for the fiftieth time.

"That's more trouble than it's worth," Cat said. "Finding a table for all of us, fitting everyone's preferences, dressing up? Pfft. Anyway, Ellen's bringing her barbecue chicken."

Megan's stomach rumbled. This was why she couldn't argue with Cat. The woman always had a point. Megan loved eating at her house, and the only way to mitigate the guilt of all the work it caused Cat was to provide as much food as possible.

"Of course I'll bring the brownies," she promised. She had nothing else to do on a Sunday morning, especially without projects to finish up at work. "What else?"

"I'll tell you if I think of something."

Megan would bring wine and fancy Italian beer for Antonio, Cat's husband, but any other idea she had would end up in the back of the refrigerator, ignored, judging Megan for her presumption.

"Okay, gotta go make dinner," Cat said. "See you Sunday at eleven."

Megan noted the time diligently on her calendar, as though she'd forget. Sundays were sacrosanct at the creaky old Fielding home where Cat and Antonio lived, forty minutes out of the city. Megan could try to be late, but she'd just get the Wrinkled Nose of Disappointment, and Kane would start up about how Cat was too harsh about everything. It was easier just to be on time.

"Bye," she said, but she'd hardly pressed the button on the phone before she became aware of a person standing at her cubicle.

"Hey, Megan?" Britney, her coworker, asked.

"Yeah?" she said, spinning around in her chair.

"You doing anything right now? I wondered if you could help me with this conference next week."

"You're not worried about it, are you?" Britney had trained under Megan this year and was going in her place. Megan was *fine* with it.

"Well..." Britney flopped into the chair in the next cubicle.

Megan gave a subtle glance at her computer clock. Nine minutes to get packed up and all the way downstairs. "See, I know I did good on the Northwest Regional presentation materials, but they haven't asked me to write a speech for next week, so I must have done something wrong."

"You're the queen of PowerPoint, Britney," she said. "Everyone knows that. They're using your strengths. And I've been writing most of Kane's speeches this year. That's just how it's shaken out." And, of course, Megan knew Kane's every mannerism, and she knew his cadences better than anyone, except Leo.

"But you're leaving soon, and someone will have to write your brother's speeches. I want to work with your brother more. And Leo started asking more of the rest of us to—"

"You're right." Megan patted her knees with her hands in the classic *it's time to end this conversation* manner. "You're absolutely right. I'm sure your speeches will be great. You should talk to Leo about it."

"But you have a great way with words. Can I take you out to dinner so you can help me with Leo without shooting myself in the foot?"

Now Megan fisted her hands in her lap. "I'm so sorry, but I can't. I have plans."

She *never* said no. Her skin began to crawl as Britney frowned at her. "I'm so sorry," she repeated.

"Who with?"

"A—a friend." The skin crawling got worse. Everyone knew what "a friend" meant. And Alessandro wasn't that. Those two words could start a rumor that would be around the entire ninth floor by seven o'clock the next morning. "I mean, a—a client."

Britney was still frowning up at her. "Outside of work?"

The Studio was a client, right? Right. "A charity that needs my help."

The clock showed 5:23. "In fact, I have to get going." She stood, hoping Britney wouldn't follow her. "They're sending a car."

That didn't help. "A charity is sending a car for you?"

"Well..." Crap. "It's not in a great neighborhood, apparently, so they're sending a cab."

She leaned down to pick up her purse, and when she straightened, Britney was right next to her. "I'll come down with you."

Great. Megan hoped to hell that Alessandro wouldn't get out of the car. For his sake. Not hers. Better yet, that she'd have to stand outside for a few minutes until Britney was definitely gone before he showed up.

They gathered their coats and scarves in the break room. Megan tried to give Britney a few encouraging words, but afterward she wasn't sure what she'd said. It being the time for everyone to go home, they weren't the only ones waiting, and the elevator took forever to show up. Megan rarely allowed herself to show frustration, but she heard herself emit a small growl when the closest elevator stopped for a full minute at the floor right above theirs and then showed up packed to the doors.

By the time they got into the elevator, it was five thirty. Megan fidgeted all the way down, even though it made Britney glance worriedly at her a few times. She all but burst through the doors on the ground floor, following the stream of employees making for the exit. The lobby was full of movement, suits, and briefcases.

Except for one person, talking to security, a dripping black golf umbrella in his hand. He wore the same coat and baseball cap as yesterday. No glasses.

"Shooooot," Megan let out on a long breath. Why was he in the building? Why wasn't he in the car where he said he'd be? She wasn't late yet. She stopped walking, causing people to *tsk* from behind her and Britney to pause along with her.

"You okay?" Britney asked.

"Uh. Yeah. I'll see you, okay?" Megan walked straight toward him, hoping to leave Britney in her dust, but the younger woman followed.

She broke through the crowd and approached the security desk. The security guard said, "Oh, there you are, Ms. Fielding. I was just going to call you."

Alessandro turned to her. Then his glance flicked a foot to her right, to Britney, whose mouth and eyes were big giant O's. Megan winced. Yep. She recognized him all right. And who wouldn't?

"You're, you're..." Britney stuttered.

"Hello," he said. And could he not? Even one hello from him was sexy.

"I thought you were going to wait outside," Megan said, not moving her mouth much, as though that would stop Britney from hearing her.

"It is sleeting outside. You did not have a hat or umbrella this morning."

Megan could *feel* the other woman's eyes all but pop out of her head. "We met at a coffee shop," she said quickly. Jeez. The man was a walking promise. He made "we met" sound like "it was fate that we meet."

"Oh," Britney said. "But you *are* Alessandro Rosselli?"

"Yes, I am afraid so," he said.

"Oh my God." Britney fumbled with her purse. Megan twisted her mouth with embarrassment. Did Alessandro think she'd brought Britney along on purpose?

"He can't do a selfie," she said flatly. "We have to go. Sorry."

"Really? Wow. Okay. I just... no one's going to believe–"

Should Megan tell her not to tell anyone? That would just

make it all worse. Alessandro had done this by walking into a public building at the busiest time of day. *Incognito, my left foot.*

"Nice to meet you," he said and reached out a hand to turn Megan toward the exit. To do that, he had to touch her elbow, and Megan felt—guided. No, not guided. Nurtured. And Britney obviously translated the touch as that of a boyfriend. Not someone who was just Megan's ride to the Studio.

"Bye," Megan said, though it was really a sigh. All she could do was allow Alessandro to steer her out of the building, under his now-open umbrella, and into a waiting black car. Britney wasn't the only one noticing them as they left.

"Why did you come inside?" Megan asked again when they were safely closed off from the world. "Everyone saw you! After all the cloak-and-dagger this morning, why ruin your privacy now?"

Alessandro sat back in the black leather seat, and Megan watched the streetlights flicker over his face as the cab pulled into traffic. He was wearing a thick parka with a sheepskin collar, and the sleet had left sparkles all over his hat and coat. He was exceedingly distracting.

"It is not polite to make a woman come out into bad weather for you," he said. "And I... I guess I do not agree with my manager on this one." He turned to her, and did she notice that their knees touched? Yes. Yes, she did. "I was thinking about what you said this morning: Jaelyn and I are the big draws for the event. How can I help them if I stay in my hotel room for two weeks? Is it not better that I go around *telling* everyone about the Studio while I'm here?"

"Oh." He'd remembered something she'd said? He'd been thinking about it? "Well, okay, then." And it did make sense from a marketing point of view. "So, what's the plan now?"

"That is up to you, Megan."

There he went again, making everything sound like a promise.

The auction, her mind stuttered. *He's talking about the auction.* She couldn't even see him looking at her in the uneven lighting. Could she?

"We'll see what Etta and Susie have to say about it," he added, "but I will see if I can get an interview on one of the morning shows. Radio, too."

"That's what I'd have you do," she said. "I know a few people at the stations. But—" His publicity team would have their own contacts. "You don't need me for that, of course."

"Let's not say that yet," he replied, and the light disappeared from the car so she could hear only his voice. He sounded amused. Megan was getting too excited. She didn't even know if she would get along with these people.

They drove in silence through the rush hour traffic and pulled up in front of a brightly colored, low-slung building with a couple of bare trees and a snow-covered swing set out front. A churro truck stood in the light coming from floor-to-ceiling windows on one side. The rest of the neighborhood was rundown, but Megan got the sense this was the life force of the place. Her heart immediately lifted as Alessandro ushered her to the door.

"So what's your secret surprise?" a short white woman with high blond hair asked as soon as they got inside.

"Charlene, meet Megan," Alessandro said. "Megan knows about publicity and is going to help us now that Melanie is gone."

"If I can," Megan put in.

A woman with a buzz cut came out of an office. Alessandro introduced her as Etta and a green-haired woman as Susie. He didn't have to introduce Jaelyn Jones, though of course he did. She'd almost gotten used to Alessandro's star presence, but with Jaelyn, Megan had to start all over again. Soon she had three women and Alessandro looking at her around a dinged-up conference table with a laptop between them all.

She swallowed her starstruck tendency and began. Once she started talking, though, she lost all timidity. She put her phone in the middle of the table, and they all leaned over, squinting at their own website and social media profiles while she told them what was going wrong and how easy it would be to put it right. Every question Susie answered gave Megan more ideas, more visions, more certainty that the Studio and the community center could do so much more with their social media—and that Megan could help them do it.

Etta handed over the passwords to everything without a blink. She must really trust Alessandro's judgment. Megan would do everything she could to earn that trust, too.

She drilled down on how much Jaelyn could do to help the cause between filming her series. Susie gave Megan a list of alumni who'd made it to the big time, and Megan swore she'd chase them down for quotes. "Really? Him? Her?" she said several times. The Studio should be legendary, not struggling, if it was connected to these people.

And Alessandro? "What can I do?" he asked.

"If you're serious about not staying in your hotel room," she told him, "you can get into a TV studio. Yesterday."

"Whatever you say, boss." He saluted. The others laughed, but Megan didn't.

"Watch what you agree to," she said seriously. "You're the one without a day job right now. I'm going to be taking every spare hour you've got."

"They're all yours," he said.

Megan would have loved to take a second to examine exactly *how* he'd said such an innocent phrase, but she was looking at the SEO settings on the website.

"After the fundraiser, you'll have to make sure we keep these updated for all the programs you run every week." She tapped the screen with one finger. "The kids might be learning this in school. You could use them to keep it fresh."

"Don't bet on them learning anything in school," Etta said. "Not that they're not trying, you understand. But the funding for enough computers for everyone?"

"Oh. I'm sorry, that was stupid of me." Megan thought fast. "Do you have a computer lab here?"

"I refer you," Etta said in a dry tone, "to my last comment."

"Right. Right." Megan mentally kicked herself. "Well, I can certainly keep up with that for you if you'd like. What are you doing with the money from the fundraiser?"

Etta and Susie began talking at once. Jaelyn interrupted, and Alessandro put up his hands to stop them talking over each other. Megan laughed. "Okay! There's a lot to do, apparently!"

Susie grinned sheepishly. Etta spread her hands out on the table. "You see our problem."

"So," Megan said. "We'd better make sure we bring in as much money as possible."

"And you'll help us?" Susie asked.

"As soon as I get home tonight."

Jaelyn ran around the table to hug her. "Thank you, thank you, thank you! This place is so special. I knew you'd see it as soon as you came."

"I knew already from what Alessandro told me," Megan said, hugging her back.

"Good job, 'Sandro." Jaelyn put her hand up for a high five. "The Drummer saves the day."

Alessandro rolled his eyes but didn't leave her hanging. As he leaned over the table to high-five Jaelyn, Megan caught his scent, and some of her reticence returned. He looked so good, even in the unforgiving lights of the gymnasium, which only set off shadows and planes on his sculpted face.

"I'm so glad I can help," she said. "Thanks for asking me, Alessandro."

"I am glad I came into the coffee shop yesterday," he replied. Megan's cheeks warmed and then really heated up when he said, "If you really plan to start tonight, let me get you some dinner first."

"Oh! No, that's not—I don't need—"

"You have to eat," Etta said mildly, smiling in a way Megan didn't want to translate. Then Jaelyn started smiling too.

No. Megan could *not* sit in front of Alessandro at a restaurant for another hour while fighting her fangirl crush. Even if she had known him since way before the rest of the world. "Thank you, but I have leftovers at home from last night," she lied. "And I really do want to get started on fixing up the website."

A set of double doors at the other end of the gym slammed open, and a handful of teenagers burst in, making them all jump.

"Hello!" Etta called.

"I told you," a girl in the front hissed.

"What class are you looking for?" Susie added.

"We..." a blond girl behind the braver one stammered. "We... uh, thought it was acting class tonight."

"That ended at six o'clock," Susie pointed out.

"Oh!" The students looked at each other, and apparently, made a silent decision. "Well," the brave one said in a rush, "we just wanted to know if it was true that Jaelyn Jones and Alessandro Rosselli were here."

"It is true," Alessandro said. "Come on in, guys."

Needing no further invitation, the gaggle of kids came into the gym, and Alessandro, closely followed by Jaelyn, met them in the middle. Megan stayed at the table. Etta and Susie stayed with her. "It was bound to happen," Etta said.

"Sooner or later," Susie agreed.

"Better get it over with."

"It's wonderful," Megan put in, watching Alessandro talk easily with the children. "Look how they're lighting up."

Jaelyn was already taking selfies with some of them, and Alessandro was soon pulled in. Their voices crossed over each other until Megan couldn't hear what they were saying, but she loved how Alessandro looked at each student as he spoke to them. From what she'd seen of his interactions with the media, he always appeared somber and standoffish. But that was obviously just for the professionals. He smiled so widely now that Megan had to stop herself from staring at him. His charisma, alongside Jaelyn's, filled the room. Megan took a few photos herself. She would send them to Alessandro and Jaelyn later and get permission to post them.

"How do you handle parental permission for the kids' photos?" she asked. "This is gold."

Seriously, it was a crime that this center wasn't drowning in donations, with the story it could tell. With the smile currently on Alessandro's face alone.

"We'll check the waivers we have on file," Etta said, writing down the kids' names. "I'll let you know what you can post."

The students got their photos, and the actors got their promise to tell everyone they knew about the auction. As the small crowd left the gym, Megan stood. It was a good time for her to leave as well. She began her goodbyes and looked on her app for a cab.

Alessandro joined her at the table. "My car can take you home."

Another promise. Why was *everything* he said a promise?

He only meant that he'd make sure she got home safely. She needed to get a grip.

"No, I can get a cab. You should go straight home."

"My car is much safer than an Uber." He frowned.

"My Uber is safer for you. Low profile, remember? At least until you get on those morning shows."

"Megan."

Ooh, he'd said it again. Lord, he was his own worst enemy. "Think about it. If your car pulls up to my apartment building, people will get all kinds of ideas. No, Alessandro. Tomorrow I'll bug you for all kinds of help. Tonight, let me help you by sending you back home in your own car."

"I did not think about it that way," he conceded. "I apologize. Let me escort you outside at least."

His sudden capitulation was sexier than a quarter hour of arguments. Megan hid her hot cheeks by putting on her coat and grabbing her bag. She said goodbye to the others, promised she'd call tomorrow with updates, and let Alessandro usher her outside.

The temperature was as cold as ever, the air just as perfumed by the cinnamon sugar from the churro truck. "Would you like a churro before you go?" he asked her politely.

"Sure. They smell so good." In fact, she was beginning to regret saying no to dinner. The smells were making her stomach grumble loudly.

"I absolutely insist," he said when Megan went to pay. He handed her a paper cone of churros. "I do not know if you know this," he added, picking up a napkin, "but I get paid for what I do."

"I know you do," she said, blushing despite the cool air. "But I do, too." She wasn't going to tell him that she was probably worth more than him, no matter his recent success.

"That is true." He seemed to consider the concept. "Can I buy you a churro because it would make me happy to buy you a churro?"

"That's not fair," she said. She couldn't wait any longer to pull out the delicious pastry and take a bite. "Ohmigod."

Alessandro was grinning at her.

"Don't look so pleased," she said with her mouth full.

"What?" He cupped a hand behind his ear. "I couldn't hear you."

"Don't look so—mmm. Never mind." She took another bite. The cinnamon sugar warmed her from the inside out. "I officially allow you to buy me churros whenever I come here."

"That sounds as though you will be back."

"Of course I'll be back. I told the others I'd be back."

"But you are very polite."

"I meant it." Then his words distracted her from licking the sugar off her thumb. "Hold up. What do you mean by that?"

"I have always noticed this about you. You work to make everyone have a better day. You choose your words carefully. You smile at everyone, but sometimes I think..."

She stared at him. Those silver-gray eyes wouldn't let her go.

"I wonder," he said, "what you would say if someone asked you to do something you *didn't* want to do. I wonder if all this making others happy is tiring for you."

"I—" The emotions bubbled up so fast, she didn't know which one to throw at him first. Megan didn't get to put herself first. She'd chosen this. Infuriated with Cat and Kane's fights? Smile and make a joke. Frustrated with Kane's restrictions on what she could do at work? Smile and tell him she was happy with the work she had. Move away from a department whose projects made her heart sing? Nod and smile and make sure the coffee machine was running.

And this man, who hadn't seen her in five years, had seen enough—remembered enough—to see what she'd hidden: that her ease around people always came with a cost.

"H—How do you know that?" *No one* was supposed to know that. Even her family didn't know this. If people knew that she had to work to make them happy, that it wasn't, in fact, something she did easily? No. Megan couldn't countenance it. They would be disappointed. She would let them down. She would fail.

"I saw it whenever you came into the coffee shop," he said. "I saw it behind your eyes. It is what actors do when they are preparing for a scene."

"Oh." Shit. That was why he'd been looking at her so hard. "You remember all that back then?"

"Yes. I remembered you."

His voice had changed. It was now like warm syrup in the cool night.

There was nothing for her to stagger against, but she wasn't sure if her beautiful kitten heel boots were going to hold her up. "Oh," she said in a very small voice.

"Megan," he said, drawing her away from the light of the churro truck. His hand was light on her arm, but she would have gone wherever he directed her. She couldn't misread the intensity in his eyes this time. Nor the meaning of him remembering her from all those years ago.

"Hey!" A cacophony of voices broke into the spell he was drawing around her.

"*Merda*," he mumbled. Megan breathed in, almost gasping, as the cold air rushed back between them. "Excuse me," he said and left her all but hyperventilating as he joined the students, who had all left the building at once.

"Hi!" they said, now obviously his best friends. "Buy us a churro?"

"Of course," he said, nodding to the man in the truck. "Whatever they want."

One girl sidestepped the others and joined Megan in the half shadows. "Are you an actress, too?" she asked boldly.

"Oh, no!" Megan laughed at the possibility. "No, I'm just a regular Jane."

"So why were you in the Studio?"

"I'm helping with the fundraiser. I'm Megan."

"Rochelle."

"Nice to meet you. Do you want to be an actor, too?"

"I already am an actor." Rochelle put her hands on her hips.

"Right." Megan nodded. "Alessandro thinks so, too."

Rochelle's whole body seemed to swell with pride. "One thing they always tell us at the Studio: we've gotta have faith in ourselves."

"That's right. Well, I have faith in you, too, if that's any help. I hope I see you again soon."

"You're coming back? Then you'll see me. We're here pretty much every afternoon after school if we don't have to work."

"Ready?" Alessandro said. A car had pulled up. Rochelle moved away to place her order, and Megan and Alessandro were alone again.

The smell of cinnamon and sugar and Alessandro made her dizzy.

"Thank you for a really fun evening," she said. Why did he seem taller now?

"Thank *you* for meeting with me. For all your help."

"Um." Her hand went to the tips of her hair. *Be brave* warred with *don't cause any trouble.*

"*Guarda,*" he said and touched her fingers before they reached her hair. "Your fingers are sticky."

"Oh."

Alessandro was only touching her fingers with his, but the sparks from it reached all the way up her arm. After a second, he lifted his hand, but she didn't pull away. Couldn't pull away. Didn't *want* to pull away.

He put his hand back. His fingers crooked over hers, trapping her in the slightest, most delicious cage.

She glanced at him again. His mouth was slightly open, his eyes darker than ever.

"Megan," he said.

"Mm-hmm." Her throat was thick with anticipation.

"Will you let me know how your work goes tonight?"

"Oh." Not what she'd thought he was going to ask her. But what could she expect? He'd only stopped her from getting sugar in her hair. She was reading signs that were not there. "Oh, sure, yeah. 'Course."

"Okay. Thank you again."

The car was spewing exhaust all around them, but Megan couldn't smell it as long as he stood in front of her. Only when he opened the car door and used his hand on her arm to get her inside could she breathe again. He closed the door. Megan gave her address to the cabbie and looked out the window at Alessandro.

He licked his fingers. He licked the churro sugar from *her* fingers off of *his*.

Megan's heart did another lap around the block before joining her back in the cab.

♦

Chapter 5

Alessandro couldn't sleep.

Did Megan know that the way she looked at him was driving him crazy? Was he misreading the way she alternately treated him like a work colleague and blinked up at him like a lover?

She'd taken on his problem at the Studio, and all he'd done was nearly kiss her.

Dimenticalo, idiota. Forget it. She was there to help the Studio—the focus she'd held when talking to Etta and Susie proved that—not to spend more time with her ex-barista. And she'd told him in simple words even he could understand that she could not live in his world.

But then he remembered that little shiver she'd given when he'd stopped her from touching her hair. And maybe Alessandro could tell himself that he tended to do that to women when he first met them, but the problem was, he'd felt a spark reach up his arm. He'd wanted to hold her hand properly, to warm those fingertips, to stroke her hair flat against her coat, to smooth out the raindrops until they chilled his heated skin. To lift her chin so he could see the light reflected in her eyes.

Gesù Cristo. Get a grip. You just haven't been with a woman in too long.

No one had reminded him that having a relationship with Nikki that only extended to the cameras would mean he wouldn't be able to date anyone *else*. He'd been too busy with filming and interviews to think about it, always believing he'd end their arrangement after *this* project or *that* one. Now that they were a continent away from each other and he'd met

Megan again—the one woman he'd never been able to get out of his mind—the ridiculousness of him and Nikki had become abundantly clear.

At first, he'd enjoyed their differences, and they'd dated for real for three whole months. He'd met talented singers he wouldn't have known any other way; he'd learned a lot about the music industry from watching Nikki's recording sessions and his backstage pass to her concerts. In return, she'd been invited to movie premieres she wouldn't have gotten to by herself, met his friends, and become a fixture on morning shows.

She'd taken him to more clubs than he could remember the names of, and his social media hits became more about his outfits than his acting. Nikki even kept him around when the top designers would send her racks of clothes to choose from before her shows. She told him not to question his own talents, and he praised her songwriting and made fun of the charts whenever her numbers dipped.

And that was the problem in the end. They had more fun being friends than they did as lovers. One night, they'd stopped in the middle of having sex and just laughed at each other.

Alessandro turned over in bed and punched the king-size pillows. They didn't help him get more comfortable, but he liked the release of energy.

They'd broken up but kept up their genuine affection for each other in front of the cameras. Alessandro was content to trail Nikki to her clubs and concerts, and she was happy to join him on the red carpet. They backed off from discussing their relationship in interviews, answering any questions with knowing smiles and assurances that their other half was wonderful. They'd been doing this for most of the last year—longer than they'd actually dated. It had worked. But now it didn't. And Alessandro found himself itching to make a change.

He was going to disobey Yasmin again. Tomorrow he would have to call Nikki and figure out a way to officially break off their "romance."

Once he'd decided on that, he fell into a sleep that was broken at three a.m. by the ringtone he'd assigned to his manager.

"Mmph?"

"Okay, who is she?" Yasmin's very wide-awake voice said.

"Um—who?"

"The woman in the viral photograph you let someone take last night!"

Alessandro woke up, fast. He pulled the phone away from his ear and looked at his notifications, which he always muted at night.

Alessandro Rosselli Welcomed Home by Mystery Woman

"*Merda!*"

Someone had taken a picture of him with Megan in front of the churro truck. There was no mistaking the intimacy in their look, even before you flicked over to the one of him holding her hand. Jesus. He'd had no idea the light from the truck would make them so visible.

One of the students must have taken it. Megan had stopped him from messing up her no-camera rules only for him to blow it by touching her in front of a crowd of phone-wielding kids.

He had to call her. He hadn't wanted this. *She* hadn't wanted this.

He clicked onto another link, putting a hand over one eye as though that would help block it out. The photos of him with the girls in the gymnasium had all been posted. They were normal pictures—electronic squeals of joy at meeting a real-life movie star.

"I told you to stay in your hotel room!" Yasmin said.

"I couldn't. I told you this fundraiser was coming up. Megan was just helping me—"

"Megan? Megan who? You know better than this, Alessandro."

As soon as he told her Megan who, he would change Megan's life no matter his best efforts. He'd known since his coffee shop days that Megan Fielding's brother was the Kane Fielding made famous for dating several A-list actresses while Alessandro was still in Italy. She'd filled in the rest of the story this morning, and it made him glad he'd never asked.

"Can I… not tell you that right now?" he asked. Useless question.

"If you don't tell me, someone else is going to find out and tell the press, and you won't be able to control the narrative," she said as though teaching kindergarten. "You know that."

He sighed, and in the brief silence while he readied himself to tell her, she added, "Well, you look fucking amazing. Both of you."

"That's not the point."

"It's always the point, Mr. Sexiest Man Alive. Don't be naïve."

"I don't want to bring her into this. Her family has bad history with publicity."

"Well, now you really have to tell me who she is."

He imagined Yasmin at her desk, despite it being midnight in LA, pushing her glasses back up her nose.

"Her name is Megan Fielding," he said, as though at the top of a roller-coaster dip. "She is Kane Fielding's sister."

He heard tapping on keys. Looking up Kane's name, he assumed. Then "Oh."

Alessandro didn't like that knowing *oh.* "So can you understand why I do not want her name to get out there?"

She was silent for a moment. probably scrolling through pages. Or Megan's Instagram account. The photos of her sister's wedding—yes, he'd looked at them, too—were right there for everyone to see, showing her handsome brother and her equally stunning sisters.

"Alessandro," Yasmin said. "I sometimes forget how few years you've been in this industry. This is already out there. Don't you see the reposts on their wedding photos? TMZ even took the shots for their site. Not front page news, sure. Kane Fielding hasn't been important for years."

Alessandro winced. Yasmin's version of important was always so mercenary. He remembered how Megan's face softened when she talked about her brother. Kane was important to a lot of people.

"But it's out there nonetheless," Yasmin went on. "By morning, they'll know who she is. And *you*," she paused dramatically, "are supposed to be dating Nicola."

"I know," he said. "I was going to—"

"And Papier just asked me if you're planning on breaking your no-controversy clause more than twice before shooting starts."

Papier was the production company behind his next movie. He'd fucked this up good. Just because he couldn't stop himself from touching her.

"Hold on," Yasmin said. "Here's Donna. I'll patch her in."

"No, don't!" He did *not* need to hear about it from his publicist as well. Unfortunately, Donna worked for Yasmin or at least answered to her more than to Alessandro, given his relative newbie status in the business.

"How many times," Donna said once she was on the call, "have I told you to tell me before you make any big decisions—big *public* decisions?"

"I did not make a decision!" he protested. "I was just trying to stop her from getting churro sugar on her hair!"

The women on the other end of the phone treated him to a heavy silence. He scrubbed his hand over his stubble and walked over to the window. Boston was as quiet as it was ever going to be. If he craned his neck, he could see the Custom House clock illuminating the night. Boston hadn't changed in five years, but his responsibilities had. And he'd pulled Megan into them without thinking through the consequences to her.

Of course, there wouldn't have been any consequences if he hadn't given in to the wish to touch her.

"I have to call Nikki's publicist," Donna said.

"Don't call her until I talk to Nikki," he begged.

"They're nine hours ahead of us," Donna pointed out. "It's daytime over there, and she'll already have seen them. She wasn't sleeping through her damn career like you were."

"*Porca puttana*," he growled, ignoring her dig. "*Vi richiamero*."

He hung up before he realized he'd switched into Italian and they might not understand that he was going to call them back.

He hit Nikki's number and put it on speaker, checking his texts while the line rang with an unfamiliar tone. Yep, she'd been texting him.

"Nikki," he said, then was interrupted by a string of Polish and could only let her run herself out before he would be allowed to speak. He didn't blame her, but it was still three a.m. and he was getting a headache.

After what sounded like one long sentence, she remembered to switch to English. "I won't be made a fool of, 'Sandro."

"That was not my intention," he said. "There is no story here. She is a woman I am working with for the Studio fundraiser. That is all."

"Is she an actress too? Because if she isn't into you, she's doing a damn good job of pretending she is."

Alessandro winced again. Nikki was very good at gazing at him the same way Megan had last night. But Megan had had no reason to do it. Apart from what his stupid heart hoped was the truth: she liked him.

"No. She is not in the industry at all. I was just getting some—you know what?" He couldn't spin the churro sugar thing. He might as well quit protesting. And Nikki was a friend. "Truth time, *bella*," he said. "I like her. I met her years ago and again by accident a couple days ago."

"Of course you like her. She's gorgeous. You make a cute couple."

"We are not a couple. You and I are supposed to be a couple."

"Well, we'd better do something about that, and quick. You're not telling me she wouldn't be interested in you. She's not looking for a career as a celebrity girlfriend, is she?"

"That sounds so mercenary."

"It's a job. And so is being a celebrity boyfriend," she pointed out.

"I am glad you remember that. I was worried you regretted our agreement."

"Not at all. My sales skyrocketed on New Year's Day, and they went up again last night. Sympathy for the poor, jilted Nikki means mucho moolah, baby." Nikki's slang vocabulary was much better than his.

She did sound quite bouncy about the whole pseudo-cheating thing, now that Alessandro thought about it. "I just wish we'd talked about this before I left," she added.

"Our people were determined to keep us apart."

She called them a name he couldn't translate. "Like we're goddamn children."

"I have messed up, though, without Yasmin to tell me what to do," he admitted. "And brought you into it."

"I knew you'd be back on social media. Your fundraiser."

"Right." Alessandro sagged against the huge window frame. "Nikki, I think—"

"You want to chase your mystery woman? You go ahead, *kochanie*."

"No, I won't chase her." A small part of his heart thumped with grief at that decision, but he wasn't going to give Megan any reason to avoid him *or* the fundraiser. "I know I made you look foolish, and I am sorry, Nikki."

"It's no bother," she said. He imagined her waving an expressive hand at the air. She talked with her hands like Italians. "I hated being stuck at home. Now I will go out and get drunk and find a friend and have a hot night of wild passion, and our publicists won't be able to say anything about it."

One of her songs was called "Wild Passion." "We will need our publicists to make a joint statement."

"I'll let you handle that," she said. "I'm going to lunch. A long lunch that might take me through the night. *Ciao, bella.*" She blew him a noisy kiss and hung up.

Was that it? Would he never see Nikki again? Alessandro would miss her fun. Then he remembered the club and the police and the night in jail getting eyed by men a lot bigger than him. Maybe he wouldn't miss her that much.

He called Yasmin back. "You can tell Donna to put out a statement that we broke up right after the arrest."

"Of course she's going to do that," Yasmin said impatiently. "What about Megan?"

"Nothing about her. She's helping with the fundraiser, and apart from that, I won't be seeing her."

"You sure? Hollywood loves a romance. And so might Papier. You can tell them you guys simply couldn't help yourselves."

"I am an asshole right now, remember? No one will be happy if I start dating someone else right away."

"Memories are short, Alessandro. And having someone on your arm for awards season is always useful."

"After the arrest, you told me I could not attend any of them."

"Not for that long, honey. Once you get nominated for the Oscar—"

"*If* I get nominated."

"You'll get nominated," she said stoutly. "Being in the press for something wholesome will keep you in front of the judges. Romance sells. It just does. If she's interested, there's no reason not to keep it going." Alessandro winced at her clinical description. "I'm not saying you have to invite the cameras into your bedroom or anything—"

"Thank you."

"I'm kidding, Alessandro. You've been in this country long enough—you have to learn when people are teasing you. I'm saying that if you two give the press a few well-placed publicity opportunities, they'll satiate their hunger and your profile will stay high. Which you need at this point in your career."

"Yasmin," he tried again. "She does not want to be in front of the cameras, even if we know when it's going to happen. You just read what happened the last time someone in her family got famous."

"That was her brother! And he came out great in that—Boston hottie for a few years, then he got the sympathy of the public. He could have parlayed that into all kinds of speaking gigs."

"I am pretty sure he didn't *want* any speaking gigs," Alessandro said.

"I'm just saying. I wonder if he had a manager," she mused. "They would have handled the whole thing better. Gotten his girlfriend protected."

He let out a breath he was sure she could hear. "I do not know if you are right. It was years ago. But Megan told me this morning that she does not do cameras."

"I'm always right," Yasmin pronounced. "So I guess the only question is, do you want to convince her that I can make this work for both of you? She's a businesswoman, right? The publicity would be good for her, too."

Alessandro turned away from the lights outside, which suddenly hurt his eyes. "I'm not going to try to convince her of anything. If I am lucky, she will still help the Studio. That is all I can ask."

"Okay," Yasmin said in the tone that meant *you're crazy.* "What are you doing today?"

"Apologizing to Megan. Several times if necessary. Then I will call the producers."

"Don't. I'll call them."

"Thanks for the vote of confidence."

"You can call them when you have a better story to tell."

He shook his head at her. She hadn't listened to him at all. "Then I'm going to go film the kids at the Studio."

"That's sweet," Yasmin said. He wished he could believe that she meant it. "I'll call you tonight," she went on. "This isn't going to go away just because you ignore it, Alessandro."

Now he sighed, and she could definitely hear it. "I know, I know. I will deal with it."

"Good. Talk to you tonight," she reiterated and hung up.

Alessandro looked at the clock. Three hours before he could even think of calling Megan. Thank God he'd gotten her number yesterday or he'd have had to go through the switchboard at work, and she didn't know his code name, so he'd have had to use his real one.

He wasn't going to sleep now, thinking about what he'd say to her, so he changed into workout gear, then grabbed his keycard and his phone, which had started lighting up with notifications as soon as Yasmin hung up. He headed to the basement gym. At this time of night, he'd be alone, and he needed to keep up his training anyway before rehearsals for the next movie started in March.

From the gym, he used the pool, and by six thirty a.m., his muscles shaking from effort, he was back in his room and back on his phone.

Chapter 6

Megan worked on a dummy website for the Studio until well past midnight before staggering to bed in her sweats. She also updated their Facebook page to show the correct information, created a couple of flyers and Instagram posts—Alessandro and Jaelyn's faces most definitely front and center—and made a list of sites they could use to advertise the fundraiser in a hurry. She hoped she could talk to Etta and Susie at some point today to get their approval for the changes. Then she could start hitting everyone in sight and getting those tickets sold.

She bought two tickets herself, of course. She could drag Kane along. He'd bring a few of his business friends. The ticketing process could use some streamlining, too, but she'd deal with that later. Apart from the churros, she'd eaten only a bowl of ramen and five chocolate chip cookies that had gone stale after her trip, and she was exhausted.

So when her phone rang at six thirty the next morning, she moaned loudly enough to ring off the plate glass windows in her bedroom. If this was Cat, she was going to kill her.

When she saw it was "A," however, she sat straight up in bed and began smoothing her hair off her face. As if she would put anyone on video at this time in the morning.

"Hello?"

"Megan," Alessandro said. "Am I calling too early?"

"N-no." *Yes, you Italian loony.* "I had to get up soon anyway."

"Ach, I am too early. I am sorry, but I had to apologize as soon as I could."

Megan was already twirling the tips of her hair, since being alone meant she didn't have to pretend she was in control to anyone else. At his words, she stopped, then smoothed down the ends.

That moment last night! He'd touched her hand. That was all. And been kind enough to think of the sugar on her fingers. In one way, she supposed he should apologize, as he'd gotten into her space. Then again, she'd been pretty far into his space, too, and God knew she hadn't thought about getting out of it.

"It's not a big deal," she said. "You were right; my fingers were sticky all the way home."

"No, not that." She heard him give a low laugh. "I would not—anyway. You have not seen the photographs?"

"The ones you took with the kids? How did they come out?" And why should he have to apologize for them? Was she in the background? She'd told him she was camera-shy, but she wasn't going to blame him for a couple of angles with her twenty feet away.

"There are other pictures," he said. "Of us outside. Here." He gave her an Instagram account. Rather than take the phone away from her ear, she went over to her laptop and pulled up the site.

In beautiful chiaroscuro lighting, she and Alessandro stood a foot apart. Alessandro's hand was holding hers—she could feel the warmth of him even now—and they were looking so hard into each other's eyes, even the camera could pick up on the charge between them. "Oh," Megan said, and her fingertips tingled.

"I did not know they were taking it," he said. "I would never let someone take a photo of you if I knew. Especially after you told me—"

"It's okay," she said automatically. She looked at the views. One point two million views. Five hundred thousand reposts. "Is this anywhere else?"

She heard him sigh. "It is everywhere else."

"Oop."

"I am sorry, Megan."

"It's not your fault. It's mine, honestly, for—" She couldn't end that sentence in a way that would stop her face from glowing hot.

She looked at the picture again. Her green coat was lit by the churro truck, and her hair spilled down its collar and her back in what she had to admit was a very satisfactory way. "They got my good side, at least," she joked weakly.

"You only have good sides," he said.

"You're very kind." She googled his name and came up with a string of sites with the photo and others like it, along with the shots of the students, Alessandro, and Jaelyn. Unfortunately, his open smiles with the kids only highlighted the intensity of the moment she and Alessandro had shared.

"They don't know who I am," she commented. "That's something."

"They will find out. My manager is going to release it so we can control the information. As much as we will be able to, anyway."

Megan felt as though she were throwing her stomach down a very dark hole. "That's a hell of a way to think of it," she said, hoping she put some amusement in her voice. She didn't blame Alessandro for her name getting out there, but he didn't know her family.

"Your family is going to be upset," he said. Oh, now he could read her mind?

"They always find something to be upset about," she said. She put her hand on her belly. "Last year, it was Thea, then Sam. It's my turn."

"Still. This was my fault. I should not have... asked you to come to the Studio."

"I enjoyed going to the Studio." And being out on that ice-cold sidewalk, being taken care of, for one second, by Alessandro.

"The press release will not give any information other than your name," he said.

"But they'll only have to google me for a second before they find Kane."

"Yes."

Megan's lips twisted. "I'd better call him now."

"Please tell him I apologize."

"Sure." Looking at that picture, Megan doubted Kane would feel charitable toward the man holding his little sister's hand like she was his girlfriend.

Girlfriend. "Oh no!" she yelped. She stood, almost falling over the bedsheets in her agitation. "Nicola! She must think–" God! That picture! "Alessandro, I'm so–"

"Nikki is not my girlfriend," he interrupted. "She never was."

"Oh." How many *ohs* did that make now?

"She was, at first," he corrected himself. "But for a long time now, we have been friends. We kept up the romance for the cameras."

"Oh." Dammit, there she went again.

He isn't dating Nicola Kulik! So when he'd looked at her like that last night and briefly yesterday morning, she didn't have to feel guilty about it.

He. Isn't. Dating. Nicola. Kulik.

"The press release is also going to announce that we broke up after the Perfection fight."

"God." She quickly looked up a picture of Nikki. "I'd be mad, though, if I were her. If–" *If my pretend boyfriend was looking at someone else the way he's looking at me.*

Why had he looked at her like that? She hadn't imagined it. Was it just a man's wish to seduce? Megan knew she had a lot to thank her genes for.

But he wasn't acting as though he'd only wanted to seduce her. In any case, she was too chicken to ask him outright.

"She was… surprised. But it is okay."

"Are you sure?" Megan didn't want a temperamental artist like Nicola Kulik, or her fans, coming after her.

"I am sure." He paused.

"I knew it," she said. "It is not okay!"

"No." He laughed. Megan loved that sound. He made her laugh, too, even though she was imagining hordes of teenage Nicola fans knocking down the security guard downstairs. "Megan, I promise that Nikki is fine. Maybe one day you can meet her and find out for yourself."

The silence that fell seemed to darken the room even more than the predawn gloom outside.

"I forgot," he said.

"I can't be in your world," she said.

"Yes. I forgot that for a second. I wish—"

"Better you don't." She leaned against the desk in the corner of her room. He wished. *He wished.* And maybe she did, too. But if wishes were horses, or whatever the phrase was.

"I have to ask you one more favor," he said. "Will you still help the Studio?"

"Of course I'll still help them."

"That's good. But you may want to stay away from the Studio itself." He paused. "And from me."

Oh. "I guess that would be… a good idea."

"You spent an hour with me last night and this happened. If they see us together again, they will assume we are… together. This way, they will move on in a couple days."

"Right. Right." She hoped she sounded as though she was all for this. That she hadn't, for a moment, wished as hard as he had.

"I will be at the Studio today, filming the kids for promos. If you want to meet with Etta and Susie again, I will make sure I leave before six o'clock."

"Don't worry about that," she said. "I was going to email them everything I've been working on anyway. It's all online. If you send me the videos you take, I can edit and post them. I don't really have to see them again." *Or you.*

So. Aside from never seeing Alessandro again, she didn't have to show up at the Studio. She didn't have to develop her relationship with the wonderful ladies she'd met last night. This was a world of Zoom and emails and WhatsApp groups. She didn't even really have to show up next week to the fundraiser if she sent a donation instead.

She rubbed at a sore spot on her chest. How had she hurt that? Crouching over the laptop last night? She'd been having so much fun, taking the Studio's words and making their story shine. Now she could finish the job and go back to her normal life. And never see Alessandro again.

The sore spot got worse.

"Well," she said. "I'd better call Kane."

"Yes. Thank you again for helping me, Megan," he said. "And I am sorry it has led to this. Tell your brother, too, that I apologize."

"I will. Bye, Alessandro."

"Goodbye, Megan."

She shivered and hung up. Her face reflected back to her in the windows, whose curtains she hadn't even closed last night. There was a hint of light over the harbor, which was probably what made her look so pale and sad.

She opened the picture of her and Alessandro one more time. He had been so pretty to look at.

Then she closed the app and dialed Kane's number.

"Hey, Meg," he said. "Everything okay?"

"Kind of." The scratch in his voice, a holdover from the fire that had nearly taken his life years ago, hit her even harder today. "Did I wake you?"

"No. I was up. Say hi to Rosie."

Kane's youngest child was two and a half and perfect. Megan loved when she got to play with all her nephews and nieces. It was easy to smile with the children all day.

Megan heard a toddler's babble through the phone and cooed at her in turn. But the sweet moment was interrupted by another call coming in.

"You have to go already?" Kane said.

"No. It's Cat." They must have released her name. "She's calling for the same reason I'm calling you."

"You sound serious. Hold on, let me put Rosie in her high chair." There was a pause, and then he came back to the phone. "Okay. What's so terrible that both you and Cat are up at this hour without a baby as an excuse?"

"I had to tell you that you're probably going to be—"

"She's calling me now."

"Yeah. That's why I had to get to you first. I'm sorry, Kane. I didn't plan on anyone—"

"Spit it out, Meg! You're starting to scare me."

"Okay. I was with Alessandro Rosselli last night, and someone took our photo. Then—"

"Alessandro Rosselli? The actor?"

Megan walked from her bedroom to the kitchen. How she'd survived this many minutes without her first cup of coffee, she didn't know. "Yes. The actor. Which is when someone took our picture. And now it's all over the net. And they know who I am, so pretty soon they're going to connect me with you, and then *you'll* be all over the net."

"I see."

Megan's phone beeped with texts. Probably Cat, infuriated

that she was being ignored. Megan cared more about the tone of Kane's voice. Was he mad? Hurt?

"I'm sorry, Kane. I had no idea anyone would take our picture."

He laughed. "My experience tells me that happens when you hang out with movie stars."

"I know, I know, but we weren't *hanging out* like you're thinking. He asked me to help him with a charity he supports. It's just that... other people knew he was there."

"Hold on," Kane said. Megan put the phone on speaker and put the coffee on to brew. It wasn't as good as Roman's, but it got her out the door in the morning. God, she still had to go to work today. Deal with people who'd all probably know about the photos by nine o'clock. Deal with *Britney*. Could she call in sick?

"Nice photo," Kane said. He must have pulled it up. "You're not seeing this guy?"

"No."

"Does he know that?"

She gulped on a laugh. "Yes."

"Huh." He paused. "You might wanna check on that."

"I'm sorry, Kane. I told him this isn't happening."

Kane was silent again. Megan distracted herself by getting milk and sugar out, but she did it quietly while she attempted to hear his breathing.

"So it was an option," he finally said.

"No. He knows about our history." Wow, the sugar was fascinating today. She realized she'd been scooping it in and out of the bowl, frozen in place with regrets and might-have-beens.

"Well." Megan heard a voice in the background. Ellen, Kane's wife. Who'd also been hurt the last time a Fielding got famous. Kane's voice grew quieter as he told her the situation in a couple of sentences.

"Is Ellen mad?" Megan had to ask.

"Of course not."

But she couldn't stand how subdued her usually gregarious brother was being. "Kane. Talk to me."

"I don't have anything to say," he said. "I mean, this is *your* life, Meg. I don't want something that happened to us to interrupt your social life."

But he was okay with it interrupting her professional life.

Megan rubbed her chest again. This time the stab had been pure, unadulterated guilt. Kane had done everything for her and their sisters. So she didn't give speeches. So she avoided cameras. It was a small price to pay for his peace of mind.

"It hasn't. It won't. We're just working together on this fundraiser, and that'll be it."

"Okay. Thanks for giving me a heads-up. I'll talk to Leo."

His right-hand man had been so helpful the last time. Then again, that situation had ended in near disaster.

The only thing they could do was hunker down and ride this one out.

"You'd better call Cat," Kane said, and finally she heard amusement in his voice.

"Yippee."

"Are you going to be there for her birthday?"

"Couldn't miss it. Like, literally, can't miss it without fear of losing a limb."

Finally, she got him to laugh. "That's right. We'll see you there."

"Can't wait. Are you in the office today?"

"Yes, but I'll be in and out." So she wouldn't be able to see him in person.

"I'll see you on Sunday, then," she said. "Love you." Then she shouted, "LOVE YOU, ELLEN!" so Kane would get it right in the ear.

He yelped, and she heard Ellen laugh and reply, "Love you, too!"

Megan hung up. Phew. Crisis averted. All she had to do was not regret her decision.

♦

Chapter 7

Megan left the house later than usual and hoped that her early starts for the last few days would keep people from judging her for it. She wanted to get on with her life, that was all. Finish up in PR, move into manufacturing. Take the steps that had been laid out for her.

Two people with professional cameras called to her as she left her building, but she didn't look at them. There was no story here.

However late she was, she had to stop at Roman's. She was disconcerted, but she wasn't dead. The baristas' reaction to her joining the line inside the door, however, did not help. Sophia danced her fingers against each other and bounced on her toes a couple of times. And Grace said, "Yup, here she is," which made the entire line turn around and stare at her.

"Thanks, ladies," she said, aggrieved.

"You are welcome," Sophia said seriously. Megan supposed she had a point, since Megan had met Alessandro here in the first place.

The crowd continued to stare at her, so she assumed they recognized her from those photos. At least her outfit would pass scrutiny. Today she wore wide-leg black pants and a houndstooth silk blouse under a long black padded coat. With less time to style her hair today, she'd opted for a loose side braid. She'd chosen her pointiest, shiniest black boots, feeling that she might need some kind of metaphorical weapon against the world. Especially as the coat didn't have a hood, so there was nowhere for her to hide. As a final layer of armor, she was wearing three of her mother's gold chain necklaces; their icy touch against her neck from the wind helped her stay calm.

"It's not what you think!" she called over the heads of the crowd—or it felt like a crowd, with all those pairs of eyes looking at her.

"That's what they all say," Sophia replied with a sly grin just as Megan heard a phone camera click somewhere down low. She didn't want to look down and see that the people in front of her were sneaking pictures of her. Hadn't she just promised Kane she would stay out of the spotlight? That this would blow over? The more pictures taken, the more this would stay right where it was.

"I'm not interesting," she tried again. "Nothing to see here!" She caught a glimpse of the phone a kid was holding by their waist, hoping to catch her on the screen. She put her hand out to block the shot, which was probably pointless, and widened her eyes imploringly at Sophia.

More phones began to rise up, making the photo op more obvious. "No photographing the customers," Roman growled suddenly from the coffee machine. "Megan, come through."

Megan gratefully stepped out of line and over to the counter that Grace had lifted for her yesterday—only yesterday? Her world had become unrecognizable since then. "Hey!" said the customer who'd begun photographing her. "She's cutting the line!"

"Typical celebrities," grumbled another.

"I'm not—" Megan began hotly but stopped herself. She *was* cutting the line. In fact, Grace was nodding to the back hallway just as she had yesterday, and Megan was grateful for the respite from the other customers.

"I'll bring you your coffee here," Grace said. "And you can leave through the back door." She waved to the end of the hallway, past Roman's office where Alessandro had touched Megan's knee with his.

"That okay?" Grace said.

"Hmm? Oh, yes. Thanks, Grace." Megan slumped against the bare beige wall. Her heart was thumping, and her hands were tingling. Was she having a panic attack? No... she didn't think so. She didn't feel like she was dying. In fact, the fizzing in her extremities might even be described as... excitement?

Impossible. Megan was upset about this. Right? She didn't want to be photographed. To be associated with scandal and movie stars and charities she'd never heard of before yesterday.

That wasn't true. She'd loved helping the Studio last night. She'd *loved* staying up late, only the blue light of the screen and Miles Davis keeping her company. She'd had to stop every few minutes to scribble down more ideas for how the charity could keep raising its visibility in the future. As the list grew, it chided her for her enthusiasm. She was only there to help for one event.

And the event would only raise more money if she raised its visibility. And how could she raise its visibility hiding in a corridor behind a coffee shop?

Megan stood up straight, brushed down her outfit, and smoothed her braid. She walked back into the shop and let herself through the counter flap. The line was just as long as before. Her audience even included a couple of people at tables.

"Let's make a deal," she said to the first young woman who'd taken her photograph. She might have been college age, or just above it. "You can share that picture of me if you tag the Community Center in Allston. You know it?" The woman shook her head. Megan didn't expect her to know, but she wanted the excuse to give them all the link. "Well, look it up. The tag is at CCAllstonMA." There were maybe ten people in line—not quite the crowd she'd thought when she'd arrived. Now she wasn't nearly as afraid of them.

"They're having a fundraiser for their actor's studio," she went on, making sure she was standing in a flattering pose: one hand on her hip, casually revealing her outfit under her coat. "And Alessandro Rosselli is going to be there. That's why I saw him last night. I'm helping out. So you can tag him, too. And maybe he'll share your post. *This* post." She pointed down at the coffee shop floor. "There's the tag for Oh Beans!, too." She waved the same finger at the chalkboard wall and the links for the shop. "Next thing you know, you'll be an influencer."

The woman's eyes grew as large as the coffee cups around them. "You got all that?" Megan asked. Someone else was obviously videoing her. "You got all that?" she repeated, and the man dumbly nodded. "Good. The fundraiser. Don't forget. Alessandro Rosselli learned everything he knows from them. Worth a donation, don't you think?"

Everyone nodded this time. Megan didn't expect them to follow through, but she'd been looking right at that video camera when she said it. If she was going to be a trend on social media, dammit, she was going to make sure she got to say what *she* wanted to say.

"What's your handle?" the video recorder asked.

Megan smiled at him. "I'll find you. Don't forget. Hashtag, Boston Arts. Hashtag, donate." The other tags that had come to her last night were right at the front of her brain, and she reeled them off easily. "Oh, and my outfit is from Soodee in Beacon Hill. In case you're wondering." She lifted her chin and swept a leg to the side, as though she were at the end of a catwalk. As she'd hoped, they all raised their phones and took a shot—even the ones who were still frowning as though they didn't know who she was. They might not know her, but they sure the hell knew who Alessandro was, and she'd just given the Studio a boost they could ride for the rest of the day.

"I got your coffee, Gisele," Grace said behind her. Megan broke her pose and became herself again. But the buzz she felt remained. She'd looked good, she'd gotten her point across, and she'd controlled the situation. Okay, these were regular people, not the paparazzi. But Megan gave them all her biggest Fielding smile as she went to pay for her coffee and Danish. She walked back past them and shook the bag. "Get the pecan Danish. It's the best."

And she left the store, her heart racing, her cheeks warm with exhilaration. That feeling fueled her fast walk all the way to her office building, through the lobby, where a few eyes turned, and into the elevator. The five or six people who squeezed in with her kept glancing at her, but she held her eyes in front and her chin high, and no one tested her.

She turned right out of the elevator and said her usual breezy hi to the receptionist.

"Megan!" the receptionist exclaimed and half rose from her seat.

Oh no. Megan did not want to get into anything in the lobby with everyone coming and going around her. "See you later!" she called and walked into the open office that contained her cubicle—her familiar, safe, sensible cubicle.

Familiar, but not safe nor sensible. Britney skidded around the corner. "Hi!" she said in the kind of gushing tone Megan was really good at mimicking.

Not today. "Morning, Britney," Megan replied, knowing what was coming.

Britney pulled up a chair from a nearby cubicle and sat in it, leaning her elbows on her knees and her chin on her hands. "Is it true?" she said.

"Um, which part of it?"

"I mean, I saw you with him, and I mean..." She raised her eyebrows to the heavens. "He's even taller in real life! And his eyes!"

She made a valid point. Those eyes.

"And this morning, those photos appeared—wow! So you really are dating him? I mean, you just got back and he just got into town and the whole Nikki Kulik thing!"

"He is no longer dating Nicola Kulik," Megan said, in a very clear and very un-Megan-like voice.

"Oh! But when did that—did you—"

Megan stared her down, and Britney seemed to lose her nerve. Maybe Megan should use that voice more often. "No, I did not," she said. Did not break up Alessandro and Nicola. Did not plan on getting photographed and videoed. Did not kiss the man, which was a big mistake. If she was going to get into all this trouble, she could have at least gotten a smooch for it.

But Britney looked so hurt, Megan couldn't take it. "Welp," she said in her normal tone. "Now I have to get back to work." She pushed her chair back from Britney's and closer to her desk. "See you later? We can talk about what you want to say to Leo if you'd like."

Britney looked frustrated but resigned. Megan continued to smile at her, and the woman slid her chair back and left.

♦

Alessandro slept late—or he didn't want to get out of bed and face the day. One of those. He turned off his phone, kept the curtains closed, and hid his head under the pillow until hunger forced him to move. Thank the Fates for room service.

When he turned his phone back on around eleven o'clock, he found himself tagged in a set of photos and a video he'd never seen before, though with a backdrop of rough wood and blackboard walls he recognized at once. And there, obviously knowing exactly what she was doing, was Megan, posing for the cameras with that 500-watt smile, looking like she'd just stepped out of her day job to do a spread for *Vogue*. When he clicked on the video and heard her familiar voice admonish the camera to mention the Studio, he found himself grinning as well. She'd told him she didn't like the cameras just five hours ago, but clearly the cameras liked her, and she'd decided to embrace it and do some good at the same time.

"Thank you, Megan," he said to his phone. Megan's name and phone number promptly replaced the video. God, he'd love to call her now and thank her for coming out of her comfort zone for the fundraiser. But people who lived in the real world had jobs, and she wouldn't appreciate him interrupting hers. He clicked off the phone app and went back to the video.

He listened to his own name on her lips. He liked it. And he liked the braid she had today. He liked the way she gave her listeners clear instructions so that she was the one controlling the moment instead of being a victim to it.

Did she know how good she was at this? Was it her job training that made her like this, or was she naturally camera-ready? Alessandro would say the latter. Her brother had certainly slid into the celebrity world with ease. Like Yasmin said: maybe if he'd had a manager, none of the bad stuff would have happened.

He checked his texts and found several from Etta, Susie, and Jaelyn. *Ticket sales have doubled!* Etta said. *Donations are way up thanks to your amazing friend!* Susie gushed. *How come all anyone wants to talk about today is your friend rather than you?* Jaelyn said, adding a smiley face.

That was fine with Alessandro—if Megan could handle it. And it looked like she could. His mentions were through the roof as well, always connected to the fundraiser. Etta reported that two news channels had already contacted her for an interview. He didn't even have to have Yasmin twist arms to get him on the shows. Megan had done that with one smile and a quick hashtag.

Speaking of Yasmin. It was eight o'clock in California. Time enough to be calling her.

"Well," she said when she picked up, "your friend sure has been busy."

"I know." Alessandro felt an unearned surge of pride.

"I thought you said she didn't like being in the public eye."

"That's what she told me," he said. "But I guess when she did not have any choice, she ran with it."

"Is this the coffee shop where you used to work?"

"Uh-huh."

"She even got *them* more publicity. Quite a neat little package. You sure she's not looking for management?"

"I do not think so."

But Alessandro was beginning to wonder. He looked at the picture again. She'd controlled the room so well. Maybe she hadn't been thinking of her family when she'd rejected him yesterday. Maybe she'd just... rejected him.

He'd spent a lot of his life around people who used him for their own purposes. In LA, even the most warmhearted, sincere people in the business would give him a good two or three seconds of stare while they sized up what he might do for them. He'd learned to navigate it the way he'd learned to accept the dismissive waves from casting directors at auditions.

But in Boston, for a brief few hours, he'd felt safe from all that. People either liked him or didn't. He couldn't do much for them except give their social media a brief boost. Roman, Susie, and the others had liked him before he became famous. He didn't have to prove anything to them.

Megan had been like them. She'd jumped in to help *him*

without any thought of what he could do for her. In fact, she'd helped him at the expense of her own comfort.

That was what he'd thought. But here she was, loving the spotlight. Managing to sell her coffee shop, her favorite clothing store, and the Studio, all in one speech.

So maybe those big eyes and the flush on her cheeks when he'd touched her fingers had been an act. A damn good one. "Yeah, maybe," he said to Yasmin, getting off the bed and stalking over to the bathroom. He shouldn't be disappointed. His chest shouldn't feel like it was caving in. This wasn't a rejection like all the others. Like his parents. He'd gotten what he wanted, hadn't he? Help for the fundraiser? He didn't have to see her again.

And now he didn't want to.

◆

Chapter 8

Megan called Etta at lunchtime and got an ecstatic tribute to the new website and social media pages. "Make that website live immediately!" Etta yelled into the phone. "It's so freaking gorgeous! Thanks, Megan!"

Then by four o'clock came the email that told her the new website and social media pages, along with her video that morning, had led to a completely sold-out room for the event. And more donations were coming in all the time. "We have a waiting list!" Susie enthused. "We've *never* had a waiting list!"

Megan focused as hard as she could on her own work, but at five o'clock she gave up and made another phone call.

"Hey!" her sister-in-law, Ellen, said, flipping them to a video call.

"Hey." Thank God. Ellen's "hey" had sounded welcoming, not furious, and her smile was relaxed, not hiding anything. Kane hadn't thrown Megan to the wolves... or to his wife. "You're home already?" Megan recognized the tricked-out kitchen of Kane and Ellen's imposing house in Chestnut Hill.

"I only work till four these days, unless it's one of our big events. What's up? Has Cat given you more instructions for Sunday?"

Megan laughed. "No, not yet. I'm calling to ask a favor."

"Sure." Now Ellen's face betrayed uncertainty. Megan rarely put her hand up to ask for things. Usually, she was the one offering. Which had been what she'd signed up for. It had been *fine*.

"You know this fundraiser I've gotten involved with?" She

didn't pretend that the family phone lines hadn't been buzzing all day with judgment for her sudden social media fame. "They've now sold so many tickets, they're out of space in their building."

"Wow. How long did that take?"

"I don't know how long the tickets have been open, but the other night they were less than half filled."

"I'm impressed. Maybe I should steal you over here."

"Well, that was kind of what I wanted to ask you. I don't suppose The Rosette has a big room available next Friday night?"

Ellen ran events at one of the most prestigious hotels in Boston. The kind of space a struggling community center in Allston could only dream of.

"It just so happens that yes, we do. How big?"

"Um... I think they said they were hoping for two hundred people. Maybe I could rent a room for three hundred? They're getting more donations for the auction, too, so they'd need lots of space."

"What do you mean, you'd rent it?"

"I mean, I'll pay for it." Megan coughed to give herself an excuse to look away from the camera. She didn't want to spell it out. Ellen knew her finances as well as her husband. Even with Megan's love of good clothes, she couldn't spend nearly what Kane had husbanded for her and her sisters. Her trust fund had been waiting for her to figure out what to do with it for years.

"Meg," Ellen said slowly. "I don't think you know what you're offering. You want it catered as well? Decorated?"

"I do know," Megan said firmly. "I want to do it for them. If they'll accept it."

The Studio might have reasons to stay local. The Rosette was all the way over on the other side of town. Megan would have to follow Etta and Susie's lead. But she couldn't make the offer without first finding out if it was possible.

"Well then, yes." Megan knew Ellen had the hotel's event schedule memorized. "We have a banquet room that can seat three hundred and give you space for tables for the auction items."

"And a stage. There are presentations or something."

"Right. I think I heard somewhere that Alessandro Rosselli is going to be there?"

Megan felt the thump of guilt in her chest again. "Ellen, I really am sorry about all that. This morning was a surprise, and I just thought—"

"I'm teasing you," she said and gave an un-Ellen-like snigger. "Kane's a little shaken up, but he would be."

Megan groaned. "That's *exactly* what I've been trying to avoid. He doesn't need—"

"He needs to take care of the business he has now. Not the one from almost ten years ago."

"Are you afraid?" Megan asked. She hadn't checked the media all day, not wanting to know what she'd started this time.

Ellen paused before she answered. "Look. I'll admit I don't like it much."

"Ellen, I'm—"

"I know, I know. Stop apologizing. You told Kane you didn't plan that photo, and I believe you. This morning's video... that was different. You opened the door with that one."

"I guess I did. They were taking my picture already. I figured I may as well get control of the situation."

"Something Kane and I didn't do back then." Ellen rubbed her forehead.

"How could you?" Megan knew this role. This, she could do in her sleep. Encouragement. Support. Smoothing the wrinkles of her family's lives. "You guys were incredible. I remember when that picture of you flipping the paparazzi the bird came out."

Ellen choked. "Oh yeah. That was a great idea. It just made them more rabid."

"And you dealt with that, too. Look at your lives now. Your marriage and your kids are the best revenge you could ever get. It could so easily have gone the other way."

Ellen laughed. "You don't know how close it came to doing exactly that. Anyway." She swept a hand in front of the screen. "We're talking about you. Do you want to meet at the hotel this weekend to look at the room?"

"I'll call the organizers now and see if they're comfortable with the idea. I'll text you back. Thanks, Ellen."

"No problem. It'll be nice to see you somewhere other than with the family. We should have lunch one day."

She was right. They worked a few blocks from each other, but Megan never saw her unless there was a family event. "That would be awesome! Give the kids a kiss from their auntie."

"Will do."

Megan clicked off and called Etta right away.

◆

Megan sent a car to the community center to pick up Etta and Susie and bring them to The Rosette that Saturday. In the meantime, she posted nothing of her own on social media and heard nothing from Alessandro. On Saturday morning, he and Jaelyn appeared on the local morning shows. So they hadn't needed Megan's contacts for that after all. Good. That was good. It was *fine*.

Megan also saw the videos he'd recorded over the last couple of days and posted on the Facebook and Instagram accounts she'd cleaned up. He stayed behind the camera and the videos weren't edited, but no one could mistake that rich, warm voice and that accent as he talked to the students about what the Studio meant to them.

She wished she could get the raw video from him and do a little tweaking to get the message across more quickly. But she texted him once or twice and he never responded.

It didn't matter. The big picture was, by the time Etta and Susie's car rolled up to The Rosette that afternoon, they had already texted her that the expanded seating was selling fast.

Megan and Ellen were in the lobby, in navy leather chairs that cushioned them from the crowds around them. The hotel was buzzing on a normal Saturday afternoon, with a line for the receptionists and a good crowd settled in at the restaurant. Megan had never been to Ellen's workplace, so she looked with interest at the décor, which included clean lines but was much more traditional than most hotels Megan had been into. The Rosette obviously saw itself as a bastion of Boston Blue Blood convention.

A *bastion of Boston Blue Blood convention*, her brain repeated. Now that would be quite the party.

Megan laughed and covered it with a big grin as she received a hug from Etta and Susie.

"Here's your knight in shining armor," she said.

"I can't even!" Susie gushed, gripping Ellen in a death hug so tight Ellen squeaked. "Thank you so much for doing this!"

Etta was a little more composed, but she kept Ellen's hand after she shook it. "We could never in a million years have expected this. You are literally saving our work."

Ellen waved her free hand. "Honestly, it's not that big a deal for the hotel. You're helping *us* with the publicity."

That wasn't entirely true, as The Rosette was a global brand and the Allston Community Center decidedly was not, but Megan loved her sister-in-law for the kindness.

"Come on," Ellen said. "Let me show you the space, and we can talk about how to set it up."

She led them to the right, past soft couches and roaring fires and babbling groups of guests, and over to a corridor leading off the elevator hallway.

Behind the elevator bank was a door that led to the emergency stairs. It opened as they passed, and Alessandro Rosselli stepped out.

Megan hadn't seen or talked to him in three days. "Oh!" she said, then, "Hey! How are you? It's been a while!"

And Alessandro, for some completely unknown reason, considering he'd all but had her finger in his mouth the other night, frowned at her and then said in the most noncommittal voice known to man or beast, "Yes. I have been busy."

"'Sandro!" Susie crowed, hugging him. Megan stepped back. What the hell was that? Had it been anything? She was the one who'd said they couldn't be more than colleagues for this one project. He was probably just reacting to that.

"And this is Ellen Fielding," Etta said, and Megan realized there'd been a short pause while they waited for Megan to introduce her sister-in-law.

"Oh, yes," she blurted out too quickly as Ellen shook his hand. "This is Ellen, my sister-in-law. She, um, she's going to show us the room we'll be using."

"Using for what?" Alessandro said, looking at Etta. Not at Megan.

"I told you this, didn't I?" Susie said.

"I have not seen you," he said. "I just did the videos and uploaded them. I only saw Charlene and the kids. Using for what?"

"Megan had the greatest idea, and Ellen set it up," Susie went on. "We're holding the auction here! Isn't that incredible? A bigger space, better sound, better equipment, better *food*... everything!"

"And The Rosette is paying for all of it," Ellen put in.

"No, you aren't," Megan blurted out.

"Yes, *they* are." Ellen smiled at her. "They insist."

"But I—"

What? What was the problem? Did Megan want the kudos for paying for the event? What did it matter who covered it as long as the Studio got what it needed?

They were all looking at her now. "That's wonderful," she said, kicking herself for how *not* wonderful her voice sounded. She could use her trust fund in a million different ways. So what if this one had felt personal? If this one had made her feel good in a way that all the helping her friends and family didn't?

"Was that your idea?" she asked Ellen.

"It came up in conversation," Ellen said enigmatically. So yes.

"It's good publicity for the hotel," Alessandro said. "And a tax break."

"I didn't—" Something was definitely going on with him. The way he said "publicity" while looking at her. Megan *hated* not being able to read someone. And Alessandro was a closed book right now.

"Alessandro, come with us," Susie said. "Are you doing anything else right now?"

"I was going to visit you," he said, lifting his hand, which held a baseball cap and the glasses Megan remembered from her first day back. "I usually take the staff entrance."

"Makes sense." Ellen nodded.

"Well, we came to you for once!" Susie said.

"Come on back," Ellen said, "and I'll show you my ideas for the setup."

Why should Ellen notice that he wasn't smiling the way he had the other night? Or that he hadn't looked at Megan again?

Alessandro let Susie pull him along. Megan trailed behind the small group as Ellen led them down the corridor and into a shadowy banquet hall that looked as large as the lobby outside.

"Wow," Etta said and mimed staggering back into Alessandro's arms.

Ellen turned on some lights, and the wow became even wower. Cream-colored paneled walls reflected the lights of a dozen chandeliers over a navy carpet that had to take hours to vacuum. Ellen opened a couple sets of navy drapes to reveal arched floor-to-ceiling windows with a view of a terrace outside. At the far end was a raised level, almost a stage, with a microphone and more draped curtains behind it. A lighting assembly peeked out from the ceiling.

"We'll do round tables in this area, then have rectangular tables for the auction items on this side," Ellen said. "There's a staging area, and the kitchens are over there. We can talk about the menu, but I was thinking bite-size hors d'oeuvres your guests can eat while walking around the items. Are the kids coming? Do you want to keep it alcohol-free? We have a list of virgin cocktails you can choose from instead."

Etta swayed, and Alessandro quickly grabbed a chair from the wall behind him to put her in. "I'm fine," she said faintly. "I'm fine."

"This is so beautiful," Susie said, a catch in her voice.

Megan started thinking about using the venue as a backdrop for online ads. "Can I take some photos?" she asked, and when Ellen nodded, she moved away from the group, letting them talk details while she photographed the chandeliers, the windows, and the stage.

One thing the recent videos hadn't done was focus on Alessandro as the MC. Megan turned back to them, ready to walk over and ask him if she could take his picture in front of the windows, only to find that he was staring at her, ignoring the others completely.

Her hands wanted to stray to the ends of her hair. If she didn't know better, she'd say he wasn't staring, he was *glaring*. She took her phone in both hands to stop her weakness from showing.

But wait. He'd already seen it. He'd stopped her doing it before. She shivered. Had he seen that? Now that he'd closed off to this extent, Megan didn't want to show him any more of herself. She lifted her chin and walked back to Ellen and the others. She didn't need no stinking pictures of Alessandro Confusing-as-hell Rosselli.

"What about getting all the donations here?" Susie asked Etta. "We'll have to set up a day."

"I can help," Megan said at once. "In fact, why don't we rent a truck and people to do it for you? That way, you don't have to negotiate traffic back and forth, and you can get everything here at once."

"Great idea," Ellen said.

"And this one's on me," Megan said to her. Ellen laughed and cocked her head in acquiescence. "I can get more social media posts up tonight, too."

"I'll get the hotel to advertise it as well," Ellen said. "And you know Kane's already started strong-arming his friends. No one's going to forget about your community center from now on."

Etta put her hand to her chest. "Do you know what the budget was for this fundraiser?" she said. "The thought that we can put it *all* back into the center... Suze, we might be able to update the heating!"

"Wonderful!" Megan said. "I'll leave you guys to it." She hugged Ellen and the other women goodbye before realizing that *not* hugging Alessandro would now be weird.

But there was no part of him that radiated hug-me vibes.

Unlike the other night, he was giving her nothing but leave-me-alone. "Bye, Alessandro," she said instead. "Thanks for bringing me in on this. Good luck with it."

She didn't wait for him to answer. If he couldn't be civil after a woman had rejected him—for very good reasons—then forget him.

She was halfway up the corridor to the lobby when she heard him behind her. "Megan."

May-gan. She couldn't resist it. She turned around. "Yes?"

He'd lost the jacket he'd been wearing to go outside, as well as the hat and glasses. His hair was scruffy and gorgeous, his eyes silver in the light from the hallway sconces. His hands were in his jeans pockets, like a teenage rock star.

And for a second, he didn't say anything. Megan waited, then put her hands on her hips. Dammit, she was getting mad! And not just because her heart wouldn't cool its jets whenever she was around him. "What is it?" she said.

"I just have to know," he said, choosing his words as he had the other day in Roman's office. Only without the warmth of that day. Megan had no intention of letting her knee get anywhere near his anymore. "You made that video the other day."

"Which video?" She'd watched a dozen videos in the last couple of days.

"The one in the coffee shop."

He paused, so Megan prompted him impatiently. "Yes? What about it?"

"It was... very good."

What the hell did that mean? "Thank you?"

"You are a professional at this," he said. "More than you said you were."

"Well, yes," she said, not seeing the problem. "I told you. I've been in PR for two years and involved with Kane's public life for years before that." Wasn't that the whole reason she was here?

"You are now..." He looked away, as if searching for words. "You are now famous."

"Am I?" She had stayed away, turning off her notifications and only working from the community center's social media pages. "I think it's more like the Studio and Oh Beans! are famous."

He stared at her so hard, she couldn't stop her fingers from touching the tips of her hair. "No, Megan. You. Are. Famous."

"Well." She thought of Kane first. Then Ellen, back in the banquet hall. Then Cat, who would slam her hard for bringing the press back into their lives.

"That wasn't my intention," she said. "I was stuck with all those people. They were already filming me. So I used the opportunity. Wouldn't you have done the same?"

He shook his head, slowly. "You did it very well."

"All right," she said, letting her annoyance show in her voice. Her hand fell back to her side. "You make it sound like *you* have a problem with it. Didn't it get you what you wanted from me? Publicity for your fundraiser?"

"What I wanted? Megan, you told me you do not do publicity. You told me that you could not... that we could not... because you had to stay away from the cameras. And then the next minute, you're out there giving a virtual press conference."

Her mouth dropped open. She felt it. "I was just doing what I had to in the moment! What would you have me do? Run away? How would that have helped anyone?" She held up a finger. "I told you the truth. Why else would I—"

Suddenly, she noticed that they were barely a foot apart and her words were echoing up and down the corridor. She looked up at him. He seemed to surround her, even though they weren't touching. For a second, she just held his eyes with hers, hoping she could show him that she hadn't been lying to him without giving away any more of what she felt about him.

"Why else would you what?" he asked, his voice softer.

"I–" She didn't want to say.

"Megan," he said in a frustrated groan. Then he looked to the side, to a door they'd stopped in front of. The next thing she knew, his hand was on her back, gently but firmly drawing her into a conference room lit only by the late afternoon sun coming through less palatial windows than the banquet room. He closed the door behind them.

Her heartbeat skipped up two levels. He moved his hand away from her back, but now he was holding her forearm, keeping her close. "Megan," he said again. "In all these days I've known you–for years, in fact–you have never told me what *you* want."

"I have too!" she protested. "I want everyone to be happy."

He shook his head again, but this time, finally, he smiled. "That is a fine ideal, but I want to know what you want for *yourself*. You helped with the fundraiser because that is what I wanted. You fixed the website because that was what *Etta* wanted. You told me you did not want to see me because that was what *your brother* wanted."

"No, that–"

"Megan."

She closed her eyes. She might have moaned as well. When she opened them, he was right there, right in front of her, his hand now cupping her upper arm. She could feel his breath on her suddenly dry lips. "What do *you* want?"

She dropped her purse, freeing up her other hand so she could put it around his neck. Alessandro put his arms around her waist, and now she was where she'd wanted to be for years: pressed against the most beautiful, kindest man she'd ever met.

And all she could do was close the inches between them and kiss his waiting mouth.

◆

Chapter 9

Dio mio. Alessandro couldn't believe she'd answered him like this. He hadn't meant to set her up, but God, he was thrilled to feel her waist beneath his hands, to have her lips on his, taking exactly what she wanted.

She was just as he'd imagined: soft and firm and hot and cool. Her knees buckled; he caught her, relishing the weight of her in his arms at last. Megan's head fell back, and he followed her, diving into her mouth, flattening his hand on her back to support her. God, she felt perfect.

But this was about her. "*Cara*," he whispered against her lips when he could take a breath. "This is what you want?" He moved to her cheek. "This?" He kissed her under her ear. "This?" He trailed his lips down the cord in her neck, and she shivered. "This?"

"Yes," she breathed. "All of it."

"*Anch'io*," he said against the curve of her neck and shoulder. "For so long."

Megan shivered again. He bussed her skin, then let his tongue dart out, leaving a wet mark and eliciting a moan from her that made him laugh.

Since he had most of her weight already, he bent down and swept her into his arms. She gave a small "eep!" and he turned fast to stop her long legs from hitting the wall. He carried her the few steps to one of the comfortable conference chairs beside them, settling himself with all of Megan's beautiful, lithe body tucked onto his lap.

Better. Also, thank God he'd been keeping up with his

workouts. Of course he could have carried her out of a burning building if he had to, but his exercises were certainly useful for taking this beautiful, smart, funny woman into his arms.

He kissed her again, letting their tongues play, before finding the spot on her neck again and nuzzling it. Megan groaned.

"That is my favorite sound in the entire world," he said against her skin.

She ducked away from him, and the next thing he knew, he was the one groaning as she found a spot behind his beard and below his ear. How did she know that was one of his most erogenous zones? *He* hadn't even known that. The effect of her lips made him shift in his seat, as though that would stop her from knowing how badly she was turning him on.

Megan laughed, low and sexual. She backed up and touched his beard with her fingers, outlining its shape. "Such a difference," she said. "You grow beards fast."

"Sicilian blood," he said. "I drive my makeup artists crazy."

Her fingers moved down to his lips, so Alessandro did what he'd wanted to do the other night: he captured one precious tip in his mouth and touched it with his tongue.

"Gah!" she said, but then she offered another finger. Alessandro obliged. Megan sighed and dropped her head onto his shoulder.

After he'd made love to each of her fingers with his mouth, he kept her hand in his and put them in her lap. For a moment, they sat in silence. Alessandro could feel Megan's heart rate slow to normal.

"This," she said, "is going to get complicated."

"Mm."

After another silence, he felt brave enough to say, "It could be worth it."

Her breath paused. He missed feeling it against his open shirt. "It could just be a nice dream."

He held her more tightly. Would she slip back into that Megan who did everything for everyone else, and this Megan, the soft, sexy, selfish Megan–*his* Megan, and now who was being selfish?– disappear?

"I never want to come between you and your family," he said. "But Megan... Ach, I am going to say this wrong. When are you going to start living your own life?"

"Oof." He'd done it now. She put space between them.

Alessandro hated himself. "I knew I would say it wrong."

"To be honest," she said, "until this past year, I thought I was."

He noticed she hadn't taken her hand away and took heart. "Do you think your siblings want you to give up everything for them?"

"Of course not. And I'm not giving up everything. Or anything!" she corrected herself at once. "I love learning about the company. I love writing Kane's speeches. I love meeting everyone and working with the different departments."

"Which is all good. But you said this past year has made you question that."

"Not question, just..."

"Megan."

She laughed, thank God. "I don't know. Don't you have any family you owe something to?"

He should have seen that coming. He should have just dropped it. Enjoyed her kisses, held her for as long as she'd allow it, then let her go.

"No."

"Oh. No one you left in Italy?"

She was looking at him, her hand on his chest. So open and caring. He could trust her with this, what he wanted to remove himself from in the media. "I've been on my own since I was seventeen. They threw me out when I told them I wanted to be an actor."

"That's—" Her eyes widened and she searched his face. "That's—positively Victorian!"

He smiled at her. "They live in a world of high culture. My father is a conductor; my mother is a world-class cellist. My brothers play instruments in orchestras around the world. My kind of art did not... did not live up to their standards."

"Alessandro," she said. "That's terrible. I'm so sorry."

Oh hell. Her eyes were wet. "No, no, no, no," he said quickly. "I am used to it. Do not cry. Now I wish I had not told you."

"Don't wish that." She smiled and pressed her fingers to her eyes. "I'm glad you told me. It explains... well, it explains that darkness I've seen in you."

"The 'darkness' is for the cameras."

"Some of it."

He looked away, to the far end of the conference room with its large black screen reflecting their images to them. "Sometimes, I do not know how much of me is the actor and how much the boy from Rome."

"You said you were from Sicily."

"I was born there, but we moved to Rome for my parents' careers when I was very young."

"Don't they know who you are now? Don't they watch your movies? No one can say what you do isn't high art."

He looked back at her. Compliments came so easily to her. Perhaps for this one minute, he would believe her. "I do not know if they watch them or not. We have not spoken in years."

"Not even your brothers?"

"Not even them."

"That's awful," she said. "I mean, I know my family is a pain in the butt, but I can't imagine..."

"Maybe you can," he said, recapturing her hand. "You lost your parents far more completely than I did. And you were younger."

"But I had my siblings. They're..." She put her hand over her own heart. "They're vital to me. I'm so, so sorry you don't have that."

She threw her arms around his neck. The chair rocked backward, but Alessandro didn't care if they landed in a heap on the floor. He took her hug, her warmth, took it for the extra minute he could believe in it.

He knew on a logical level that some people could love their siblings, could rely on them for anything. But he'd spent so long living his life without his, knowing—telling himself—deep in his bones that he didn't need anyone, that the lone wolf act had become part of him. Megan loved her brother, sure, but was she going to put aside her own wishes for the rest of her life to make him happy?

Megan held him for a long time. Alessandro had lost track of when they'd come into the room, and she didn't seem to care either. The evening fell early outside the windows, leaving them in shadows. Only a light in the corner blinked green. Alessandro closed his eyes against it, burying his face in her long thick hair. It might be his favorite thing about her. If it wasn't for all the other things he loved about her.

Megan took her arms away suddenly. "I have an idea," she said.

"I have no doubt you have." He smiled.

One side of her mouth turned up. "We could kill a couple of birds with one stone if it works."

"Those poor birds," he murmured, kissing her cheek, "getting in the way of one of your plans."

When he backed away this time, she went pink. So of course he had to do it again. Then his kiss found its way to her jawline, and his mouth opened wider so he could touch her again with his tongue. She gasped. "Don't you want to hear my idea?"

"I also have an idea." He groaned into her ear.

Her belly laugh shook them both.

"Okay." He let go of her and folded his arms between them,

though that just meant his forearms were pressed against her breasts. Megan kept her hands on his shoulders, so he guessed she didn't mind. "Tell me," he said.

"Well, I was wondering about your girlfriend."

"Not my girlfriend," he pointed out.

"Right. Your not-your-girlfriend. The papers have been kind of mad at you both, haven't they? First because you punched out that reporter—"

"He was a pap, and I did not punch him out. I just pushed him away from Nikki. With a closed fist."

"Oof. So okay. They're mad because of that, and then they were mad because you two broke up. At least, that was the impression I got after my video. Which I'm sorry for again, by the way," she added quickly.

"Don't." He cut a hand across between them. "Do not apologize for that anymore. I apologize. I overreacted. I should have known better."

"Okay. We're equal on apologies. So anyway, I was wondering... what if we use my family's history and do some good in the meantime?"

Do some good. That was all he'd come back to Boston to do. He'd somehow managed to screw it up. And now here was Megan Fielding, offering a solution as easily as she'd offered her help the other day.

"You have already done good," he said. "The fundraiser tickets and this hotel."

"Yeah, but that was easy. That was my background. My contacts. And this way, you and I might be able to see each other. Without being hassled by my family or attacked by the media."

He stared at her. What was she talking about? Nothing could make that miraculous scenario happen.

He must have been silent for too long because she reached

for the tips of her hair and ducked her face. "If you want to see me—a little, that is."

He groaned and kissed her again. "Megan, *cara*. I want nothing *but* to be able to see you."

She'd gone pink again. "Okay, well, that's good. So what if we do what you and Nicola did? Date for the cameras? Now that my name's out there anyway, I can use the publicity to help Fielding Paper. And you can use it to help the Studio. We can't put this genie back in the bottle, so let's make it work for us."

To be able to be with her? To hold her hand where other people could see? "I love the theory, *cara*, but I see many obstacles."

"Kane?"

"To start."

"Would your manager be willing to orchestrate this? Give us some staged events, like the fundraiser, so that Kane can see we're the ones in control?"

"The fundraiser is only one event. I want to see you more than that."

He wasn't going to think about the fact that they lived on different sides of the continent. He had a month, if that, before he would be called back to start training for the next movie.

If the producers still wanted him.

He had a window of opportunity here, and Megan was letting him open it. He'd do whatever she said, for as long as she told him to.

"Right, so." Her cheeks were getting redder. "I thought that if your manager is willing, we could tell Kane all the events we're going to. So he could calm down about them."

"What other events?"

"Just dinner or a play or something. Something where we know they're going to look at us and we can prepare."

"Megan," he said. "If we tell them we are dating, they will *always* want to look at us."

"Yes." She bit her lip. "And we can control what we look like when we go where they will see us."

"So... no sweats?"

Megan released her lip. Alessandro wanted to kiss the light swelling there, but he let her answer. "I know you're joking, but yes, sweats. Just sweats that fit." She looked at his chest, and Alessandro laughed at her.

"You are thinking like a publicist."

She smiled on only one side again. "I guess so. It's what Kane did before he got married."

"You watched him a lot back then."

"And now. I watch a lot of people."

He ducked his head to catch her eye. "Did you watch me?"

She blushed all the way this time. "Of course."

He took her fingers and brought them to his lips. "Did you watch Grace and Sophia and Roman like you watched me?"

"Actually, yes," she said, then caught her breath. He'd been kissing her fingertips, but at her answer, he bit down gently on one. "Well, it's the truth!" she protested. "I need to watch them to know—"

She brought herself up short. Then, to Alessandro's deep regret, she got off his lap. While he mourned the loss of her weight against his thighs, she went to the windows and looked out at the darkness.

He didn't speak; he didn't want to say the wrong thing again. She knew that he knew she was an observer of people—he'd told her that the other day. A thousand years ago. But he wasn't going to ask her to share more with him now. They'd come so far in these few minutes. He would wait for the rest.

"I don't want to just observe this time," she said to the window. "I don't want to watch what I say to make sure it doesn't stand out." She began stroking the ends of her hair. "I want to see what it's like to enjoy a moment because I enjoy it. Like you said."

Alessandro walked over to her but didn't touch her. "As an actor, all I do is observe people. Learn their ways. We are more alike than I realized."

That made her look at him. "I'm not acting."

"You can call it something else," he said. "When you are mirroring what people do and searching for their responses to cues—*cara*, that is what actors do. And it is okay," he added quickly at her frown. "You know your way to exist is just fine—as long as it does not make you tired or make you do things you do not want to do."

Megan sagged against the window frame. "I *do* enjoy the events I go to. I enjoy my friends. Afterward, I'm tired, yes, but I can be both."

"Your video the other day shows that you are a professional at being both. If we do what you suggest, I hope you will enjoy it." Megan looked up at him and rolled her eyes with a sideways smile, and Alessandro laughed. "I will make sure you enjoy it very, very much."

Now she shivered, and he dared to put his arms back around her. Megan allowed it but lowered her head. "I want to see more of you, *cara*. I want to help all the people you want to help. I want your brother to accept me—or perhaps not to reject me just because of my work. But my manager told me this world loves a romance. She meant it as a good thing, but if we go public, you will be subject to the kind of publicity you can't always control."

Megan leaned into him. "So I can have some time with you and scrutiny. Or you and I forget about this, and I go back to what I do."

He waited, rubbing one hand up and down her arm. This was

probably going to go horribly wrong. But what she lacked in knowledge, he could make up. He and Yasmin would make it work, and he could be with Megan as long as she allowed him.

"I keep going back to what you asked me," she said. "I haven't wanted to answer that. But now I do." She lifted her head and touched his beard with her fingertips, drawing him in for another kiss.

"What the hell," she said. "Let's give it a try."

◆

Chapter 10

Schedule for Megan and Alessandro

Sunday: no contact. Megan to sister's. Alessandro in hotel.

Monday: Studio and dinner. "Sources" release acknowledgment Nikki relationship is over. Megan walks to work: "Candid" photos.

Tuesday: Walk in Beacon Hill (weather permitting).

Wednesday: A. on *This Morning* (questions attached); dinner at The Rosette.

Thursday: A. and Etta on WGBH; M. at Studio to dress students; Phoenix concert (aftershow photos booked).

Friday: Fundraiser (red carpet-style entry; A. leads interview with M. present—questions attached).

"Look what she's already got planned," Megan said to Cat, who was staring at the email in disbelief. "She did this in less than twenty-four hours. On a weekend."

Cat looked at her as though she didn't recognize her. That look, by the stove where Cat was cooking up a batch of chili large enough to feed the entire basketball team, where her own birthday cake sat in the refrigerator awaiting last-minute sprinkles, in the middle of all the familiarity that was the home Megan had grown up in, made Megan reach for the tips of her hair.

"You're out of your mind," Cat said. "This isn't going to work. Like, at all."

"Look," Megan said desperately, pointing to the interviews. "The questions are preapproved. And they're just puff pieces. It's not Sunday morning on CNN or something. And this is exactly what we do for Kane's interviews. It's worked for him. Why not for us?"

"Because!" Cat spluttered. "Because Kane isn't as famous as Alessandro freaking Rosselli!"

"He was pretty famous back in the day, right?"

"Right, and look what happened there!"

"Yasmin said that's because he didn't have a manager to control his—"

"A manager?! Who—why the hell did he need a manager? And who's Yasmin?"

This was not going well. Thankfully, the kids and Cat's husband were all outside having a snowball fight, and no one else had arrived yet. Megan had gotten up early to make her brownies and get to Cat first. The kitchen island was covered in bowls and platters of snack food in various stages of disarray, thanks to the twenty teenage boys' first five minutes in the house.

A timer dinged, and Cat shoved an oven glove on her hand as though she were about to reach into a beehive. "Yasmin's Alessandro's manager," Megan said to her back as Cat pulled another tray of pigs in blankets out of the oven. "And mine now."

Cat spun around so fast, some of the pigs slid off the tray and onto the floor. The family dog, a young golden retriever called Bofur, happily skidded into the room and snapped them up. Megan bent to pet him while Cat said, "Bofur, no!"

Now Megan had annoyed Cat on two fronts.

"You have a damn manager?" Cat said, all but throwing the rest of the pigs into their bowl. "What's next? You got a perfume line yet?"

Megan knew that Cat's reaction to unwelcome news was always to get grumpy and judgmental. She knew that Cat loved her and worried about her. She'd seen Cat's stink eye hit Ellen as well as Thea and Sam's husbands in their time. Everyone always allowed it and waited for her to calm down.

"Yasmin knows the business that Alessandro's in. She's controlled his image for a long time—she and her publicist—"

"Oh, now you're going to have a publicist." Cat threw up her hands. "Am I going to have to make an appointment to see you on Sundays, too?" She nodded to Megan's phone.

"No," Megan said patiently. "We tell Yasmin what we want to do. She makes it work. That's her job."

"What does she get out of this?"

"First, don't you want to know what I get out of this?"

Cat waved her hands around. "I know what you get out of it. I'm not immune to that boy's looks."

"He's the same age as me," Megan pointed out. But what did that matter? Cat was fourteen years older than Megan; she could only ever see her as a child. "And you married an Italian. What do you have against Alessandro when you haven't even met him?"

"Meg," Cat said, as though talking to a very simple person. "He. Is. Super. Famous. You're going to get caught up in his world, chewed up, and spit out. Those people aren't normal. You're being naïve thinking you'll be able to make this work."

Megan's patience began to send biting sparks down her arms. She kept the smile on her face. "I'm working with the people who do know how to make this work so I won't be spit out. Didn't you go through some difficulties when you and Antonio met? And you overcame them. I'm just looking to spend time with someone who wants to spend time with me. You're acting like I'm being unreasonable."

"Ugh." Cat stalked to the other end of the kitchen with the bowl of pigs in blankets, opened the back door, and put the bowl on the deck table someone had cleared off. "Food!" she shouted to the two teams huddled behind three-foot walls in the backyard. Megan, drifting out after her, saw an unwise boy raise his head too soon and get a snowball in the back of the head. She laughed but sobered when Cat scowled at her. "Stay on topic," Cat said, slamming the door.

Megan's patience ran down to her fingertips and stayed there, hovering. She let go of the ends of her hair. "You haven't even met him," she said. "Don't you think you should before you tell me he's not worth it?"

"I don't get to meet him, remember?" Cat pointed out, jabbing a finger at Megan's phone. "I'm not on the schedule."

Megan's patience ran all the way off her fingers and was lost. She opened her mouth, but someone said, "What schedule? Who aren't we meeting?" and Thea and her husband, Liam, walked into the kitchen.

Megan hadn't heard the front door open. Thankful for the few seconds she needed to slow down her heart rate, she hugged her sister and Liam. Cat allowed a hug from Thea and a kiss on the cheek from Liam, then went right back into her rant. "Do you know who Megan's decided to date?"

"Alessandro Rosselli," Thea said seriously. "Well, duh, Cat. Did you see that photo of them? Where did you meet him, Meg? And where's the wine, Cat?"

"I didn't get to it yet," Cat snapped, as though that was Megan's fault, too, at eleven o'clock in the morning.

"He used to be my barista in the city," Megan said, glad to have a distraction from her oldest sister. Thea was the next oldest and always calmer than everyone else, except Megan. She'd had her own struggles in life, and Megan was thrilled to see her relaxed and happy with her stoic, protective husband. "He asked for my help with a fundraiser he's doing, and... well, things escalated."

Cat let out a "chah!" from the pantry.

"Nice job." Thea smiled, tucking herself into Liam's side while he rolled his eyes. "I can't deny he's easy on the eyes. So why's Mother Cat up in arms today? She knew about this when the photo came out, no?"

"When that photo came out, you told me it was a *mistake*," Cat retorted, carrying two bottles of red wine out from the pantry. "You said nothing was going on. You told Ellen that, too. If you remember."

Megan felt her jaw lock. She never got this wound up around her sisters. Why was Cat pushing her buttons today? "I changed my mind," she said in the mildest voice she could muster.

"And now she's going to put all of us back in the limelight, just like before, and she doesn't remember what happened back then, so she thinks it's all going to turn out just fine and—"

That word triggered Megan. "I don't think it's going to be *fine*," she interrupted, making Cat's mouth drop open. Oops, Megan sounded mad. And she never sounded mad. "I think it's going to be a start. Something I want to explore. I don't know where it's going to go. He's surrounded by the most beautiful women in the universe. He has to go back to LA soon. He has a movie to shoot sometime. And a career to manage. So I'm aware that there are any number of things that could go wrong. But I will try to get to know him anyway. Because I *want to*."

Cat did the big-eyed shock face again. Thea left Liam to hug Megan, who had just realized her face was hot. She didn't want to talk about this in front of Liam, because while she loved him for loving her sister, she didn't know him well, and she didn't want the first thing he knew about her to be that she supposedly had the hots for some actor.

Well, she did, but that wasn't the only reason she'd signed up with Yasmin.

"Okay," Thea said, her voice soothing. "He seemed kind of grumpy to me, but if you like him, I trust you. Is Cat right that we don't get to meet him?"

"I don't know." Megan sighed. "Maybe. I guess you can. This schedule is only for this week. After the fundraiser, we could get together if he doesn't have to go back to the West Coast right away."

"There," Thea said. "See, Cat? We'll meet him, and we can make up our own minds. But if Megan likes him, that's good enough for us. Right?"

"You are all missing the point," Cat said, pulling a drawer open so hard something got stuck inside it and shook the entire island. "Dammit!"

"Let me have a look," Liam said quietly. Cat folded her arms and backed up. Liam disentangled the utensils inside and got out the corkscrew. He then calmly opened both bottles and found glasses for them, while Cat turned her back on them all and stirred the chili.

"What's the point?" Thea asked after Liam had handed Cat her glass and she'd had a big gulp. Megan drank, too, and appreciated the light burn of the alcohol entering her system.

"The man could be a damn saint," Cat said. "The *point* is that his world is one this family already dipped their toes into, and you remember how that turned out."

Thea's lips thinned. She relaxed at once, but Megan saw it. The guilt swept in, replacing her irritation. Was being with Alessandro worth all this?

She hadn't even slept with him yet. No matter how hot he was, Megan wanted to spend a little time getting to know him more before she committed herself to that level of intimacy.

Maybe you should commit sooner rather than later, though.

"That was different," Thea said. "Ellen didn't know what she was getting into."

"Neither does—"

"I did, actually," Ellen said. She and Kane and their daughters came into the room. Again, no one had heard the front door.

Megan's face burned. She hated for Ellen to think they'd been talking about her behind her back.

"That's what you call that?" Cat said. Unlike Liam, she'd known Ellen for years, and their ease of relationship was clear by how hard Cat leaned into her now. "The fire and the mugging and—"

"Yes, thanks, Catriona. I remember all of it."

"Ooh, full names, now," Ellen's older daughter, Libby, said. "You in trouble now, Aunt Cat."

"I am not," Cat said crossly. "Give me those platters and go tell the boys to shovel the driveway. It's started snowing again."

"No snowball throwing around Rosie!" Ellen added.

Libby and her younger sister handed over their plates of cookies and veggie sticks and ran out the back door, grabbing a hug from Megan on the way. Megan's heart thumped at the sight of them so carefree, so safe. Libby was only a couple of years away from Megan's age when her father had died.

She went over to Kane and hugged him extra hard. "What's that for?" he asked when she at last let go.

"I—I'm just... happy for you all." She smiled at Ellen, who smiled back quizzically. "And you," she added, turning to Thea and Liam. "I jus—" Dang it, she was welling up. "You're giving your kids what we didn't get. That's a cool thing."

"Honey," Ellen said, pulling her in for a hug. "It *is* a cool thing. And you've been a huge part of the safety our kids feel. You know that, don't you?"

Megan nodded in Ellen's shoulder. "Sorry, I—"

"And if you want to find some of that happy for yourself," Ellen said, "you are absolutely allowed. Right?"

Megan assumed the "Right?" was addressed to the people behind her. She didn't dare move.

"I'm going to guess that this has something to do with you and Alessandro disappearing and not reappearing last night?" Ellen said.

Megan choked. "Nothing happened!" she said fast. "Well, at least, not what you're thinking." Now she really was hiding her face in Ellen's neck.

"You're a grown woman," Ellen said. "You are at liberty to do whatever with whomever. Isn't she, Cat?"

Such a quelling tone, one Megan wouldn't have dared use with her sister.

"She's going to get hurt," Cat said. She sounded as though she could hardly move her lips.

"Maybe," Ellen said. "Maybe not."

"The press are going to bring up what happened with you and Kane," Cat added.

"We're ready for it," Kane said. Megan felt his hand on her back and let out a sob she tried to stifle. "We've talked about it. Megs, listen."

Megan left Ellen's safe arms and quickly wiped her eyes before looking at her brother.

"Be happy," Kane said. "Be safe."

She hiccuped again and gave up on stopping the tears. Could she be both at the same time? She wasn't sure. "I'll try," she said.

"Okay, then," Kane said. "Hey, Liam. You got any more of that wine?"

♦

Chapter 11

Since Megan was the one giving up her privacy for him, Alessandro had to be the most grateful for any moment she spent with him. She couldn't possibly feel the kind of warmth he felt when he looked at her across the table of a quiet restaurant in the North End. They were getting looks from other patrons, but a burly man in a black suit, hired by Yasmin, sat at the next table and discouraged anyone who might have had ideas of approaching them.

Alessandro saw the surreptitious flashes of camera phones, but he didn't care. Well, he almost didn't. Megan looked incredible tonight. His mouth had gone dry when she'd removed her thick fleece coat and revealed a figure-hugging black-and-white geometric-designed dress. A thin gold necklace highlighted the pulse in her throat, and her dangling gold earrings made him want to move them out of the way and kiss the spot below her ear that had made her shiver the other night.

"The students are so excited," Megan said after the waiter had delivered her lemon drop cocktail and Alessandro's Milano-Torino. "I can't wait for them to get pampered."

"I had to stop some of them from skipping school to get ready," he said.

"Very hard to do. Do you think they will anyway?"

He shrugged. "We can only give them a good night and hope they have learned the rest. *Salute.*"

Had she chosen that drink because the yellow contrasted with her dress so perfectly? Her gold jewelry glowed brighter in the dim light of the restaurant. And the spark in her eyes when she talked about the students from the Studio really undid him. She'd adopted them as easily as if they were part of her family, and when they'd arrived together at the community center the other night—after a photograph outside her building and another at the entrance to the Studio—the kids had treated her with the same lack of admiration they treated Alessandro. Megan seemed to be happy with this. Then one of them asked her what they should wear, and he lost her to a chattering group in the corner for half an hour. By the next morning, Megan had contacts at three local department stores ready to dress them all. Yasmin's team got approvals from the kids' caregivers, and they were going to run a red carpet at The Rosette.

Megan had made that happen. She'd made more people happy, without even blinking.

So Alessandro wanted this dinner to be for her. And that meant giving her something back.

"When did you move to America?" she asked.

"When I turned twenty." He glanced behind them and lowered his voice. "This is just for us. Not for the plan."

Megan's eyes widened and she leaned in. "You're scaring me."

"It is not a big deal," he said. "The older I get, the less it matters. But when I started out, I did not want to be associated with my life in Italy. I thought it was hard enough to be taken seriously, so I hid it."

"Okay, so I'm not scared anymore, but you're killing me with the hints."

He smiled, and she smiled back. And if the cameras caught him reaching up to stroke her jaw for a second, then that was what they caught. "When my parents and I first... agreed I needed to leave, I had very little training in acting. Only what I could get around my school. But I did have something else that I could... *monetizzare*. What is that? Make money with."

"Monetize, I guess."

"Oh." He laughed and shook his head. "Sometimes I say an Italian word and people think I'm speaking English. Some days I do not know which language I'm speaking."

"Do you dub your own movies into Italian?"

"And French. I learned when I was modeling."

He looked at her very hard, but her expression only showed comprehension. "That's what you did?" He nodded. "Well, of course that's what you did! Alessandro, I'm still getting over the fact that your parents threw you out when you were still a teenager! They're lucky you didn't get a way worse job than modeling!"

"They didn't see it that way. We were still talking then." He leaned back and took a sip of his drink. The bitterness matched his memories. "I can say it was my only choice, but it was not. I knew it would piss them off, and I loved that."

"You were so young. You fought back the only way you knew how. Who did you model for?"

He gave her a few names. "I was afraid you'd recognize me when you first came into the coffee shop. I could tell you knew your designers." He nodded respectfully to her dress.

She brushed a nonexistent speck from her dress. "My one vice."

"That is not much of a vice, *cara*."

"You say that because you lived in that world. My sister Sam wears cargo shorts to every event."

He laughed because she did, but he heard the pain in her voice. Now he didn't want to meet her family, because he was really beginning to dislike them for putting doubt in her mind about her worth.

"So you modeled and saved enough money and came to America?" she asked.

Megan wasn't the sunny innocent she put out to the world. Yet he still hated to allow the more sordid realities of a model's life into hers. She didn't need to know about his move into studio photography and the sleazy photographers who thought their fee included free access to the model.

"I grew," he said instead. "Got too big for the runways."

"Too tall?" she said.

"Too... big," he repeated, gesturing to his chest. Half the guys he worked with had eating disorders to keep to the weight requirements, but Alessandro wasn't about to damage his health when his future career depended on it.

"I know," she said, covering her mouth. "I just wanted you to point it out."

"Oh." He'd been moving back into a dark place in his mind, to the fear that had gripped him when he'd taken that final flight to New York and left his agency. But Megan was teasing him back to the present with her mischievous eyes and that hidden, sideways smile.

He laughed at himself, and she rewarded him by taking her hand away from her mouth. "What made you choose Boston?"

"A friend of a friend had an apartment where I could stay," he said. "And I like it here. I like being close to the water but still in a city. I liked the people. And I liked that I got a job." He smiled. "That was a big plus."

"For a few of us," she said. So what else was he going to do but lean across the table and kiss her?

He kept his hands to himself for the rest of the meal but was happy to help her with her coat and have her take his arm when they left. One brave customer found a way around the bodyguard and asked for a selfie. Alessandro found it much easier to smile for this picture than any other. Megan stayed to the side, though she gave him a proprietary look he wished he could take his own photo of.

A sleek black car picked them up outside the restaurant and drove them back to Megan's apartment. The car had a black partition between the driver and passengers, which Alessandro took full advantage of, stealing Megan's lips for the entire trip, until she was giggling and pushing him away. "The car stopped, Alessandro!"

Yasmin had insisted he leave her chastely at her door. "Moving slow will look good for you right now," she told him. He didn't need her Machiavellian plans, as Megan had made it clear she wasn't about to leap into bed with him. But he could give the planted photographer and the guard at her building a show when he kissed her one more time.

And it worked. The stories the next day gushed over their "romantic evening," how "Rosselli has found more from his trip home than a catch-up with old friends." And "Megan Fielding's style fits the celebrity lifestyle of new flame, Alessandro Rosselli."

Just as Yasmin had promised. He just wished he didn't feel so much like a pawn in a chess game.

◆

Megan liked her wardrobe. She loved finding clothes that fit her body type but were also comfortable. She loved her shoe collection. She had what the sample-size world would call big feet, so some of her shoes were custom made.

The rack that sat in the middle of her living room was packed full of clothes—sleek evening gowns, avant-garde pantsuits with pointed hips, maxi dresses hand-embroidered from shoulder to hem, palazzo pants, and structured blouses. All gifts from designers. All beautiful. Sent over by Yasmin's team with a note. "Pick some, make note of the designers, and enjoy."

Megan stared down the rack of clothes. She hadn't chosen them. Hadn't gone to boutiques, chatted with the saleswomen, spent a happy Saturday afternoon picking out accessories.

She already knew which dress she wanted to wear tomorrow night. She'd gotten it from one of her favorite stores. She and Alessandro had visited it just the other day. Another opportunity she'd had to make this... arrangement work for people she cared about.

Yasmin had explained that Megan's idea of photo ops to give her and Alessandro more time out of the cameras was a long game. "For this week, let them see you. Don't change the story by sneaking around, Alessandro." Alessandro had rolled his eyes at this. "Yes, I'm talking to you. I can't help you if you don't let me help you. So use the cars, go to the restaurants I gave you, and let them take their shots. It'll pay off later. I promise."

He'd raised an eyebrow at Megan. "It is up to you," he said. "I understand if–"

"I'm still in," she'd said at once. She'd already gone against the wishes of her family. She was damned if she was going to let a little thing like the celebrity game stop her from being with Alessandro. So she could wait a week to really be alone with him. A week wasn't much, was it?

♦

Chapter 12

Megan had wanted to get to the fundraiser early to help Ellen and the others with the setup, but they had vetoed the idea. "You helped those kids get dressed up," Ellen said. "Go enjoy their moment. And have one of your own with your handsome young man."

Although he was already living at The Rosette, Alessandro came in the usual black car to pick her up that evening. They timed their arrival to coincide with the bus that had been hired to bring the students from the community center, but they hung back, not getting out of the car until the kids had walked the short red carpet into the hotel. Megan laughed in delight as they nailed their poses; at the same time, she had to stop herself from tearing up at their beautiful outfits, hair, and makeup.

"Okay," Alessandro said beside her, where they'd been looking out of the blacked-out window. "Our turn."

The driver, whom they hadn't shut out this time, came around and opened the door so Alessandro could step out. Cameras flashed, the crowds babbled, and Megan's heart rate skipped up. He gave the cameras a wave, then reached inside to help her out. She put her hand in his and followed him into the cacophony of sound and light.

For a moment, she was blinded, but Alessandro's hand squeezed hers. He pulled her to him for a second and whispered, "You got this," and she took strength in his belief and stood straight next to him. She was ready.

She wore the dress she'd already picked out, and the hell with those designers who didn't even know her. She'd gone with a bias cut dress in a shimmering green shot through with gold threads. The diagonal cut meant that the shape of the dress changed all the time. The dress was tight in the bodice and sat off one shoulder, the long sleeve on her right arm ending in a medieval-style point. She wore a gold and emerald solitaire ring from a costume shop and no other jewelry. Her hair was up in a sleek braid that wrapped around her crown. *Like Leia at the end of* A New Hope, Sam had texted when Megan had sent her a picture a half hour earlier. *I hope your Han deserves you.*

Megan stole a look at her date while the flashes made her eyes buggy. Turned out, he was looking at her. And the admiration he'd held in his eyes ever since she'd met him in her lobby made all the strain of the last few days worth it. Now he took the hand he hadn't yet relinquished and kissed it before backing up so the cameras could take her picture alone. They hadn't scripted this, but Megan struck her pose anyway—the kids wouldn't want her to let down the team—and gave her biggest, brightest, most carefree smile.

And the more the cameras clicked, the more she looked around and popped her hip, the more Alessandro gave her that proud smile, the more natural it began to seem. Megan loved pretty clothes, and these people wanted to see them. By allowing the public into her life, she got to show off what made her happy and help others at the same time. Where was the downside?

She laughed all of a sudden, and Alessandro came back to her side. "Together!" someone shouted.

"Yep," he said, then looked at her. "You okay?"

"I'm grand." She smiled and put a hand on his chest. His tuxedo was so finely made, it almost had no texture. She laughed again and he laughed back at her, though his brow furrowed in confusion.

"Let's go make lots of money," she said so only he could hear, and they walked the line into the hotel.

One face in the crowd in the lobby stuck out to her. Her annoying, wonderful brother, looking front-page ready in his custom tux. She hugged him, and he stood her at arm's length to inspect her. "At least one sister gets my sense of style." He grinned. "You look good, Megs."

"You're not so bad yourself," she said. "You wanna meet Cat's nemesis?"

"Happy to." Kane shook hands with Alessandro. "Good to meet you."

"And you. I hear you were personally responsible for a quarter of our tickets selling out within twenty-four hours."

"That's an exaggeration," Kane said. "But let me introduce you to a few of my friends."

"Megan!" one of the students called from behind her. Megan turned around and was called to admire all the outfits of the group who'd huddled near the hallway. They took photos of her and each other, and she worked with them to make sure all the hashtags were included as they uploaded them. When she looked around her again, Alessandro and Kane had disappeared and an usher was shooing them out of the hotel lobby and into the banquet hall.

Ellen was waiting for them in a stunning black-and-white ombre sleeveless gown, her blond hair around her shoulders shot through with silver jewels. Megan went through a long round of introductions before a man in waiter clothes whispered in Ellen's ear and pulled her away. The students melted into the crowd, and Megan was alone.

Usually, she was the one making sure everyone was having a good time. At Fielding events, Kane was the star and she was the one in the waiter outfit—well, not quite, but at least something unobtrusive. She'd already lost count of the number of photos people had taken of her tonight. She giggled to herself at her "transgression." But boy, did she love this dress. Why shouldn't she show it off?

Etta appeared out of nowhere in a shiny black jumpsuit and braids gathered up in a half pony, showing off the most palatial earrings Megan had ever seen. Susie was similarly glamorous, and Megan's heart swelled. These women, of anyone in the room, deserved a night to be the stars.

Megan perused the auction items and bid on a few. Kane's influence was here, too, but Megan observed with pride the display of dresses from her favorite boutique—not that she had a favorite boutique in Boston; that would be like choosing her favorite niece or nephew. But this one, like the others she'd asked this week, had donated or lent all the clothes the students were wearing, and for that they deserved all the hashtags in the world.

The grand prizes, however, were Alessandro's props. A traditional drum he'd played in *The Drummer*. A pair of boots he'd worn in his second movie, with the soles signed by him and his co-star. Even the mug he'd used in one scene already had a list of names and bids on its sheet.

As the evening went on and the guests sat down to dinner, Megan found herself in the unique position of not doing the talking. Everyone was having a perfectly good time without her having to chivvy them along or cheer them up. She kept a small smile on her face, in case anyone looked at her, but after the first flurry of photographs, no one did. The students were divided up among the tables, and they made corporate CEOs sit back in their seats, gripped by their stories. The students did more to advertise the Studio than any social media post Megan could create.

She barely glimpsed Alessandro, who was in crowds of women and men, chatting in a way that would do serious damage to his brooding reputation. She loved this side of him: this enthusiasm, this need to give back, this determination never to forget who had helped him get where he now was. If her job tonight was to sit back and let him do his thing, then she was satisfied.

But then he got up on the stage, and Megan suddenly found herself extremely *unsatisfied*. He'd taken off his tux jacket and rolled up his sleeves and, holy Italian hell, had she been a forearm woman before? Because she sure the hell was now. His tux was a midnight blue that brought out his eyes, but now his white shirt against his olive skin and dark beard drew everyone's eyes to him. And made Megan recollect their last private kiss, stolen in that car before the more photogenic one they offered the cameras. God, what would she give to mess him up right now.

"If I could have everyone's attention," he began, and the music that had been playing in the background stilled. "We are going to do a few introductions, then you will have fifteen more minutes before the bidding closes."

There was a flurry as people found seats. Kane flopped into a seat next to her. "Hey," he said.

"Hey. Did you eat?"

"Doesn't matter. I got into a bidding war with Joaquin Turner on that TV."

"Kane," she hissed. "You have three TVs."

"I know." He grinned. "I'm going to give it to the Studio."

She shook her head. "You big softy."

"Isn't that why we're here?"

"Yeah, yeah." She leaned so they could touch heads. "Thanks, Kane."

She didn't just mean the fundraiser.

◆

Alessandro looked out over the crowd. The lights were up, so he could easily spot Megan a table or two back, her head resting against her brother's. That was cute. She really did love her family.

"First," he went on, "I would like to introduce the women who are the reason I'm here. Who let a clumsy kid who barely knew which end of a stage was which into their classes and encouraged him—and chided him"—he smiled at Etta and Susie in the front row—"to be the best he could be. I literally would not be standing in front of you without them. Please give it up for Etta Mayer and Suzanne Jackson."

He led the applause and stepped back to let Etta and then Susie take the podium. They began with a blush-inducing rundown of his own achievements, during which he had to stand there while the audience gave him a standing ovation. He put his hand to his heart and then held it out to them, as he'd seen the American actors do with such ease. He thought it was *sdolcinato*—for God's sake, Keanu Reeves had done it in a rom-com to show what a perfect boyfriend he was just by being himself—but if it showed his appreciation for his mentors in a way they'd understand, he'd do it.

He looked over at Megan and let Etta's other words wash over him. Megan's beauty shone out in the room, alongside that incredible dress. She'd told him she'd chosen it herself and she'd catch hell for it when Yasmin found out tomorrow, but that was one of the things he loved already about Megan—she knew her style and stuck to it.

She wasn't touching Kane any longer, just sitting with that half smile Alessandro had learned was her neutral face, the one expected of her. He loved that he'd seen her natural expressions—both happy and pensive. And he'd seen those lips bruised and flush from his kisses. He suppressed a sigh. The evening was far from over yet.

One hand turned her wineglass around and around. Occasionally, her brother would say something to her and she'd laugh easily. Alessandro couldn't remember the last time he'd held a light conversation with his brothers. He was the youngest, like Megan, but unlike her, arguments about his future had begun before he was even out of middle school. His brothers knew where their parents' affections lay, and he didn't blame them for wanting to keep them. Whatever rebellious streak he'd been born with couldn't be talked or threatened out of him, and when he'd told them he wouldn't be continuing with school after sixteen, they'd stopped speaking to him.

Megan's body language showed how comfortable she was with her brother, and he'd seen the affection she and Ellen had with each other. What was that like? And was Alessandro going to break that with this crazy idea of wanting to spend more time with her? Kane had been perfectly friendly to him, and Ellen had accepted him right away, even speaking Italian to him. But what would happen when he went back to LA? He already knew he wanted more time with Megan than just this week. They'd barely scratched the surface of all he wanted to know about her. At their last dinner, they'd talked about childhood summers, agreeing without words to focus on the good times, before Megan lost her parents and Alessandro's walked away from him.

Megan lit up when she talked about her family, but she also lit up when they discussed the work she'd done for the Studio. There was no denying the animation in her face when she talked about making other people look good. Feeling good and making others look good were one and the same for someone as generous as Megan, and she had the means to do it. Perhaps some of her optimism would rub off on him.

But who did he think he was to break into her life like this? What was a shift in career to the comfort and love she received from her siblings?

"...and I have to mention Megan Fielding," Susie, who had taken over the podium, said. "Our Amazon in shining armor, who came in at the last minute and not only kicked our promotion into high gear but got us this incredible venue. Stand up, Megan!"

She did so and gave that clear, uncomplicated grin that made Alessandro grin in return. She was born for this kind of work. Dressed to perfection, bowing out of the limelight when needed, stepping up when required.

He was vaguely aware that people's heads were turning between the two of them, since Megan wasn't taking her eyes off him except for a second to bow to Etta and Susie. His own big grin wasn't going to win him any most-grumpy-movie-star awards, but he didn't care. He was the one who'd have ten minutes in a car with her at the end of the evening. Not a whole lot, but he'd take it.

Etta thanked The Rosette and Ellen next, and Alessandro watched Kane stand at once to applaud his wife. Thank God they'd made it through that situation all those years ago.

Etta and Susie wrapped up, and Alessandro directed everyone back to the auction. He stepped down from the stage and joined Megan's table. This time, he was determined to stick by her side until absolutely required not to.

Kane stood as he approached and relinquished his seat. "Time for me to mingle," he said. "Also, I think that rat bastard Turner is about to steal my TV."

"What TV?" Alessandro asked, taking Kane's seat.

Megan put her hand in his. "One of the auction items. He's in a bidding war for it."

"So... I shouldn't double the last offer?"

She laughed. "No! Well, you can. But we're trying to make Kane like you, remember?"

"True." He looked into her eyes. "I might do it anyway, but I don't want to leave being right here."

Megan went pink and ducked her head. "Me too. Where did you leave your jacket? You don't want to lose track of it."

"It was gifted," he pointed out. "It'll turn up."

"Well," she said. He caught a deepening in her tone. "You look pretty good without it."

"Thank you." He took a chance and nuzzled her neck. In front of God and everybody. She smelled so good, lemony and bright. She rewarded him by giggling and also shivering. Alessandro got a surge of frustration he could assuage only by breathing her in and stealing a kiss on her one bare shoulder.

Megan shivered again. "Keep doing that, Mr. Rosselli," she whispered, "and you might not make it to your next speech."

"You promise?" he said against her skin.

She shook him off with a laugh. "Come on. We have work to do. Well, you do. And if you could maybe cover up a little, it would make it a lot easier for me to concentrate."

"My dear Ms. Fielding," he said. "Are you ogling me?"

"I've been ogling you for ten years," she admitted. Alessandro cracked a laugh, and she gave him a gentle swipe on the arm. He caught her fingers and kissed them, watching as her eyes went black. Turning Megan on in public was his new favorite pastime. There was no masking with this activity; she was as open to him as his own loosened bow tie.

Yet, unfortunately, she was right. He had work to do. He could have sworn he'd met everyone in the room, but Etta was soon there, dragging him off somewhere else. He took what felt like a hundred more selfies before he could beg off and go back to the podium.

The announcement of the winners was just for bragging

rights. The winners would stand in their seats, accept applause, maybe pump the air in victory. Alessandro's props got gasp-inducing donations. Kane got a cheer when he won the TV. Megan won a spa weekend in the Berkshires, which she was going to give to Etta. Alessandro wondered what he looked like when he read her name. He was a good actor, but his own personal stake in what made Megan happy must have shown on his face. He couldn't resist blowing her a kiss, and the audience ate it up. *Sdolcinato* be damned.

Susie had been frantically calculating the numbers from the auction sheets and now came up to the podium in tears. "Three hundred thousand dollars!" she sobbed. Alessandro had to hold her to help her stay standing. The audience freaked out, the stage got mobbed, and he barely had a chance to grab the mic and thank everyone before he was buried in backslaps and handshakes.

◆

Chapter 13

"Goodbye! Yes, goodbye! Yes, it was wonderful. Yes, I'm so glad. I know! So much money! Yes, we'll talk tomorrow. Okay, okay. Goodbye!"

Megan lost count of how many times she said goodbye—to the same people—before she and Alessandro finally got out of the hotel and into the waiting car. Alessandro had the same problem, only he did it in two languages, so it sounded way better. He handed her into the back seat, followed her, and the driver closed the outside world on them.

There was a moment of silence when they just panted a little and looked at each other. "That was fun," she said.

He laughed and dragged his hand down his face. "So much fun. So much fun I could sleep for a week."

"When's the last time you gave a speech?"

He thought about it. "Never." He scratched his beard. "The salon convinced me to put something in this, and it itches."

Megan took his face in her hands and felt his beard with her fingers. "Mm," she said. "Maybe you used a touch too much." She scooched closer to him. "Let me see."

God, she wanted to be close to him. His PDA at the event had been a giant tease. He hadn't put his jacket on until they were about to leave, so she'd had to look at those forearms, the gentle play of tendons and muscles when he held her hand or even took a drink.

She had it bad.

She'd told him she wanted to get to know him a whole lot better before she let him into her bed.

Yeah, forget that. She knew what she needed.

She kissed his lips slowly, tantalizingly, not deep, just playing with him. Then she used the tip of her tongue to touch each of his lips in turn, making him groan. The partition window was closed, so Megan felt not the slightest embarrassment. She felt powerful.

Continuing to tease him with her mouth, she grazed her fingernails along the edge of his beard, feeling the cord in his neck tense and harden. "Meg," he begged.

"'Sandro," she replied against his lips. He groaned again. She kept her fingers exploring his hot skin, fluttering under his loosened collar, feeling the rigid muscles under his shoulder. She pushed aside the collar and touched the skin with her tongue. Alessandro gasped, but she laughed and captured his lips again, still light, still teasing, but he had no ability to do anything but what she wanted.

Thank God her skirt was full so she could straddle him on the deep car seat and work on the other side of his neck. The prickle of his beard on her hands, the contrast between that and his lips, made her want to open a window to cool her heated cheeks. But she wouldn't because this was where they could be entirely themselves. No one else could come into their world for now. For tonight.

He put one hand on her hip to hold her on his lap, and then it was Megan who gasped as he began to knead her butt, squeezing and releasing, rocking her into him and away so that, in the end, she couldn't help but drop her head back and grind down on him.

Now he had the control, and he knew it. He took her hips and pushed them down harder before feeling for the hem of her dress and grabbing at her calves, then her thighs. Megan moaned and tipped her hips up to let him get even closer, and—

The car stopped. And didn't start again.

"*Gesù*, that was quick," Alessandro growled.

"Are we home already?" Her voice seemed to come from very far away. But when Alessandro began to remove his hand, she sat down harder on him.

Despite the darkness of the shaded car, she could see his impossibly light eyes, melted with desire and frustration.

"This hairstyle," she said.

"What about it?" he asked gruffly.

"I might need some help taking it down."

"Meg." He tipped his head forward until their foreheads touched. "Don't kill me. Don't, please, don't."

"'Sandro," she said, putting one finger to the corner of his mouth. "Come upstairs with me."

He turned his head and sucked on her finger, drawing it fully into his mouth. Megan let out a peep of pure lust. Gods, if he didn't get her upstairs right now, she was going to make the driver roam the streets of Boston all night.

"It is not in the rules," he said, though he didn't let go of her finger.

"I think I found a new vice," she whispered, replacing her finger with her mouth. "Come home with me."

"*Cara.*" He let go for two seconds, nodding to the world outside. "They will see. Are you sure?"

"God, yes, Alessandro." She was still sitting on his lap, and she knew he would go home a very injured man if she gave in to Yasmin's rules right now. And she would go home a lonely, frustrated, pissed-off woman. So.

"Yes. I'm sure."

She got off his lap and began to straighten him. Her hair was already beginning to fall out of its braid, but she couldn't help that. She arranged her skirt back around her ankles. The driver hadn't even gotten out of the car, but when he heard Alessandro open the door, he opened his. "Don't worry," Alessandro said loudly through the closed partition and got out. "I have it."

He sure did. The cool air hit her burning cheeks. She didn't care if they burned. She didn't care who saw. She was inviting the man who made her feel sexy into her bed. And he wanted to go. That was all that mattered.

"You can go home," she told the driver through the passenger window, which he'd opened. He betrayed his surprise by only a slight contraction of his brows.

"Certainly, madam," he said. "Have a good night."

"You too!" she sang, because shit yeah, she was going to have a good night.

Before the car could drive away, she and Alessandro were past the scheduled paparazzi and inside her building, and she was smiling at the night guard.

"Good evening, Ms. Fielding," the guard said.

She was all done with small talk. "Hi, George. Have a good night!"

The moment the elevator doors closed, she pushed Alessandro against the wall and kissed the bejeezus out of him, just in case he was thinking of changing his mind. Didn't seem like he was.

She kept an arm around him when they left the elevator and went into her apartment. She turned on a couple of lights but kept things dim so they could see the view from the floor-to-ceiling windows in the corner.

And now they were alone, really alone. And Megan suddenly got shy.

She walked to the windows, keeping her back to him.

"What is it, *cara*?" he asked behind her.

"I... haven't done this in a while," she said to the windows.

"We don't have to do this at all," he said softly.

She turned to him. "No. Not that. Just..." She shook her head.

Alessandro took her into his arms with a tenderness she wouldn't have believed she needed. "It is a conversation, *cara*," he said. "A wonderful, joyful conversation. You tell me what you want, and I provide it to you. And if you do not agree with the subject, we change the subject."

She laughed at the metaphor. "That sounds good." Which was when Alessandro's arms around her drew her to the couch that faced the windows. He sat her down and instructed her to put her head in his lap–face up.

"I believe you needed help with your hair," he said. He began by pulling out a few pins, until her braid lay in his hands. He gently pulled off the hairband that held it together and then slowly, tantalizingly, separated the strands. Once he had her hair freed, he began to stroke it, laying it down against her shoulders and breasts. He didn't outright touch her breasts, but Megan had to bite her lip not to arch into his delicate touch.

He felt in her strands for more pins, then just massaged her temples. Megan moaned with pleasure, her eyes fluttering closed, helpless. Alessandro's strong fingers worked their way over her scalp, turning her to mush in his lap.

She couldn't let him do all the work. "My turn," she said, pushing his hands away. She stood and pulled him with her into the bathroom. Alessandro cocked one eyebrow when she began to unbutton his shirt to reveal his chest and those shoulders she'd wanted to kiss so badly before.

"You didn't have to get off the couch for this," he said, but Megan shook her head.

"I don't want to get that lovely shirt wet." Alessandro barked a laugh, and she cocked a hip at him. "Hold still." She began running water in the sink, testing it with her hand until the temperature was perfect. Then she wet her hands and ran them over his beard, moistening it. The thin channels of water that ran down his neck and onto the hair on his chest–oh shit.

Megan paused to take in his chest. Hairy, like his beard. God. She was going to explore that in a minute. But first...

She worked soap through her hands and then began to pat it through his beard. Alessandro hummed with pleasure, making her grin. She massaged him the way he'd done her, then moistened a washcloth and wiped off the soap.

He was shaking now, and Megan felt her power anew, no longer afraid that she would mess something up or not be what he needed or some other nonsense. She cleaned him up and then ran her mouth along his jawline and down his neck to his chest, finding his nipples with her tongue until he sagged against the counter. "*Merda!*" he growled.

She knew what that meant. In this case she guessed it was a good thing. She ducked her head and let her hair play over the sensitized nipple. Alessandro twitched, and now his hands were vises against her upper arms. He pulled her back to his lips, and this was no kiss for the cameras. This was messy and wet and ferocious, and Megan was bent backward with the force of it. He picked her up without breaking the kiss and began to walk out of the bathroom.

"Wait," she said against his lips, then opened her condom drawer, something she hadn't done in two years. Alessandro grinned and carried her back to the couch.

He felt behind her back for the zipper, and Megan might have gone on teasing him, but she couldn't stand the wait herself after that kiss. She said, "It's on the side," and reached for it.

"No," he demanded. "You must let me do it."

Megan obediently put her hands to her sides. And Alessandro tortured her by unzipping her inch by careful inch, kissing each sensitive morsel of skin as it was revealed from her ribs to her hip. His other hand felt for the dress' shoulder and slid it off her arm, and the dress slipped to the ground, leaving Megan in a strapless bra and panties and a great tidal wave of want.

"You are," he said, touching her stomach, setting a finger under her panty strap but not pulling, "so beautiful, *cara.*"

Like he wasn't? Sitting in winter moonlight, dressed only in dark pants, his chest rising and falling with the same want she had coursing through her? "This conversation," she said through gritted teeth while his hand continued to do and yet not do what she really, really wanted it to do.

"Si, *cara?*"

"Maybe we could make it more of a... ah!" His hand had dipped low, and Megan's knees came up involuntarily, making him laugh, low and dirty. "Quick chat," she managed to finish.

"Sure," he said, sliding his hand down and back again. "Tell me what you want, Megan. Tell me everything you want."

Was it his accent? Was it her previous hookups that had been predicated on none of them lasting more than a few weeks? She had never been so turned on in her life. She directed him to her breasts, to the removal of her bra, to the removal of his pants, to a glorious moment where both of them were naked and Megan had to writhe on the couch with sheer joy at it all.

"Now," she said, trying to put authority back into her voice—which was difficult when Alessandro's hand was stroking the very, very top of her thigh—"you need to let me put this on, and then you need to stop teasing me. Dammit!" Because of course as soon as she said *tease*, his fingers flicked out to touch her even more closely. "You are a devil," she gasped.

"I am your devil," he promised, and he looked as though he might be, darkness and light in the shadows, danger and safety and the naughty sparkle in his eye. Megan put the condom on him and then sank back into the couch, willing him to lie on top of her without her having to ask.

Seemed as though their conversation was going just fine, even without words. Alessandro stretched on top of her, kissing her breasts on his way. Megan raised her knees again, and he kissed her mouth and entered her at the same time, catching her joyful gasp in his mouth.

"Devil man," she scolded, making him laugh, and when he began moving, she realized that she apparently had gone over to the dark side because she never, ever, ever wanted him to stop. She told him that and he swore he wouldn't.

"Never, ever, ever," he said with the rhythm of his hips, and she caught it and repeated the words back to him, and now one of her feet was on the ground and she was bucking into him, and he was swearing in Italian and English. He bit her shoulder and Megan scratched his back and tilted her hips and he shuddered and yelled and that last bit of movement made her cry out as well as the moonlight shattered around them.

◆

Chapter 14

Alessandro woke up in Megan's bed before light. His muscles were Jell-O, but he wouldn't have missed this workout for anything. Her hair spread out between them, so he kissed the tips and drew them to his nose to smell that intoxicating scent that was hers alone.

He couldn't help but smile at the effect he'd had on her. She'd gone from sunny, cheerful Megan to dirty, demanding Megan. And all he'd had to do was take off his jacket.

But there was nothing wrong with sunny Megan, and he didn't want her to go away. He didn't want Megan to change for him.

He sat up and wrapped his arms around one knee. Last night, she'd said he was her new vice. Would sunny Megan regret giving in to that vice this morning?

It would be much better for her if he thanked her for an incredible night and left. The fundraiser was over. They'd raised an inordinate amount of money. He could go back to LA. She could go back to her family, to a life he hoped would now include her own dreams made reality. She didn't need him for that. She didn't need him for anything.

His calves cramped, and he straightened out his leg with a hiss. Well, maybe she could use him for *something*.

His movement made her stir. She looked at his pillow and then his seated figure. "You okay?" she said, her eyes wide.

"Very okay," he smiled. "You?"

"Very okay," she repeated, then winced. "Sore. In a good way."

She sat up next to him, rubbing his back. He loved her touch.

Loved how she cared. He might not deserve it, but he loved it nonetheless.

He dug his knuckles into his calf until the cramp subsided. Megan went to get water for them both. "Too much wine and not enough hydration," she chided, handing him a glass.

He took the glass and drank from it.

"Okay," she said. "Something's wrong. Tell me."

He tried not to get distracted by her naked body kneeling next to his. Her breasts and hips were perfectly in proportion, perfectly rounded. Her body on his, the second time they'd made love right here in this bed, had been the ideal blend of heavy and pliable. Shit. He was getting *really* distracted.

"Nothing is wrong," he said. "I would like to know if... What will happen now? And I don't think either of us has the answer to that." She might, of course, if the answer was to throw him out forever. But he couldn't say the words.

"Where's your phone?" she said in a non sequitur. "Actually, where's my phone? I didn't take it last night. Where did I leave it?"

"I—how does that answer me?"

"We'll see what the reaction was to the fundraiser. And if anyone cares that you stayed over last night."

"I do not want to make decisions based on what the public says about us," he complained, knowing he sounded like a petulant child. He'd signed up for this, and it was his fault if he'd given in to her last night and broken the rules.

"We won't," she said. "But the reaction will tell us *how* to go on making our own decisions."

He wasn't sure he followed her, because that "vice" comment was still racing around his head. If the press was up in arms that he'd spent the night here so soon after "breaking up" with Nikki, would Megan use that as a reason to send him away?

But he'd follow her lead until he could ask the question

directly. Megan opened her phone, and a cascade of pent-up texts began to ping onto her screen.

"Yasmin," she said resignedly. "Yeah, she's a little mad."

"Not *that* mad or she would have called."

"I guess so. The usual I-wish-you'd-tell-me-first story."

"Like we planned this."

Megan gave him her halfway smile. "Maybe I did plan this."

He laughed and stroked her arm. "You are not that artful."

"Is that a bad thing?"

"It is exactly what you should be."

"Good. Because I—" She looked down at his hand on her arm. "I would be real, real happy to do it again."

He had to ask. "To prove to Yasmin that you can't be controlled? Or because you want to be with me?"

She started back. "You think that's why I invited you here last night? To put one over on Yasmin?"

He knew he was fishing for compliments, for assurances. But Megan's opinion of him *mattered*. He didn't want to be just a step on her journey to independence. He wanted... he didn't know what he wanted. Just not to be pushed aside when she found it convenient.

Megan's face was serious as she looked away from him, and then her hair fell over her shoulder and hid her. Alessandro moved it back; he didn't want any partitions between them right now.

She shifted so she faced him again. "I invited you in last night because I wanted very, very badly to. Honestly, I wasn't thinking much beyond that at the time. I wasn't thinking about Yasmin or my family—"

"Thank God," he put in, and she smiled.

"Right. So, honey," she said, taking his hand in a more tender than suggestive way, "I choose you. I don't know what happens next. But right now, I choose you."

Alessandro couldn't speak. Her words sank so deep, they stole his voice. He gathered her into his arms, burying his face in her loose, thick hair. "I choose you," he repeated.

"Good," she said matter-of-factly, but she sank into his embrace.

◆

Megan knew they were going to hit hell when they let themselves leave this room and this paradise of understanding. They could ignore the outside world all they liked, but it wasn't about to ignore them. After they'd made love again and he'd put coffee on—complaining about Megan's perfectly good coffee machine as he did so—and toasted a couple of bagels, she allowed him to scroll through their mentions while she scrambled eggs. They had agreed not to talk to Yasmin until they'd eaten.

"Most of it is the fundraiser," he said. "The official photos aren't up yet, but the gossip sites have theirs." He angled the phone toward her. "How do you like it?"

Megan paused and looked at the photo of the two of them on the red carpet. "Hey," she said. "Look at us."

"Flawless. *Impeccabile.*"

She had to agree. Whatever she'd learned from her years of scrutinizing fashion and how celebrities chose and wore their outfits had paid off. She allowed herself a pat on the back for how good the dress looked and how good she looked in it. When she was done cooking, she would have to make sure she tagged the store. They deserved their own post.

"What about the kids?" she asked, and Alessandro found shots of the students posing, laughing, pouting, and having the time of their lives.

"That's wonderful," she said sincerely. "I'm so glad. Do you think the community center can give them what they need to graduate from high school?"

"With the money you helped them raise? Yes. And the adult classes, too. I know Etta wanted to make a pathway for homeless people to get work skills. Now maybe she can do that."

Megan's PR brain jumped to press releases, updates, polls, photo opportunities. Then she remembered that, aside from a few official thank-you posts for the Studio, her work with them was officially done. She wasn't prepared for the disappointment that swept through her.

"The eggs, *cara.*"

"Shoot." She pushed them off the heat so hard, the pan almost fell off the stove.

"It is no problem. I like them a little crispy."

"No, I'll remake them."

"Don't." He reached across the counter and grabbed her hand. "You have cooked for me. I will eat whatever you make."

Blushing hard, she turned off the heat and checked on the eggs. Only the very bottom was crispy. She plated them up and gave him his.

"What made you look so sad?" he asked as she came around to sit with him at the counter.

"What? I wasn't sad," she said at once. "I was... distracted." She nodded at his outfit, which consisted of his tuxedo pants and nothing else.

He smiled. "Nice try. Tell me."

"I was just thinking... Well, but it doesn't matter."

"It does matter. Do not fall back into those patterns. Tell me what you want, Megan."

"Oh, sure. Sit there looking like an entire snack and ask me what I want." He shook his head at her. "Okay. I was just thinking... wondering, really, if there are other charities that could use a little bump. I hadn't thought about the fact that not everyone knows how to build a social media presence like I do. Maybe I could do that in my spare time. It didn't take much to help the Studio. I couldn't make a fundraiser like that happen again, but..."

"It sounds like you're passionate about this. So do it."

"Okay. I'll put out some feelers. I don't want to offend anyone."

"You have not been around charities much. They are dying for help. You only have to offer."

"Okay, I will."

She'd been involved with the foundation Kane ran, but that was a slick organization with paid employees and top-tier graphics. She blushed again at her assumption that everyone had that kind of help.

They ate in silence but side by side so they were always touching. Alessandro kept scrolling, and Megan weaved dreams in her head. When her plate was empty and Alessandro's coffee was refilled, she retrieved her own phone. Ignoring the messages from Cat and Yasmin for now, she found a photo of her and Alessandro and tagged the store that had sold her the dress. When she got back to her profile page, she was shocked to see she had gained a hundred thousand followers overnight. "Lord," she said.

Alessandro looked over her shoulder. "You're an influencer now," he said.

"But... I'm not ready."

He laughed. "You were born ready. Look at you."

All she was wearing was a soft cream-colored lounge suit—a tracksuit, basically, but looser and in a fine cotton fabric that draped just the way she liked it.

"You could walk out of this building dressed like that," he said, "and you'd be better dressed than most of the people in the city. You've got style, baby," he added in a terrible impression of...

"Was that supposed to be Frank Sinatra?" She frowned. "Elvis?"

"I don't know," he admitted, which cracked her up. "My point is, you achieved something on your own."

"With some pretty good eye candy on my arm," she said. He inclined his head in thanks, and she went back to checking out the reactions.

In another minute, she found her first negative review. "Oof," she said, and the punch to her gut did indeed feel physical.

"Do not read the opinion pieces," he said. "They have nothing better to do than tear you up."

"Down," she corrected absently. "So you saw this?" She turned her screen to him. His face told her that he had.

Another Fielding Gets Famous by Standing Next to Someone Famous, the headline said. Megan closed one eye, as though that would soften the blow, and read the article. They had gone into the archives, and most of the pictures were of Kane and his old girlfriends. And they were determined to give both her and Kane hanger-on status.

"Your brother knew what he was doing," Alessandro said.

"He told me it was just a happy accident, meeting Didi Ravello. The company was in trouble back then, and his name being in the media helped." She glanced sideways at him. "And I might have only been in college, but even I knew he was having a hell of a lot of fun at the same time."

Alessandro barked a laugh. "I hope she did, too."

"Ew." Megan shuddered. "Moving on!"

"*Scusami.*"

"Anyway. I guess they were right. That was why it was so hard for Ellen when she came along. Cat thought she was using Kane the way the other women did. Not 'using,' just…"

"Enjoying," he put in.

"Right."

She looked back at the article. "That is *not* what I'm doing," she said.

"I know." He hugged her. "You are not your brother. I am not an actress looking for eye candy."

Megan hoped she believed him.

Enough looking at the bad news. She opened her email instead. Today was Saturday, but Megan often spent weekends at work.

What she found, though, made her gulp and squeak, "What?"

"What?" Alessandro said.

"I've got—" She opened a few of the latest emails. "Eight—no, ten—job offers!"

"That is wonderful, *cara*. Of course people want you after seeing your work with the Studio."

"I'm not—don't they know I already have a job? I—they're sending it to my work email, so yes, they know. I can't believe this!"

"Believe it."

"I can't." She hopped off her stool and began pacing. "I'm not looking for a new job! I meant volunteering for the charities. Not a whole new job!" She clicked on one of the offers. "This is a global marketing company! This is a fashion house! These guys run a foundation like Kane's." She waved the phone at Alessandro. "I was just talking about PR for the foundation, and these guys want to *pay* me to do it!"

"It sounds as though you would love it," he said, but Megan didn't want to hear it. Why were people acting as though they knew what she wanted better than she did? She came to a screeching halt in front of the rack of clothes that still stood in her living room. Yasmin thought she knew what Megan wanted to wear. And these people sliding into her DMs thought she was desperate to leave the job she was born to do and jump ship just because of one successful campaign!

Her phone rang. Cat. Megan was wound up enough to answer it.

"Go on then," she said by way of greeting.

"Why weren't you answering your phone?" Cat began. "And I thought you weren't going to sleep with him?"

"This is why I didn't answer my phone," Megan said coldly. "And the other thing is none of your business."

"It's all over the internet!" Cat spluttered. "I don't want to make it my business, but you're dragging the family into this! Did you see that article about Kane?"

Alessandro had joined her, and she knew he could hear Cat's voice through the earpiece. He touched her wrist, gently guiding Megan to the couch so she could sit down. Which was when she realized she was shaking.

"You blame me for some asshole doing a Google search?"

Megan didn't curse. But doing so would make Cat sit back a little. Which was what Megan wanted.

"Listen," Cat said.

"*You* listen," she retorted. "I'm thirty-one years old. Do you remember that?"

"Of course I do."

"Because you've sure the hell treated me like a ten-year-old ever since Mom and Dad died."

A year ago, when Sam had come home for Thea's wedding, she'd dared to mention their father in less-than-flattering terms, and Cat had blown up. Megan had done her reconciliation routine, going after Sam and asking her to make up, keeping the status quo. Well, she was tired of it.

"I didn't know ten-year-olds got to run companies."

"I'm not running it," Megan pointed out. "Remember? You and Kane got this brilliant idea that I should be the new kid in every single department until *you* decide I'm ready for a window office."

"You agreed to that! You should have told us if you—"

"You never asked!"

"Jesus, Meg, you make me sound like a monster. You rave about everyone you work with. How was I supposed to know you didn't like it?"

Megan rubbed her free hand down her face. Her muscles were taut, strained. She spent all her time making the best of things. She was the best actress in the goddamn world.

"I..." She ran out of steam for a second. "You've got me well trained," she said quietly.

"What the hell kind of statement is that?"

"I can't have one night with the hottest man in the world without feeling guilty because you don't approve!"

"*Grazie*," Alessandro said dryly next to her.

"*De nada*," she replied, which was the wrong language, but she was too focused on her sister to care.

"It's not about him," Cat said hotly. "God, you're so naïve. Look what they're already saying about you! You think this is going to get any better?"

"That's my problem."

"It's *our* problem. Did you forget that the family's reputation is what keeps your income going?"

"Thank you, Cat. Yes, I do know that, since you remind me of it every Sunday at the family mausoleum—I mean, house."

"God. Are you drunk? I've never heard you talk like this."

"You've never heard any of us talk like this. It would do you good if we did."

Cat paused. Megan hardly knew what she was saying. She only knew the words wouldn't stop coming. She couldn't halt them. She couldn't care about them.

"Okay," Cat said, quieter now. "So I'm a monster. That doesn't change what the papers are saying about you. I didn't make that happen. You're not thinking clearly, because if you were, you'd see—"

"I'm not thinking clearly because I don't agree with you? Yeah. That's what I thought. I'm not doing this anymore," Megan said at the exact same time as she realized it. "I'm sorry I'm younger than you by a lot. I'm sorry you had to raise me. I'm sorry Mom and Dad died."

"Meg!" Cat's voice was scandalized.

"I'm sorry I got to work at Fielding Paper and you didn't."

"*Meg!*"

No one *ever* brought that up. "I'm done being the good girl," Megan said. "I'm done trying to live up to some ideal no one's even explained to me." And she hung up.

She sat for a second, her head dropped, her hands slack. Her phone began to slip out of her hands, and all of a sudden, she stood and threw it across the room. It hit the rack of clothes and disappeared into their folds.

She let out a cry she didn't know she possessed. Stalking back across the room, she clutched her head with her hands. "She wouldn't let up! It's my fault! It's always our fault! She doesn't even see it! God, I should have done this years ago!"

The raised step at the entrance to the apartment tripped her. She let herself fall, twisting so she could sit on the step, though she bruised her butt. She grabbed her hair in both hands and pulled until she felt a few hairs tear away. "I'm sick of it! I'm sick of being the happy one! Fuck, if they knew what it does to me!"

She was shaking again. And crying. She hadn't realized that. Years of tension seemed to leach out of her all at once, and all she could do was sit with tangled legs and a sore scalp and sob and cry and yell.

And if she'd been Alessandro, she'd have tiptoed around her and left the apartment.

But he didn't. She became aware that he'd padded across the

room when his bare feet appeared in her blurred vision. He sat next to her. She gulped and cried some more. Then his hand touched her shoulder and gently moved to her back. He rubbed her back with wide circular strokes. Megan couldn't resist them. Whatever chill she'd hoped he'd think she had was shot to hell anyway. She collapsed against him.

"It will be okay, *cara*," he murmured into her hair.

"I'm so tired," she said.

"Yes. You have been acting for a long time. Perhaps it's time to take a break between movies."

She laughed and the tears slowed. "I was just thinking I've been the greatest actor in the world. And that's after being in the same room as you."

His body shook with a laugh. "I get to choose when I act. I think you only just realized how little of yourself you have shown people."

He was putting it into words better than she could. She was done smiling. She was done taking her lunch hours to help people with their jobs because social protocol dictated she should.

She was done with Sundays under Cat's scrutiny.

Her sore heart shied away from making *that* decision.

"Go back to bed, *cara*," Alessandro said. "Sleep for today."

God, that sounded good. "I'm sorry," she mumbled. "You didn't sign up for this."

He squeezed her, hard enough to make her gasp. "I am honored that you allowed yourself to let go around me. I do not want to see you so sad, but perhaps this is necessary. When you don't answer the question of what you want for so many years, the answer may frighten you."

She shivered again. "I'm glad you're here," she said into his chest.

"Me too."

She might just change her name to Cara so she could hear it over and over again when he wasn't around. Because surely he wouldn't be after this meltdown.

"I will make sure you are asleep, then I will call the car to take me back to the hotel," he said.

She nodded. She'd figured as much.

"I will change," he went on. "And then I will come back with more clothes. Do you have a gym here?"

She looked at him quickly, then remembered her face had to be a puffy mess. She covered it with one hand. "Yes."

"Then I will make use of it if that is all right. I need to keep my workouts regular or my producers will *really* be mad at me."

"You're staying?"

"If you will allow me," he said.

Megan shook her head. "I'm a mess."

"You are resetting yourself. I would like to keep you company for the next couple of days while you do that. If you would like."

She flung her arms around him, sending them both to the floor. "Yes," she said. "Yes, you polite, caring, beautiful man. I would love to close the world outside and stay here with you."

"Good." He laughed and kissed her before setting her back on her own butt. "Go to bed." He pointed to the bedroom. "I will deal with Yasmin."

"What if... what if she calls me back?"

"You are allowed to set a boundary with Cat. For now. When my family and I fought, we didn't set boundaries, and we said a lot of things that were very hurtful. A... breather, I think is the word, is what you are looking for. Just for this weekend."

◆

Chapter 15

Megan slept. And slept. She roused when Alessandro brought her food but barely stayed awake long enough to eat it. When she got to a point of being able to ask what time it was, she was shocked to find it was eleven o'clock on Sunday morning.

"This is when I should be driving to my sister's," she told Alessandro while she sipped his coffee.

"Do you want to go?" he asked.

She thought about it. "I'm tired," she said.

"So rest," he answered simply. And the decision was made.

She woke again later that afternoon. Blinking motes out of her eyes, she sat up, and her hands went at once to the tips of her hair. Not going to the family home on a Sunday had drawn a line in the sand. And Megan was going to have to deal with whatever fallout it caused.

She stumbled out of the bedroom to find Alessandro in her largest easy chair, in those adorable thick reading glasses, reading a book. Even with bedhead and worrying about the future, Megan had to admire him. Was anything sexier than a man reading a book?

"Hey," she said and cleared her throat. Her voice was scratchy from disuse.

"Hey!" he answered, jumping to his feet. He was wearing black jogger pants and a tight dark-gray T-shirt and looked like a hug in a human. Which he then proved by enclosing her in his arms.

"How did you get out and back?" she asked, her voice muffled in his chest.

"I told them to use a regular car and to come to the parking lot entrance in the back," he replied. "It worked going out, but they figured it out on my way back."

Megan looked to the windows. He'd pulled down all the blinds, closing out the nighttime view and protecting them from drone cameras. "You've thought of everything."

"Not my first rodeo." He smiled. "That is the phrase, right?"

"Right. Have you had food? I don't think I had much—"

"Our driver delivered," he assured her. "Come sit at the counter, and I will make you dinner."

"Don't," she pleaded. "I can't take you being so nice when I look like this."

He stopped in the middle of pulling her into the kitchen area. "You are right," he said, nodding his head seriously. "I had not thought of it like that. I should leave."

She poked him.

"*Cara*," he said, continuing to pull her. "I have had, I think, the most peaceful weekend of my life. Nothing to do but read, watch movies, and sleep. You have given me a slice of heaven."

She laughed and sat at the counter where he directed her. "Sure. I do my best hosting while asleep."

He opened the refrigerator, and Megan could only adjust the collars of her pajama top and watch as he poured her a glass of wine and put pasta on to boil. "Wine in my jammies?" she said. "This is quite the party."

"I will also change, if it makes you more comfortable," he said, raising an eyebrow.

"No. You look okay as you are." She raised an eyebrow back, drawing a grin from him.

"*Pasta alla Gricia*," he announced ten minutes later, putting a plate of perfectly swirled spaghetti with a light, creamy sauce and dots of guanciale in front of her. Megan realized she hadn't eaten in hours and dove in. The juxtaposition of salt and cream made her moan.

"Fine. You can stay," she said, her mouth stuffed full. And they ate another meal side by side. A lot had changed since the last time they did this.

"You can tell me the rest," she said after they'd eaten and she'd cleaned up after pouring him another glass of wine. "What are the press saying now? And Yasmin?"

"The press will not have anything to say until you or I reappear. I turned off your phone when they found your number. And Yasmin is mad at both of us for not sticking to the plan."

"You mentioned your producers before. What's their part in this?"

"I can take care of them," he said at once.

They'd had such a lovely meal. Now she'd made him back off. "If we're going to keep doing this," she said gently, leaning on the counter opposite him, "we have to know who's vested in stopping us." He became very interested in swirling the wine around his glass. "So you should tell me."

He sat back on his stool and looked her full in the face. "You are right. I am sorry. The producers of my next movie were upset at the... incident with Nikki. The next movie has a strong romance in it, and they want me to be likable."

"You are likable."

"Thank you, *cara*. They want me to be likable outside this apartment." He waved around him. "That is why the photograph of us made things more difficult for Yasmin."

She took a sip from her own wine. "Sometimes you talk about Yasmin as though she's the one living your life instead of you."

He looked away, thinking. "Perhaps. Perhaps it is easier to do what Yasmin tells me. When I make my own decisions, I get in trouble."

"All you did was stop me from getting churro sugar on my coat."

"Best decision I ever made. It got me here. Right here." He tapped the counter with a finger. "Right here."

She wanted to melt. "Good. But we still have to do something about your producers. Me asking you to stay last night—"

"The other night—"

"Oh, right." God, twenty-four hours was a long time in celebrity gossip. "Well, you've been staying here since, so it wasn't a one-night stand. And we did officially start dating more than a week ago, so I think waiting all that time was remarkably restrained of us." That made him grin. "So if we stopped seeing each other now, your producers will think you're jumping from one woman to the next."

"Ouch."

"I'm playing devil's advocate. What I'm saying is, if we keep seeing each other and you don't punch out any more paparazzi—"

"I did not punch him!"

"Right, sorry. You know what I'm saying."

"*Cara*, you are giving me a reason to do what I so want to do. It seems too easy." He stood. "I think you are right, though."

"Yeah? Cool."

"You are very clever, Megan." He came to her side of the counter and slipped his hands around her waist. "Megan, *tesoro*. Will you go on a date with me?"

"Alessandro, sweetheart. It would be my pleasure."

He kissed her as his thank-you. But when he pulled away, he said, "Then for now, I will go home and let you get a good night's sleep."

"For real?" Her heart dropped into her slippered feet.

"At night, they will get less of a photograph of me, especially if I use the parking lot trick again. Will you go to work tomorrow?"

"Of course! Why shouldn't—"

She stopped. There was no "of course" about it now that she

was all over the gossip pages. "Well, yes. I do still have a job, I hope. Unless Cat's persuaded Kane to fire me," she added dryly. "And I like my job. I only have a couple more weeks to do it before I move departments. So yes. I'm going to work."

"It will be different now," he said. "The car will not want to stop for coffee."

Megan twitched her shoulders. "That stinks."

He stretched his arms up, revealing a sliver of lean belly and a hint of hip. "Yasmin has suggested you have a bodyguard," he said. "He will follow you into the coffee shop."

Ah, the stretch was to relieve his tension at mentioning the idea. "We're at that point?"

"I always have fans who are... enthusiastic," he said. "None have risen to the level of stalker. But it is something we have always had to be ready for. And Nikki's fans... might not have believed the press release."

Megan shook her head this time. "Okay, fine. A bodyguard so I can get my coffee in the morning. Right?"

"She would rather—" But Megan glared at him. "Okay, okay." He laughed. "You are frightening when you are determined."

"Well, I'm determined to get some of Roman's coffee in me before I face the music at work."

"Face the music." He frowned.

"Deal with whatever happens there," she clarified.

"Ah." He reached for a bag he'd left by her front door. "I will call you tomorrow."

Megan put one arm around him, as one side of him was taken up by his gym bag. "Okay." She lifted her face and he kissed her, slow and sweet, until it was on the tip of her tongue to ask him to stay.

But he said, "Until tomorrow, then," opened her door, and in another second, he was gone and she was alone with the life she had now chosen.

She might as well have had The Greatest Showman standing by her bed with a top hat and a bullwhip to wake her up the next morning. The circus was in town, and she was the main attraction. She'd turned her phone back on, and after listening to an eye-watering number of voicemails—including some from Kane and Thea, though none from Cat—she called Yasmin. Her new manager had some choice words about her detour from the plan over the weekend and specific instructions on her movements for the trip between her apartment and her office.

"Remember what they did to Kate," Yasmin said in a doleful tone, and Megan thought she meant Kate Hudson until she remembered the Kate who'd married a prince.

After sleeping so much, she couldn't get more than a couple of hours rest that night. At three a.m., she turned off every light in the apartment and raised the blinds, because the lack of view was beginning to choke her. Within five minutes, a shadow buzzed across the window, a tiny red light flashing in its depths. Megan, who'd been contemplating the buildings across from her and the lives of those in them, ran and hid behind a pillar. Then she lowered the blinds again.

So at Yasmin's designated time, Megan emerged from her building and walked with purpose—"But don't run!" Yasmin had said—into the fresh air. The black car waited at the curb.

Her passage was marked by maybe two handfuls of photographers, clicking away and asking her to look at them. She didn't, but she was confident that her rust-colored, high-waisted, narrow wool pants would be shown off to their best advantage in the photos. Above them, she wore a swing coat in a beautiful cream, with matching gloves. Her hair was down today, with only a small clip holding it off her face. If the wind blew it in front of her and spoiled their shots, welp. Sucked to be them.

The driver held her door, and she slid into the seat, letting her patent brown boots be the last things the media saw. Next, she noticed the bodyguard who had disentangled himself from the front of the crowd and got into the front passenger seat. He was built like the driver: thick and solid and unsmiling. As the driver got in, the bodyguard gave her a quick look to make sure she was all there, and they began to drive.

This was ridiculous. The coffee shop was a five-minute walk from her building. And she'd spent a week in the car with this driver, thinking she'd never see him again, and she didn't even know his name. Now there were two of them.

"Hi," she said to them through the open partition. "We should introduce ourselves, don't you think? I'm Megan."

"Yes, ma'am," the bodyguard said.

"No problem, ma'am," the driver said.

"Right." Old Megan might have stopped there. Maybe they couldn't share their names. But New Megan wasn't going to sit behind two men the size of a couch and not find out what they were called. "I'm not going to call you 'yes' and 'no problem,' guys. Come on."

"I'm Nelson," the driver said.

"Aye, aye, Captain." She saluted. Then she remembered that that joke would only be funny to Ellen, whose random facts about British history tended to float around the family get-togethers.

The ones Megan had just closed herself off from.

"Terry," the bodyguard said. Megan gave him a quick glance, but all he shared with Terry Crews was smooth dark skin and shoulders wider than the seat he sat in.

"It's my pleasure," she said. "And Nelson, I'm sorry I–"

"We're here," he said, and the next thing she knew, Terry was opening her door and standing like a boulder between her and the entrance to Oh Beans! A group of what looked like regular people was standing in a line outside the door. As Megan got out of the car, she noticed a couple of them had very professional-looking cameras hanging around their necks. The wood and metal of the shop were obscured by more people.

Her first thought was to get right back in the car and let Terry and Nelson hide her away. Then she thought of what Old Megan would have done: given everyone a smile. Walked into the crowd and made everyone feel good. Felt pretty good herself when she was done.

Who had she done that for? Megan paused as phones were raised in front of her. This was important. Who was she doing this for?

The wind blew her hair away from her face. She hadn't wanted to touch the ends of it once this morning. She placed an experimental hand on her hip and posed. The phones stayed up. She smiled, and a few of the people in line smiled back.

"You ready, ma'am?" Terry asked.

She looked at him, making sure he knew she saw him. Knew that if this was going to be a dog and pony show, she was going to make sure he got to enjoy it, too. "I'm good," she said. "Let me buy you a coffee."

"I can't—" he began, but she turned left, and he had to scoot to move the photographers who were on that side.

"Ma'am," he said as she walked to the back of the line. "You can go on in. They know you're coming."

"No way," she said, thinking of the office Leo had wanted to give her. And that headline, making her out as some hanger-on. If any of them did the math, they might realize that she probably had more money than Alessandro. She didn't need him. She wanted him. There was a big difference. "I can wait."

"Megan!" a voice she recognized said through the murmur

of the crowd, and Grace appeared with a large paper cup in one hand and a tray with bite-sized morsels of what looked like cinnamon rolls in the other.

"Grace," Megan said, feeling her cheeks heat. "You didn't have to come out on my account."

"To be honest," Grace said, thrusting the mug into Megan's hands and pulling a bag out of her apron pocket, "we've got a crowd-control problem inside. People are hanging around after they get their drinks to get a sight of you."

Megan groaned. Just as Alessandro had said. "Grace, I'm so sorry. Tell Roman I—"

"Don't worry about it." Grace's open, friendly face made her almost believe she wouldn't.

"I'm not the famous one here," Megan tried to explain, aiming her words at the crowd.

"That's what Kate Middleton said," Grace replied, which was when Megan realized Yasmin had given them the heads-up. She'd probably given the gossip sites the heads-up as well, hence the crowd.

"Okay. I... thanks for the coffee."

"And this is your pecan roll," Grace added, giving her the bag. Megan wouldn't get her morning banter, her whiff of the store's deliciousness, the pretense of choosing a Danish. None of those small moments of joy.

"Thanks, Grace."

"No problem. We'll see you soon."

Grace looked at her a little oddly, then suddenly launched at her to give her a back-cracking hug, almost tipping over her tray. She pulled away just as quickly and turned to the line Terry was now easing her away from. "Roman's cinnamon rolls," she said brightly, though Megan thought her voice sounded tight. "Thank you all so much for waiting."

Terry ushered her into the car, and Nelson scooted them out

of there before Megan could even process the hug and what it meant. It had felt like a goodbye.

At the office, she could barely say hi to the security guys before Terry got her to the elevator. He stared down anyone who wanted to go with her and pressed the button before stepping out. "If you plan on leaving the building for lunch, text Nelson," he intoned as the doors closed.

Well, now Megan would starve before she did that.

She got fifteen seconds to herself as the elevator hummed upward, but when the doors opened, seven people got out of the other three elevators at the same time, making her exit from an empty car all the more of an entrance. She knew them—all of them; she'd made sure of that in her years here—yet now they all gave her a curious stare as though she were behind glass at the zoo. For a second, she got an urge to strut past them with her nose in the air like a she-leopard, maybe with a shake of her tail at them as she went.

"Hi, Megan!" the receptionist said with forced brightness from behind her desk. Megan knew she was trying, but her voice was like cut glass to Megan's ears. Over the past week, she'd doled out careful snippets of her dating life with this woman, knowing it would spread over the whole company. She admitted to anything the papers had already published and smiled and shook her head if anyone pushed their luck.

But she was done smiling this time. This had gotten way too important. She'd lost too much. "Good morning," she said without her usual fervor. She just didn't have it in her.

All eyes were on her, and no one was moving. They were probably stunned that she wasn't immediately racing around the room, asking everyone how they felt and if there was anything she could help with.

She wasn't going to do that today. The very thought made her long for her bed again.

Britney stopped by, and Megan was so taciturn, she might have permanently damaged their friendship. Friendship? What had Britney ever done for her?

All morning, colleagues with various degrees of curiosity "happened" to stop by her cubicle. Most just fished for information. To the one or two who actually asked outright how Alessandro had been, she raised an eyebrow and looked at them, unsmiling. "You don't really expect me to answer that, do you?" And their eyes got big and they stammered a little, and New Megan felt a shot of power at their discomfort while Old Megan begged her to smile.

Eventually, a messenger came to her desk, accompanied by Terry, with a burner phone as mandated by Yasmin. Megan dropped it into her bag without looking at it and held her head up with her hands, closing her eyes at her buzzing computer screen.

◆

Chapter 16

Alessandro could think only of going to the Studio. He'd been the first to text Megan's burner phone, whose number Yasmin had given him "and no one else, 'Sandro!"

"Who else would I give it to?"

"Your buddies at the Studio? They know way too much about her as it is."

"Because she volunteered for them. And they like each other." He thought of what Megan had said about Yasmin running his life, and he started pacing his hotel room again. "You worry too much," he said.

"The last time I relaxed," she said with an acerbic tone, "George Michael took an unscheduled trip to the bathroom."

He laughed because she wasn't that old. Was she?

"But now you are dealing with a woman who knows where you're coming from," he argued. "She works in your world."

"The corporate world and my world play by different rules."

"So teach her the new rules. She is very clever. She will learn fast."

"'Sandro," Yasmin said. "I want this to work for you. I do. She seems like a good kid. But I wouldn't be doing my job if I didn't warn you: civilian and celebrity romances rarely work out. You've both got reasons to do this that don't have to involve any kind of commitment to each other."

"You were the one who said Hollywood loves a romance."

"I did, but I didn't think you guys were *serious*."

Alessandro paused in his well-traveled walk from the bedroom to the living room to the tiny kitchen and back to the bedroom. He was about to reply, but then he realized. Yasmin was fishing. She wanted to know what he and Megan were planning to do with their futures. Well, hell. So did he.

So with no answers for Yasmin and only a short text interaction with Megan that day, he had to accept he couldn't see her until that night, if then.

He could spend the day reliving Friday night: recollecting every soft inch of Megan's skin, moving his fingers as though he could touch the tips of her hair, remembering her scent and how she'd writhed when he ran his lips up her thigh. He'd never loved making love to a woman more. And he'd never loved sitting in bed with her the next day, talking, sharing the problem they'd created and finding solutions. Even when her family had interrupted their bliss and shaken Megan's confidence, the fact that she'd allowed him to see her fall apart—he'd loved that too. In fact, if he hadn't had only two weeks to get to know her better, he'd be tempted to say he—

Alessandro grabbed his phone and his sunglasses. He had to do something with himself instead of obsessing over Megan.

The Studio's schedule that afternoon included acting classes for the kids who'd attended the fundraiser, so Alessandro called Nelson to drive him to the community center. For the sake of Yasmin's blood pressure, he decided not to walk through town.

His reception at the Studio was gratifying if a little embarrassing. Charlene risked the height of her blond curls to all but throw herself across her counter to hug him. Susie held him for what felt like five minutes. And Etta—somehow this was worse—Etta took his hand and squeezed it, and her eyes welled up, and she said nothing at all.

"Come on, guys," he said in his best American accent. "Gimme a break, will ya?"

"Pretty good," Susie said, recovering enough to laugh at him. "You've been practicing."

"You know they speak with a different accent in LA?" he asked, eyes wide, hoping that jokes would cover his embarrassment. "I had to learn English all over again!"

Thus distracted, he got them to allow him to sit in on the afternoon sessions, and he even found himself leading the class for a few minutes—even if his presence did make all the classes start late because everyone had to go over the fundraiser, minute by minute.

His well of human excellence filled, Alessandro left the Studio at nine o'clock, and his thoughts returned at once to Megan. How had her day been? Her text had been annoyingly mundane. Did she want to talk to him as badly as he did to her? Or had real life awakened her to the insanity of being in his world?

He sat in the back of the limo while Nelson drove him to a weary night of room service. He'd call her, of course he would—he wasn't about to ghost a woman after a night of lovemaking that could make a man change his entire future—but the farther they drove, the more nervous he got. She had more to give up than he did. He only had to give up his lack of trust in people.

He used his special card to get in at the employee entrance and took the stairs rather than wait for the elevator. Back in his room, he tried not to think about how much more homey Megan's apartment was. Pale-blue walls glowed like the ocean when the sun came around to them, and a deep slipcovered couch—oh, that couch!—and thick rugs made a large open-plan living room cozy. Yes, The Rosette was a five-star hotel with a Michelin star hanging on its restaurant. Alessandro would rather be doing the dishes in Megan's well-used kitchen.

His fingers had dialed her original number before he remembered the burner phone. He was about to hang up, but her voice came on the line.

"Hi," she said.

He tried to figure out in that one word how she was feeling. Impossible. "Hello," he said instead. "I thought you turned off this phone."

"I haven't given the new number to my family yet. I don't even know which of them are still talking to me."

"Your eldest sister is the one you had the argument with. You think the others will take her side?"

"They called me on Saturday. I didn't call them back because..." She paused. "Because I didn't want to."

"Did you see your brother at work today?"

"No."

He heard the pain in her voice. "I am sure he is not ignoring you. He must have been busy."

"Yeah."

He wanted to take that pain away so badly. But he didn't know how, short of having Nelson drive him over to her apartment again, and that would just feed the gossip machine.

"He will not take Cat's side over yours. I met him, remember? I could see how much he loves you."

"Thanks."

She sounded so defeated. She'd chosen him over her family this weekend, and now she was suffering for it.

"I am sorry I am not there," he said, the words going straight from his heart to his mouth. "I would cook for you. And I would pour you a glass of wine and choose a movie with you."

"That sounds great," she said on a sigh.

"What are your favorite dishes?"

She was silent for a moment. Then she told him about Thanksgiving dinners when she was a child, before her parents died. Much as he'd appreciated his friends' invitations, Alessandro had never understood the bowls of solid, immovable baked dishes he'd been given when he'd attended their Thanksgiving celebrations over the years. The event itself had been bittersweet for him, watching his friends' families greet each other with joy, going over their family memories, showing him yellowed photographs and playing music they would all sing to. Perhaps that had affected his taste for the food.

But Megan talked about her family's staples and somehow he was brought into the scene. He could smell the cinnamon and hear her father lightly arguing with Kane about turkey legs. He could see the fireplace burning in the dining room that the kids fought to sit away from. He could picture Megan in her boosted chair next to her mother, younger than all of them, fidgeting through the conversations, asking to be excused so she could fall asleep on the squashed couch in the family room, only to be woken by the crowd coming back to watch the football game. Alessandro saw all of it, and his heart broke for her. For all of them.

"Tell me about your childhood," she said, "as the psychiatrist said."

Alessandro began talking, again giving her only the good parts, which also meant the parts before his teen years, before he began disappointing and then infuriating his parents. Before his brothers started laying into him for being "soft." He told her about his family's signature dishes, his grandmothers who were engaged in a silent but furious war for their children's and grandchildren's affection, so Alessandro and his siblings and cousins spent every weekend after church being exhorted to eat for twelve hours straight. He talked of playing football in the streets with his cousins, and how he had to find new friends when they moved from Sicily to Rome. That they'd made fun of his accent and his parents' high-culture jobs until he'd scored so many goals off them, everyone lost count. He'd discarded his Sicilian dialect as fast as possible, the first of many adjustments and compromises he'd made on his journey to becoming an actor.

"Did you ever go back to Sicily?" Megan asked.

"Once or twice, at first. But my parents did not like how we fell back into the dialect. They became Roman and did not want to look back."

"I should have guessed that Italy would have the same snobbery for some areas over others that we do."

"There is pride for our regions, like for your states, but Italy has dialects that can separate us. When I moved to Milan, I had to learn yet another way to speak."

"Why were you in Milan?"

"For the modeling."

They had stayed off the video call, and Alessandro was glad for it when he felt his cheeks redden.

"Why aren't there photographs of you all over the net?"

"Because I used a different name." Alessandro Rosselli had landed in Boston ten years ago, leaving his other self behind.

"I'm sorry, Alessandro."

"Thank you, *cara*." He sighed, and again, the words came out that he'd hidden for years. "I was ashamed of what I did. It was the quickest way to leave my parents' house and make my own money. I met many, many good friends and some creepy, exploiting men—I learned the word *creepy* my first year—and I made enough money to live, and I got to travel all over the world, and I learned English and French and Spanish and Russian. But in the end, I knew if I didn't break away from modeling, I would never become an actor. So I sold everything I had, deleted all my social media under my old name, and moved to my friend's apartment here."

"That sounds terrifying. I've never moved more than a hundred miles from home in my life."

"You have reasons to stay." And he would do well to remember it.

"Mm." He heard fabric slide against fabric. Had he made her restless?

"I am sorry I caused your argument with your sister."

"It was coming," she said. "And it was worth it."

Alessandro couldn't stop the smile that spread over his face. "Whether you mean me or Friday night, I thank you."

"Right now, I mean Friday night."

A vision of Megan, sprawled out on her bed, waiting for him, made Alessandro catch his breath. "I thank you even more."

"It's late," she said.

"Yes." He glanced at the clock glowing in his dim room. "I should let you—"

"No. That's not what I meant. If you were here right now, I'd suggest we go to bed."

"Megan." Alessandro was so aroused he had to adjust himself. But he was up for the challenge. "If I were there right now, I would gather all your hair in my hands and kiss those lips I have dreamed of for years."

"And then?" she said. Her voice was low, breathy, inviting.

So Alessandro made love to her over the phone, and her soft moans and gasped words were his entire reward. She gave as good as she got, until they were both panting and laughing, and he didn't care what time it was.

When his heart rate had somewhat returned to normal, he said, "If I were braver, I would call Nelson right now."

"You'd find only a squished noodle in my apartment," she said faintly. Alessandro laughed.

"You are welcome."

"So are you."

"Ah, *cara mia*. What will we do?"

"I don't know. Just... don't hang up yet?"

"Of course." He couldn't sever this connection between them, not for all the money he owned. "Tell me about your day."

$$\blacklozenge$$

He woke the next morning with a dead cell phone battery and the phone still on his pillow. And a peace he hadn't felt in years, if ever.

He plugged his phone in and hummed his way through his shower. When he got out, his phone was ringing. He ran through the bedroom, naked, to catch it. Was Megan looking to start again where they left off?

"Why the hell don't you answer your phone?" Yasmin shouted.

"What? I was in the shower." What had happened now?

"Get back to LA like right now. Like yesterday."

$$\blacklozenge$$

Chapter 17

"Megan." Leo came around the corner of her cubicle. "Got a minute?"

"Got a minute" were the three little words no minion ever wanted to hear from their manager. Even last night's marathon phone call with Alessandro couldn't protect Megan from the dread that clutched her heart. She stood and followed Leo back to his office. Heads turned to follow her passage. She kept her head up, but her brain was pinging around like a squash ball, trying to find the file where she kept tips for dealing with being fired from your own family's business.

"Don't look at me like that," Leo said as soon as he'd closed his door behind her. He didn't even ask her to sit. "I just want to know if you're okay."

"Oh." Megan let out her breath, which turned into an exasperated "Huh!"

"That good, huh?" Leo smiled.

"I'm sorry about last night," she said. "And this morning." She waved a hand at the floor. As though she could see down nine floors and outside to the so-called journalists who had accosted anyone who came out of the building last night, asking if they knew her. Terry had met her at the elevator and all but mowed the cameras down getting her to the car. This morning, tape was in place and extra security guards were checking building IDs before letting people through. Her circus was turning into a... what was crazier than a circus? A monster truck rally? And Megan and her colleagues were somehow stuck on the dirt, dodging the amped-up trucks, breathing in the toxic fumes of tabloid journalism and celebrity gossip.

"Don't apologize," Leo said. "But..."

She knew it.

"Look," he said. "You're the best employee I've got. Forget about your last name. I mean you."

Megan hadn't expected that. A little of the pride she'd felt at being good at her job came back to her. She'd all but forgotten it. "Thanks, Leo. That really does mean a lot. And for what it's worth, this has been my favorite department of them all. By far."

His lined face relaxed. "I appreciate that. It was going to be hard to say goodbye to you anyway. But since you were going to move to manufacturing at the end of the month and your projects here are pretty much wrapped up, we were thinking—"

We.

As if summoned, Kane threw open the door to Leo's office and strode in. "C'mere," he said roughly and pulled Megan into a back-cracking hug.

Megan hadn't realized until right then how much she needed that hug. She clung to Kane, not caring that Leo was watching. He was the father figure Kane had needed, so he was family.

"Why didn't you call any of us back?" Kane asked, pushing her away from him so he could look her in the eyes. "Not even Thea or Sam?"

Or him, she read in his eyes. "I just needed a break," she said, knowing he wouldn't understand.

"Are you mad at us, too?"

Megan looked away, shielding herself from the hurt in his voice. "No. I just... needed a minute." She didn't know how else to say it. She couldn't tell him that she now understood how much of a strain being around her family was, just as much as being around strangers. It wasn't their fault; they hadn't asked her to do it. But Kane would be even more upset if he knew, and Megan wasn't going to do that to him.

"I hoped you'd come see me yesterday, but then we got the word about the crowds, and I had to work on the security, and then you were gone. And you didn't answer your phone. Again."

"I have a new phone," she said, remembering anew as she said it. How was she going to get used to this? "I'll give you the number, and I'll pick up. I promise."

"And will you talk to–"

"No." The very hint of talking to Cat made her stomach drop. "Not yet."

Kane dropped his hands from her arms. "She doesn't understand what she did."

"She"–Megan backed away from him, reaching for the tips of her hair–"didn't do anything. Not specifically. Not on purpose."

"So why–"

"Because I can't be the good kid anymore," she said. "I need–"

Leo's desk phone rang. "Damn," he said, racing to it. "Yes?" he said into the receiver. "Yes, she is, but we're in a meeting! Tell him to–he said what?" Leo looked at Megan, and she knew then who "he" was. Her face suffused with heat.

"Jeez, okay, okay." Leo held out the phone to her. "Your boyfriend wants to talk to you."

"You're kidding," she said, though she knew he couldn't be.

"Nope. I'm pretty sure he's your boyfriend."

"Leo." She grabbed the phone, just to take that smirk off his face. "Sandro, what are you doing? I'm at work!"

"*Cara*, I have the nomination! Best actor!"

His voice overflowed with excitement. She looked between Kane and Leo, who had obviously heard everything. Leo's smirk was a little more understanding, and Kane's eyebrows were halfway up his forehead. "Well, that's incredible, Alessandro! Congratul–"

"Come with me, *cara*. Come with me to Hollywood."

The room got blurry for a second. "Are you drunk?"

"No! No, I have just had coffee and Yasmin just called and *tesoro*, come with me. There will be—"

"'Sandro!" she interrupted, almost having to shout over his exuberance. He was talking so fast she almost couldn't catch up. "Can I call you back in a couple of minutes?"

"I do not know if I can wait that long. I want you to meet everyone, and you can shop wherever you like for your dress and no one—"

"I have a job!" She pointed at Kane with the phone. "Stop looking at me like that!"

"I cannot see you," Alessandro said as she put the phone back to her ear.

"Not you!" Dear God, her life had completely exploded. "I'll call you back in a minute."

She'd never heard him like this. He'd been amused, enthralled, intense, and pleased. But never this kind of... incandescent. It was hopelessly endearing. She wished she were with him right now, to hug him, to see his serious face light up with joy. She spent so much of her time making other people's lives better. Now this important man in her life was experiencing a life-changing moment, and she wanted to be there with him.

"I will call you in one minute," she repeated and hung up.

"You can't be thinking of going with him," Kane said at once. "You've known each other—"

"Imma stop you right there," she said, putting up a hand. "How long did you know Ellen before you knew she was the one?"

"I—"

Megan raised an eyebrow at him, and he pressed his lips together.

"Actually," Leo said. "It might be a good time for Megan to go."

Megan spun around to him. "What?"

"What?" Kane echoed.

Leo held up his hands. "Calm down, big brother. We were about to suggest a couple weeks' break anyway."

"Yeah," Kane said, "but she can't leave the state!"

"Megan," Leo said. "How bad do you want to move to manufacturing?"

She opened her mouth to give the pat answer: *I can't wait.* But the gray depression that hovered at her side when she thought of it caught the words in her throat.

"I thought so," Leo said.

"You don't want to move? Well, why didn't you say so?" Kane exploded.

"Because she didn't want to disappoint you," Leo said.

"What—how would that be disappointing us? Jesus, Meg, do you think we want you to have a miserable career doing something you don't like?"

"No, I—" Honestly, she hadn't taken her thought processes that far. And while the guilt that she'd upset her family welled up inside her, again, she also noted the *we* in Kane's statement. No matter how often he fought with her, Kane and Cat were the heads of this family. They worked together. And with Sam and Thea married and having a wonderful life with their new husbands, that left Megan. Alone.

"Why didn't you tell me?" Kane asked again, his voice strained.

"I was fine!" she exclaimed. "Honest. I was fine. I didn't mind. Until I did." That was the closest she could get to expressing her feelings of the last few weeks.

Kane scraped his hand through his hair. "My sisters are literally going to kill me," he muttered. "You know the last time I had a straight conversation with any one of you?"

"I wasn't trying to hide anything," Megan said in a small voice. "These past few weeks have been crazy."

"Crazy enough that you're thinking of moving across the country to be with this guy?"

"Not moving. Visiting."

"I did that, remember?" Kane said. "I flew over. Went to the parties. Went to the awards ceremonies. You never saw the person you went with. Their lives are controlled twenty hours out of twenty-four. You'll be expected to look good and stand to the side. And even though you're not the main event, your life will be picked apart just as much as theirs."

"It already is," Leo said.

"But if he leaves her and she—"

The idea of ending things with Alessandro sent a shot of fear through her heart. "Leo," she interrupted. "I'd like to end my internship here a little early. And then, Kane, I'm sorry, but I'm going to take a leave of absence. I need some space to figure this out."

The hurt on Kane's face was worse than anything she'd seen so far. Was this better than telling him her misgivings as soon as she'd felt them? Probably not. Megan had screwed things up. She should just stay. Write Alessandro off as a lovely interlude, stay, and finish the plan the family had for her.

She couldn't. She couldn't breathe at the thought of it. "Look," she said, going to Kane and wrapping one of his arms in both of hers. "I love you. All of you. Just... give me a little space."

"I didn't think I wasn't," he said.

"I know." She released him. "Leo," she said, turning to her boss. "All I've had for two weeks is busywork. The sooner I get out of here, the better for those security guards downstairs. Don't you think?"

"You're not going today," Kane burst out. "What am I going to tell Cat?"

That made her smile. "I love that the one person you're afraid of in this life is your big sister."

"I'm not—"

"It's okay. I was, too. I'll let you know what I decide. Leo, is it okay if I leave now?"

"Sure." Leo nodded. "Your bodyguard can help you with your stuff."

"Thanks." She turned to the door but had to go through Kane first. "Don't worry," she told him. "I'm a big girl now. You don't have to take care of everything for me."

She patted his arm, and he moved to the side, apparently unable to answer. Megan closed the door to Leo's office quietly, not wanting to hear whatever Kane said next.

Back at her desk, she looked at the pictures on her cubicle, the succulent plant she'd carefully kept alive for years, her favorite mug for office coffee—now full because Terry had convinced her to forego Oh Beans! this morning—and her meticulously arranged desktop screen, with the projects she'd worked on for two years lined up in strict rows.

If she went with Alessandro, she would know nothing. Everything familiar would be upended. She would have to learn from the bottom up again. If she stayed, she could build on the skills she had and be the best at the job that had been saved for her for ten years.

She picked up her burner phone.

♦

Chapter 18

She'd chosen him. Alessandro couldn't believe it.

Okay, if he were honest, he must have thought it was possible somewhere in his mind or he wouldn't have called her first and unleashed that embarrassment of emotions all over her.

But who else would he call? Friends, sure. But whom did he *really* want to share this with? Who would be thrilled along with him? Who would know him from his first job in America and appreciate how far he'd come?

So he'd made a total fool of himself and called the office when she hadn't answered either of her phone numbers. He couldn't keep this to himself. And after she'd rightfully told him to wait, she'd called him back and *she'd chosen him.*

"I am calmer now," he said. "And I must tell you the reality of coming with me."

"Kane already warned me about some of it." She was moving around while she spoke. He could hear her breath change and things landing inside other things. What was she doing?

"Yes, he would know. But he was there for a different reason. I do not want you hurt. And they will try to hurt you. One way or another."

She paused, and something else landed in or on something. "I'm not just doing this to stand by your side and look pretty," she said.

"Which you are also very good at."

"Thanks. Okay, Terry. You can take this one."

"What are you doing?" Alessandro asked.

"Tell you in a minute. Anyway. I'm coming for me as well.

I'm feeling… buried here." She paused again, and he heard no sounds around her. He imagined her staring into space, figuring out her reasons. He could be upset that she wasn't just choosing him for him. But that would be pathetic and jealous of him.

"I need a place to get some air, you know?" she went on, her voice quiet. Could people hear her? She must still be at work.

"The air in Hollywood can be suffocating, too," he had to point out. "First, we have to get through Logan, which does not have a private terminal for commercial flights. We can have a private lounge, but you will have to be ready for people to recognize us until we get there."

"I don't mind that," she said. "If Cate Blanchett can wear a three-piece suit and walk through a public concourse to travel, then I can pull something out of my wardrobe that will satisfy them."

"I have no doubt."

"You sound like you're trying to dissuade me," she said, her voice hitching up a notch into amusement. "Having just begged me to come."

"I am begging. And I am also trying to look out for you. It is very hard on my nerves."

She laughed, which Alessandro loved. He felt that she hadn't had much to laugh at the last few days. "Okay, then. I'm going home to pack. When are we leaving?"

"You are leaving work right now?"

"Yep." He heard a drawer close.

"I thought we could leave on the weekend. Don't you have to request time off?"

"I bet Yasmin wants you there yesterday." And while Alessandro gaped at her accurate impression of his manager, she continued. "I'm taking a leave of absence. Again, not just for your sake. I'm invited to the ceremony?"

It took him a second to remember what ceremony she meant. "Yes, of course. And other events."

"Okay. Then I'm taking a leave of absence until then. After that, we'll see. I'll stay at The Rosette in LA, so that—"

"*Cara*, will you not stay with me?"

She giggled. "I might. I was waiting for you to ask."

"Of course. Would I ask you to come and then put you in a hotel?"

"You might. Okay, that's all. Oh, hi, Britney. I'd better go. I'll let you know when I get home."

She hung up on him. Alessandro stared at his phone. Somehow, he felt she was controlling this journey more than he was.

♦

No matter how hard Yasmin wanted him back in town, Alessandro did not make Megan leap on the first plane out of Logan airport. Instead, Nelson and Terry arrived at The Rosette early the next morning and drove him to her apartment. He was going to miss these guys, and he told them so.

"Thank you," they said in stony voices, but Terry looked back at him and smiled. What lives did they lead? Touching on celebrities' worlds and then circling out to land in a new celebrity's world? Who would Terry protect next?

At this time of the morning, no one was waiting for him outside Megan's building. The concierge called up to Megan's apartment, then Alessandro took the elevator and was knocking on her door within a minute.

"Hello," she said when she opened the door.

"*Cara mia*," he replied on a breath. In her loose pale-green yoga pants and a tight zip-up cardigan with a white tank peeping through, she looked ready for a cruise or a month at a spa. Old-school Adidas sneakers were on her feet, and she wore a tiny gold necklace with a moon pendant at her neck. Her hair was up in a high ponytail, showing off her slim neck.

"Good enough for the paparazzi?" she asked, her eyes sparkling.

"Good enough for the red carpet," he replied.

"Don't exaggerate." She laughed and reached behind her for her purse and her suitcases. "I'll be wearing something much better than this for the red carpet."

"I do not doubt it," he said. "Stop, *momento*."

She looked back at him with a frown. He slid his hands on either side of her face and gently held her still while he kissed her. The hell with Nelson and Terry waiting downstairs. He hadn't seen her in two days, and it felt like forever. He got to know her full lips again and her scent and the feel of her jaw against his palms.

"Good morning," he said when he broke away.

She dropped her head to his shoulder. He took the opportunity to comb through her ponytail with his fingers. Still sleek and shiny, and the ends still curled in a way that tempted him.

"I will take care of you," he whispered. "You will be safe with me."

"I'm not afraid," she replied. "It's just a lot to say goodbye to. Even if it's only for a few weeks."

"I will bring you back when you are ready," he promised. "For now, let's see where you rise to."

Nelson and Terry took them safely to the farthest end of the departure drop-off line where fewer people would see them, and Alessandro put on sunglasses and his baseball cap. Megan wore a wide-brimmed tennis visor that hid her face but let her ponytail bounce freely. Alessandro loved that visor.

A rep from the airline walked them through check-in and

security as briskly as possible, but he still noticed heads turning, people wondering. Megan didn't seem to notice, or she didn't care. Her head was high, and she grinned at him after they got through security in five minutes instead of waiting in the long line.

"I feel guilty," she said.

"Don't. If you were in the main line, you would hold things up badly."

And then a woman old enough to be his mother stopped their progress. "I'm sorry, are you Alessandro Roselli?"

"I am."

"I told her! I told my daughter so. Honey!" she called across the corridor. "It *is* him!"

The daughter in question, if that was her, rolled her eyes and then hid her face in her hands.

"Oh, don't mind her," the mother said. "Hey, congratulations! I loved you in *The Drummer!*"

"Thank you," he replied.

"Can I get a photograph?"

Alessandro glanced at Megan, who put her hand out in a go-ahead gesture. The woman pulled out her phone and grabbed his arm as though he belonged to her. But he kept his wince to himself and rewarded her with his signature glower at her camera. She took a couple of shots and then opened her mouth. But Alessandro smoothly drew his arm out of hers and said, "Thank you. Excuse me. We are late for our flight."

He took Megan's hand and all but pulled her along, the airline rep running in their long-legged wake.

"Oh," he heard the woman say as he left. Then "Oh!" She must have recognized Megan.

They had about thirty seconds to get to the lounge before the entire airport knew they were here. Alessandro made it with at least ten to spare.

"That wasn't bad," Megan said after the door was closed behind them. The few people in the lounge were intent on their computers or their children, and the atmosphere was much calmer.

"It was a miracle," Alessandro said, rubbing his arm.

The rep took them to two deep club chairs in a corner and, after bringing them coffee and breakfast, left them in peace. Alessandro could sip his espresso and admire Megan, who smiled at him and pulled a book out of her enormous purse.

After a few minutes, the rep picked them up and led them through an outside door to the tarmac, where a car took them to the plane before anyone else. A steward offered them more coffee and a snack, gave them a full set of headphones each, and implored them to let him know if they needed anything.

"I'm overwhelmed," Megan said with a grin, picking up her second mug of coffee.

"Your family does not travel first class for business?"

"We usually stick to premium economy. It depends on the airline. And we don't bother with the lounges unless it's an international flight, which it rarely is." She stretched her legs luxuriously. "Mm, legroom."

The cabin filled up around them, but again, they were left alone. Megan flipped her legs across his lap and turned sideways, tucking herself into her seat. Alessandro used the excuse of arranging her hood more comfortably around her neck to caress her jaw, eliciting a warm sparkle from her eyes and a kiss to his palm.

They slept during the flight, Alessandro still enjoying the weight of her legs on his. When they saw the skyline of LA through the window, he couldn't believe how fast the flight had gone.

"The last time I saw this skyline," he mused, "I was in a very different place."

"Are you ready to get back in the firing line?" she asked.

"You don't call what happened to you the firing line?"

"Not compared to what's about to happen," she said. "I'm trying to be realistic."

"Do not be too realistic," he said, stroking her hair. "I do not want you to lose your joy for life in this cynical town. I learned the word *cynical* when I moved here."

"I think I was too focused on other people's joy for life. I have to find my own."

The steward came right then, and within minutes, they were in a car and driving to the private terminal at LAX. There was no partition, so they had no privacy for Alessandro to follow up on her statement, and what would he say? Could she find something to be passionate about in this town? He wasn't so sure.

He had even less opportunity when they got through the terminal and out to the car that waited for them. Make that cars. Because Yasmin got out of the first one and said, "Finally. Come on. You're taking the first car. You're doing Kelly Clarkson in one hour. Megan, hi, nice to meet you in person—you're taking the second car to Alessandro's place. He'll see you later."

◆

Chapter 19

Megan had zero seconds to absorb the words that had just come out of Yasmin's mouth or even to give her a reasonable handshake in response to the firm pumping of her hand.

Alessandro gasped. "I cannot just send her to my house like… she's a piece of mail!"

"She's not a piece of mail. Steve will get her there safely, and Jacqui will give her the code for the door. Come on. No time to argue."

Yasmin pulled Alessandro by the arm. Steve, if that was who she referred to, was putting their cases in the trunk of the second car. Alessandro looked mutinous, but Megan didn't want to tick Yasmin off within seconds of meeting her. "I'll be fine," she assured him. "Go. Be amazing. You've earned this."

"I can—"

"Text me when you're on your way home. I'll be fine," she said and hid a wince at the word. Well, this time she would be fine. The air here, even with the smells of aviation fuel and exhaust, was fresh and bright and about forty degrees warmer than what they'd left behind in Boston. The sky was a clear blue, and as Steve ushered her into the car, she scrambled in her purse for her sunglasses.

She needn't have bothered, of course. The windows were blacked out. And a voice next to her made her jump and take the glasses off so she could see. "Hi! I'm Jacqui!"

"Oh my God!" Megan burst out. "You scared me! I'm so sorry! Hi, Jacqui. I'm Megan." They shook hands. Jacqui was a platinum-blonde with deeply tanned skin and teeth that made

Megan blink. She wore a cut-off T-shirt with Gucci spelled out in gold sequins, and short denim shorts that revealed diminutive but perfect legs. "Um, what are you doing here?"

"Oh, I'm Yasmin's assistant. I'm taking you to Alessandro's. Making sure you get settled in, showing you the ropes."

"But..." Megan tried to get a handle on this situation, so different from what she'd imagined. She'd imagined a slow drive through horrendous traffic, holding Alessandro's hand and seeing LA through his eyes. When she'd been here for Kane's conferences, they'd always gone to a huge hotel and stayed there for days. Instead, she had Jacqui talking nonstop and blocking the shaded view out of the windows.

And a slow drive through horrendous traffic.

"I stopped by and filled the refrigerator, got a little of everything. Are you a vegetarian? Oh, which reminds me, I have a list of restaurants you'll love."

"I thought Alessandro could—"

"Gosh, isn't he perfect? Don't tell Yasmin I said that. It's not professional. But"—Jacqui paused for a moment and tapped her pointed nails on her thigh—"phew! You get used to seeing celebs around here, but he is really... phew!"

"You're from around here?" Megan said, since she had a moment to speak.

"Oh no, I'm from Connecticut."

Megan laugh-coughed. "Hey," she said. "Not far from me."

"I guess so!" Jacqui observed her more closely. They could not have been more different. Jacqui looked as though she'd been sunbathing on a multimillion-dollar deck since her toddler years. Megan was Boston-winter pallid. And if she tried to bleach her hair the way Jacqui had, it would probably fall out.

"But you're here now," Megan prompted.

"Yeah. I went to UCLA, and they couldn't drag me back."

"So you're a West Coast gal now, huh?"

"Oh yeah. And you will be, too, in a hot minute. Alessandro lives in the best neighborhood—you're gonna love it—and he can afford the best for both of you."

"I can pay for myself," Megan interjected quickly.

"Well, I dunno. You'll be surprised how much things cost here. Oh, you gotta go to Il Formaggio. Alessandro will take you. My roommate's an actor? And she once got taken there by Meryl Streep's assistant's hair stylist? She brought home leftovers, and it was the best damn fondue I've ever had in my life."

Fondue. Cheese. Made sense. Megan let Jacqui lay out all the best places she'd eaten—or been given leftovers—around the city as they merged onto a highway and the car stopped. And started. And stopped.

Then Jacqui moved on to the best bars in town as the car surprised Megan by turning out of the traffic and into a neighborhood with small houses and stores. Forget Il Formaggio—this was more like McDonald's and Chuck E. Cheese. Despite its pedestrian look, Megan couldn't forget that they weren't in Massachusetts anymore by the palm trees that seemed to touch the sky and the strange and beautiful plants that spilled out of every tiny garden.

"And if you want to do some real celeb spotting," Jacqui was saying, "Alessandro should take you to SAE."

"Açai?" Megan asked. It didn't sound like a bar.

"No. The letters. S. A. E. Something about returning something in the mail. Anyway, it's got a great vibe, and when BTS is in town, they always go there."

"Have you been there?"

"Oh no. The drinks are like, fifty bucks apiece. I can make you a reservation though!"

Jacqui looked and sounded absolutely delighted that she was forced to get other people into this place and yet was kept out of it herself.

"Well," Megan said. "As soon as I'm settled, I will take you to SAE. And Il Formaggio."

"Ohmigod!" Jacqui exclaimed, her big blue eyes wide. "That's so sweet of you!"

Basic human decency, Megan would have thought, but she didn't have a chance to say so, because Jacqui went on. "But you won't have time for that kind of thing for a while. We've got you booked in for hair and makeup tomorrow, and pretty much every day you don't have—"

"Hair and makeup for what?"

"The Ravello Awards. Tomorrow night."

"Oh." Alessandro had said they'd have events to go to. She hadn't realized he'd meant, immediately. Megan liked to see the outfits everyone wore during awards season, but she didn't have the schedule memorized. Especially not for the Ravello Awards, which focused on international movies.

"I know, right? It's so fun. You're gonna love it. We've got dresses ready for you to choose from—"

"What?"

Not again. Megan examined Jacqui's guileless face and knew that Yasmin must not have told her what had happened the last time clothes had appeared on Megan's doorstep. "Oh yeah, and Yasmin says, after tomorrow, you can meet with a couple of stylists yourself and choose one you want to use."

"I. Can. Do. My. Own. Dresses," Megan ground out.

"But these are delivered right to you! Or you can go to our office and they come to you there." Jacqui put what should have been a soothing hand on Megan's knee. "Yasmin told me this is all new to you. It's part of the perks of being a celebrity. You'll love it! Oh, and speaking of that, if you do yoga or if you want a massage this afternoon, let me know and we'll have someone come over."

"This afternoon? You can get someone that quickly?"

"Yeah." Jacqui's tone said *duh.*

They were on another highway now, rising over the residential streets and moving toward high-rise buildings. Megan realized she'd never asked Alessandro where in LA he lived. Maybe in one of these trendy apartment buildings in the city, like she did.

Jacqui talked about the schedule between now and the Oscars, but Megan had lost her ability to listen. She said "uh-huh" and "got it" a few times, and Jacqui seemed satisfied. The road went up and down, and the high-rises fell behind. The palm trees seemed to get higher—or was that because the houses had gotten smaller? They looked like the ones she'd passed near the airport, though these were in better shape.

And before Jacqui had stopped talking and before Megan could understand where she was, they'd pulled off the highway and into a quiet, tree-lined residential area. They followed the roads up and down steep hills, the small Spanish-style or contemporary houses clinging to the sides so tightly that sometimes she could see only a set of stairs leading up to them.

"Alessandro lives here?" she said, astonished.

"Yeah. Right up there." Jacqui pointed, and Steve pulled up to a small modern whitewashed stucco house with a front wall of windows and a beautiful door in dark polished wood. A driveway for one car led up to a small garage on the right side, and a set of stairs rose to the house. Between it and the road sat a perfectly manicured rock garden, alive with ground cover and bushes even in January.

Megan could have fit this house into the yard of her childhood home. It had no large gates, no eight-foot fence, no concierge. "He doesn't live in an apartment?"

"Nope. Don't you like it?"

"I love it. I just..." She smiled at Jacqui as Steve came around to open the door. "I was making assumptions, I guess."

"Come on, lemme show you the code."

By the side of the door was a camera and a digital keypad. Jacqui said, "Watch," and Megan tried hard to memorize the code she entered so she wouldn't have to beg her to write it down.

"Who watches the camera when he's not–Oh!"

She stopped two steps into the house. The light flooded through the windows, revealing an open-plan living room, dining room, and kitchen. White walls were the backdrop to bright modern paintings and swooping organic sculptures. The dining and coffee tables had live-oak edges, and the couch, which faced the windows and a view Megan's brain couldn't even take in, was a worn denim blue that tempted her to sink into it and forget the house tour.

"Management," Jacqui said, recalling Megan to her question. "Landscapers, too. So you don't have to worry about that. Pool guys come in once every couple of weeks."

"Pool guys?" Megan asked faintly.

"Yeah! Come see."

Megan seemed to float over to Jacqui, past the shining steel appliances and concrete countertops of the kitchen, through a dining room that had two doors leading off it, and to another set of floor-to-ceiling windows that Jacqui slid to the side.

"Oh for heaven's sake," Megan breathed. The view here was even more overwhelming: treetops and tiled house roofs and, in the distance, a hint of mountains.

"You like?"

"I love."

"Good!" Jacqui did a little spin on the spot. "You can chill here today. Pool's ready, and the refrigerator out here has drinks and ice."

Megan looked down and saw she was standing at the foot of a small plunge pool that somehow had made it onto the tiny lot. Two lounge chairs invited her even more loudly than the couch. Someone—it had to be Jacqui—had even put thick blue-and-white beach towels on them.

"We left a couple of swimsuits in your room in case you forgot yours," Jacqui said.

"A couple... my what?"

"Lemme show you." And Jacqui skipped back through the open glass doors and to the right, where Megan quickly discovered a guest room with its own bathroom and walk-in closet, decorated as minutely as the main living areas.

"This is just in case you want your own space, of course," Jacqui informed her. "The master is upstairs. We made some space for your clothes up there, but some people prefer their own bathroom, so..."

"I didn't think about it." When had she ever had to wonder if she could share space before? When had she ever had the choice?

"No rush!" Jacqui sang. "You can decide whenever. And you can change your mind. This'll be your house, too."

Megan's mouth dropped open. "Is it?" she said before she could stop herself.

"That was Alessandro's instruction, yes. If you want anything changed, he said, we have to make it happen."

"I..." Jacqui was leading her up a set of white open stairs to a reading nook that had another view over the front of the house. She thought she could see the skyscrapers they'd driven past. So far from the hustle of everyone's life. Of course Alessandro had picked this. "I can't think of a single thing."

"Well, let me know. Here's the elevator." An elevator in this small house?! Yes, there it was, near the stairs, connecting the garage to both floors. Then Jacqui opened the door to a suite that covered the entire second floor. A bed faced another set of windows, with a broad deck outside. Glass walls allowed the full view to be seen from the bed. Two club chairs sat at the end of the bed, with a low table between them, perhaps for a cup of coffee as you watched the sunrise. Or sunset. Whatever direction they were facing now.

"The bathroom's through here, and here's the closet," Jacqui finished, but Megan was opening the door to the deck and breathing in the fresh air.

"Yeah," she said. "I think I'll be okay."

♦

When she'd finally assured Jacqui that she didn't need a private chef to come and make her a sandwich nor a maid to run her a bath nor a dermatologist to derm-abrade the travel schmutz from her face—though she would revisit that masseuse idea some other time—Megan finally got the younger woman to leave. Steve, to whom she made a point of introducing herself before he disappeared, told her to text him as soon as she wanted to go anywhere. Her. Alessandro had another driver, another car.

Megan took a shower, texted Kane that she'd arrived safely, made herself a charcuterie board with some of the contents of the refrigerator, and sat outside in shorts and a T-shirt, her feet in the blissful cool water. Birds chirped, the sun began to dip behind the trees, and far, far away, someone was playing Latin dance music.

When she woke up, it was because Alessandro was leaning over her. "*Ciao*," he said.

"What time is it?" she asked, blinking at him. Darkness had fallen. At some point she'd moved herself from the side of the pool to a lounge chair. "I must have slept for hours."

"Perhaps," he said with a heartbreaking smile. "You might not sleep well tonight."

Megan looked at him, feeling as though she'd only now realized how beautiful he was. "That's okay," she said, reaching up for him. "I had other plans for tonight anyway."

♦

"So how was your interview?" she asked much later. They were in the master bedroom, tangled up in the sheets on the floor, drinking wine and leaning against the club chairs.

"It went well. Then we went to Jimmy Kimmel. You can watch that one in—" He looked around him, but his phone had been left with his clothes somewhere on their way up the stairs. "A little while, I think."

Megan crawled away from him, around the corner to a bedside table where she'd seen a remote for the TV nestled into the bookshelves. Alessandro did a Roy Kent growl as her butt left his view.

He wanted to shout at Yasmin for making him leave Megan alone on her first trip to town. He didn't count the conferences, which sounded as though they'd kept her inside hotel rooms the entire time. Hours he'd had to be away, hours where anything could have happened to send her right back to Boston.

The TV clicked on, and she took them to the guide so they could see the time. "We have an hour," she said.

"Come back here," he begged. She did so, and he wrapped his arms around her naked body, loving her softness and the way she sank into him—come to think of it, the way he'd sunk into her. He adjusted his seat, and Megan gave him a wicked grin.

"I'm hungry," she said.

"Did Jacqui fill the refrigerator?"

"Yes. Enough food to feed my family and yours and everyone else in this neighborhood."

He froze for a second. She'd said *family* so easily. Because of course everyone had family.

"Oh, I'm sorry," she said, pressing a kiss to his neck. "I shouldn't have brought them up."

"It's no big deal," he said. The phrase sounded strange in his accent.

"No, I don't want to make you think of anything sad. Not tonight."

"I am not thinking of anything sad." He dropped a kiss on her shoulder. "Nothing at all."

How could he? His perfect woman was finally in his house. Her suitcases were in his bedroom. Her scent was in his shower. She was *here*. She'd chosen him.

He would have to push away the fear. It was unreasonable, irrational. And it might not happen.

Not if he fed her, anyway. "Okay." He squeezed her and began to stand. "I will find us some food. Stay here."

"Okey dokey." Megan wrapped herself fully in the sheets and picked up her glass of wine from the floor. "They're right," she said with an adorable wriggle of her shoulders. "It does get chilly at night here."

"I'll turn up the heat." In the meantime, he pulled the comforter off the bed and covered her in it, making her squeak in surprise. Then he got on the floor and puffed the comforter over both of them, hiding them from the world and the chill. Megan smiled indulgently and let him crawl over to her for another kiss before pushing him away.

"Seriously, I'm starving."

"*Si, signorina.*"

He opened the closet to find the LA clothes he'd left behind when he'd gone to Boston so suddenly. But he could hardly get into the closet for the rolling rack of sparkly, slinky dresses that filled it.

"Have you looked in here?" he called back to Megan.

"Yes. I saw it. I'll deal with it tomorrow," she said shortly.

Alessandro pushed the rack to a corner of the room and found himself a pair of pajamas. Tomorrow, as the lady said, was another day.

♦

Chapter 20

Megan woke up at four a.m. "Damn time zones," she muttered after she'd tried not to disturb Alessandro for a whole half hour. He was apparently unaffected. A lesson he'd perhaps learned from odd schedules on movie sets. He slept against the white sheets like a dark angel. Really, his eyelashes shouldn't be allowed.

She got up and found the thick white bathrobe in the bathroom along with slide-in slippers, then tiptoed onto the deck and sat watching the lights hidden in the trees become slowly overtaken by twilight, then dawn, then the brightening sky. The peace was absolute. When was the last time she'd taken such deep breaths?

At last, the sun broke above the trees, and she went back inside to make coffee. Befitting his historical status as the hottest barista in town, Alessandro's coffee machine was huge, shiny, and complicated. Megan was equal to it, but her coffee just couldn't turn out as well as his. She brought her offering to Alessandro anyway.

"Yours is better," she admitted before he could take a sip.

He raised his eyebrows at her, took a sip, and sighed in pleasure. "You are correct. Mine is better."

She aimed a pillow at him, but with coffee in her other hand and in his, she didn't let it fly.

"I am glad to be better than you at something," he said, opening the doors to the deck.

"What am I better than you at?" Yeah, she was fishing. So what? What a joy to be around a man she could tease and flirt with in total peace and safety. Alessandro had all but said "I like you. You can relax." So that was what Megan was going to do.

He looked up at the pale-blue morning sky. "Eyeliner," he said.

Megan burst out laughing. "You don't even wear eyeliner!"

"And why is that, do you think?"

"Because you don't need it, Mr. Double Eyelashes."

He grinned. "Ah, you noticed."

Megan rolled her eyes. He'd outfished her for compliments. Watching him stretch out on the chaise in his mouthwateringly tight underwear and an open bathrobe, Megan decided to forgive him.

They spent the morning on the deck in easy silence, eating fruit and yogurt and sipping their coffee. Megan didn't even try to look at her phone.

When the doorbell chimed, they both jumped. Alessandro leaped up and tightened his bathrobe around himself. "Ready?" he said.

"I'm not sure what for," she answered. "But yes."

She'd been so busy last night, she hadn't even asked him about the Ravello Awards tonight. And she had no chance to now, as the house was taken over like Katniss' before the Victors' Tour, with Jacqui, a publicist Megan had vaguely heard of named Donna, a hairdresser, a makeup artist, and a dresser, whatever that was.

"Your first stylist will be here tomorrow at ten," Donna said. "Until then, Petra will dress you."

This meant, apparently, that Petra had a huge rolling suitcase with flat drawers hiding more shapewear than a Miss Universe pageant. Megan was insulted. And then the makeup artist tsked over her lack of tan and started on a foundation two shades darker than Megan's skin tone, and she had to protest.

"Cameras, darling," Donna said, rushing past her with a handful of papers she was delivering to Alessandro and his team. "They bleach you right out. Let the ladies do their job, mkay?"

Christa, the makeup artist, took her portable light and brought it right up to Megan's skin. "Look. This is what it would look like if we didn't do this."

The mirror showed Megan a white mask with black eyes and pale lips. "Okay. I believe you." She wanted to close her eyes, but she couldn't, of course. "Do your thing."

She almost said *do your worst*, but that was a little too much New Megan for her comfort.

Three hours later, a woman Megan hardly recognized looked back at her. "We're going for a blueblood look," Petra had said. "Very East Coast. Very Ralph. Very Nantucket. Gorgeous, don't you think?"

Well, there was nothing *wrong* with it. Megan's dress was a midnight-blue sheath with a white cape that attached on the shoulders and reached just to the floor. A diamond pendant followed the neckline and stopped a modest distance from her cleavage. A tennis bracelet and a chignon shot through with more diamonds in her hair finished the look.

While she observed herself in the mirror and tried to summon Old Megan to be as sparkly as those diamonds, Alessandro came out of the guest bedroom where he'd been prepped. Megan's shoulders slumped. He looked perfect. Literally perfect. His hair was slicked back but not too far back, so she could still count the curls at the nape of his neck. They'd trimmed his beard, and he looked effortlessly hip rather than couldn't-be-bothered hippy. He wore charcoal-gray pants and a lilac shirt under a purple and gray paisley vest. He was carrying the suit jacket, but Megan hoped with a sigh that he never put it on. He'd rolled up his sleeves again.

"Wow," she said.

"I thank you," he said. "I—Megan." His face went from a grateful smile to concern in a second. "What is it? What is this?"

"It's Nantucket," she said, trying to sound enthusiastic. "It's Ralph. It's East Coast."

"*Cara*, no." He came over and looked her in her eyes. "Your shoulders are sad. You hate it."

"I don't *hate* it," she said quickly.

"You don't like the dress?" Petra said at once. "What's the matter with it?"

"Nothing."

"It is not her," Alessandro said firmly. "And all these diamonds."

Megan winced. She especially hated the diamonds.

"Come here," he said and pulled her up the stairs to the master bedroom. "I am so sorry," he said as soon as the door was closed. He kept hold of the hand he'd used to pull her and gently unclasped the tennis bracelet. "Better," he said. "Turn around."

Megan did so without a word, and he took off the necklace and unzipped the dress. "*Porca puttana*, what did they do?"

"Did you just call me pork?"

"What is this?" he demanded, putting a finger into the shapewear that enclosed her back and belly.

"The sizes were a little off," she said.

"Megan, stop. You have to take all of this off and start again. And tomorrow I will tell Yasmin to stop sending you clothes."

"I'll tell her myself," Megan said. "But what do I do now?"

He spun her around so she faced him again and slid the dress off her shoulders and down her legs, then threw it on the bed. "Find something that makes you happy."

He waved at her suitcases, which they'd never gotten around to unpacking.

"But I—"

"*Cara*," he said, holding her arms and making her look at him. "You are a beautiful, confident woman. You know what looks good on you. You have never doubted this. Today you did. And I am so angry at those people downstairs."

"No, don't be. I should have spoken up before."

"I am sorry. I was not here yesterday, and you lost some of your joyful Megan while I was gone. I did not have time to find her before they came today. But she is in there."

"The old Megan would wear the clothes they gave her," she said, her voice small.

"No. She would convince them that everyone would be happier if she wore what she wanted. That is your superpower."

He smiled at her, and tears pricked the back of Megan's eyes. When had a man ever told her he believed in her so much? Or a woman, come to think of it? "We will be late," she said, throwing up one last obstacle.

"It will not take long. Go, see what you have."

Megan knew what she had. She'd packed her cases the day before yesterday, and she'd brought only two or three dresses that could be considered red carpet material. She'd looked forward to wandering the famous streets of LA, possibly with Alessandro by her side, finding West Coast fashions that would accommodate the balmy weather and make him proud.

"Why didn't you tell me about the awards tonight?" she asked, using up precious time to turn to him, dressed only in her shapewear and heels.

"I must apologize for that," he said, sitting on the bed. "I forgot. After the New Year's situation, Yasmin banned me from the Golden Globes, and I was not nominated for a Ravello. Anyway, I was only going to go to support my friend Mohammed, who is up for best director. Until I was nominated for the Oscar, I thought I was banished to Boston for a while longer." He sighed and rubbed his hand down his beard. "I was looking forward to that."

In the light flooding the room, showing the flowering bushes and palm trees outside, Boston seemed like a story someone told children to scare them at night. Megan couldn't believe she'd been here only twenty-four hours. "Well. I would have packed differently," she huffed, putting her hands on her hips.

"I will be more sorry later, *cara*," he said, looking her up and down. "After you take off that terrible elastic and get more comfortable."

Megan tutted but laughed.

"But please keep the shoes," he said from behind her.

She aimed a silver-clad toe at him. The shoes were barely there thin straps around her feet and ankles. They were, in fact, the only part of the outfit she'd liked, and she was definitely, positively not going to take them off.

She opened her larger suitcase and pulled out garments, tossing them behind her without regard for where they fell. Ignoring the shiny dresses and fitted tuxedo jackets, she found a pair of black drainpipe pants with a thin black ribbon running down the sides. She loved them for how they fit her and that they were long, so they always looked good with a great pair of shoes. Peeling off the shapewear, taking a couple of deep breaths as her stomach went back to its usual size, then removing the shoes for a moment, she pulled the pants on and paused again.

The closet was behind her. It only held Alessandro's clothes and the decimated rack of dresses the team downstairs had gone through this afternoon. Megan pulled that rack out and pushed it as far away from her as possible. If she'd cared only a little less for the cost of the clothes, she would have pushed it onto the deck and let the elements have it.

Now free to see what was inside the closet, she walked in, running her hands over the jackets that hung on one side. The other side held Alessandro's shirts: some formal with subtle pleats and expensive details, others casual and relaxed, made to be worn untucked—or open.

Megan pulled a tuxedo shirt off its hanger. The fabric was butter-soft, the quality obvious. This wasn't from his barista days. This was a reflection of what Alessandro had achieved in the last five years.

She walked out of the closet, holding the shirt. "Where are the studs for this?"

Alessandro stared. "That is mine."

"Yes." She held it out to him and put her other hand on her hip. "Is that a problem?"

He visibly swallowed. "That is the sexiest thing I have ever seen in my life."

"Okay, good." She went back to her suitcase and pulled out a black lacy bra she particularly loved. "Could you get me the studs?"

Alessandro walked around her and came back from the closet with three different sets of studs. Megan picked the silver ones because they matched her shoes. With Alessandro's salivating help—he told her so—she hooked in all the studs and the cufflinks. Then she put the shoes back on. There was a tiny possibility that she arranged herself on the bed so Alessandro would see down her cleavage while she did so. He gave his Roy Kent growl again and grabbed his chest over his heart.

Her torture achieved, Megan stood in front of the three-way mirror in the closet and tied the ends of the shirt in a knot at her waist. The bra showed, but not too much.

"You will not button up the studs?" Alessandro asked, his voice sounding strangled.

"I don't think so," Megan said matter-of-factly, turning from side to side.

"*Cara.* You will kill me."

She giggled. "Good. Then my work here is done."

She took the diamonds from her hair and shook her head until the chignon got a lot messier. There. "Okay. We can go back downstairs."

"You always astonish me."

"Thank you." She held out her arm for him to take. "Ready?"

As they descended the stairs, the hushed, frantic whispers she'd heard since they'd opened the bedroom door ceased, and all eyes turned to her. That was what they looked like to Megan: a whole crowd of eyes. She'd wanted to follow the rules of Hollywood, but she'd failed. And following her own rules might get her Worst-Dressed prizes in tomorrow's websites. But God, she was comfortable.

"Rock 'n roll," Petra said. "Is that your shirt, Alessandro?"

"Si."

Petra put her hands on her hips. "We'll have to know the designer. It is designer, right?"

"Of course. Federica Arte."

Jacqui's phone was in her hand in a moment. "I'm calling now."

"How does she have the number?" Megan asked no one.

"She has all the numbers," Alessandro said wisely.

"I guess so. Okay, Petra. In your magic suitcase, do you have some kind of necklace that's more geometric, more contemporary? And the hugest silver cuff you can find."

Five minutes later, after a small adjustment to Megan's hair so the messiness would stay as she wanted all evening and a promise to one of Alessandro's stylists—who'd given Megan her own homemade cuff—that she'd mention her name as often as possible, they were in one of the black cars and weaving up and down the hills to the ceremony. Alessandro was still shaking his head at her, and Megan was laughing at him laughing at her. With their fingers entwined, they watched the sunset until the car pulled up to the oceanfront hotel, where a massive awning covered a long red carpet.

"You are perfect," he said, kissing her fingers. "Ready?"

Megan threw a worried glance outside the window at the reality she'd signed up for. She could hear shouts and calls, some of which sounded more desperate than professional, amid popping flashes and jostling crowds. Unlike the fundraiser, which had been a lark, a few feet of red carpet to give the kids something to play with, this was serious business.

"Uh-huh," she said, gripping his hand now. "Just don't let go of me."

"I do not intend to." He smiled, kissing her cheek. His driver, Max, opened his door, and Alessandro did let go. Megan realized then that the choice of who sat on which side had been carefully orchestrated. Alessandro got out first. Megan tried to watch how he got his legs out so gracefully without falling over his feet, but the lights were blinding her. He unfolded, facing the crowd. Now Megan could see only his legs and back, but he paused, so she assumed he was posing. Then he turned around and reached a gallant hand back to her. She scooted across the seat, glanced down at her decolletage to check that nothing was falling out, and took his hand.

The pants had been a good choice. Nothing stopped her from putting one silvery foot out after another and rising to meet Alessandro. She pushed a stray hair out of her face and looked at him. "What now?" she asked, keeping her mouth in a smile that he returned.

"Just walk and smile, *cara*," he said, putting his hand on her back. "And enjoy."

Megan did enjoy. The red carpet led them past the gamut of photographers and to a spot where reporters were allowed to stop them for quick soundbites. They'd agreed that Alessandro would do the talking, and he did so, talking about how proud he was of his friend Mohammed and the movie that had been nominated.

"It's nominated but *The Drummer* wasn't. How do you feel about that?"

"It is not a competition." He smiled. "Oh, wait."

He received the laugh he expected, and they moved on.

"Megan!" the third reporter called. This was going to happen eventually. But the first question was easy. "Who are you wearing?"

"Federica Arte," Megan said, hugging herself to show how much she loved the shirt. "It's Alessandro's."

"Oh, that's so sweet!" gushed the reporter. "You guys are already stealing from each other's wardrobes?"

"*Sì.*" Alessandro grinned. "She has a vintage Vivian Westwood I cannot wait to try on."

"A dress or a suit?"

"Either one would look great on me. Don't you think?"

The reporter gasped and laughed uncertainly. Megan got a vision of Alessandro in a Harry Styles-type kilt or a Billy Porter gown.

"I do think." She smiled. He turned to her and gave her a big grin and a wink the cameras didn't see. It didn't matter. The grin was so unlike Alessandro's usual look that the reporter stammered a moment before saying, "Well, we'll look forward to that," and an usher guided them away.

Reaching the hotel entrance with no questions more difficult than "How are you liking LA?" Alessandro immediately found his friend, Mohammed Bittar. Mohammed wore a pair of loose black pants that tightened from knee to ankle, a baggy white-collared shirt unbuttoned halfway down his chest, showing a cluster of silver and gold pendant necklaces, and a Celtics baseball cap. The green cap highlighted his hazel eyes. He shook Megan's hand and kissed her cheek at the same time. "You're the reason I couldn't get 'Sandro back to LA!" he said.

"It was more like a school full of acting students," Megan pointed out.

"And a manager who was very, very angry with me at the time," Alessandro added, hugging his friend. "I am so happy for you, Mo. You will win tonight. I feel it."

"Thanks, bro. Come meet my friends, Megan." Leaving Alessandro in his wake, he tucked Megan's arm into his and pulled her forward. She was introduced to several beautiful people, some dressed to kill, others in more subdued outfits that tagged them as producers rather than actors. In minutes, Megan found herself at Mohammed's table, champagne in hand, while the huge ballroom around them—bigger than the one Ellen had donated to the Studio—filled up with a talking, laughing, kissing crowd. A TV camera sat at each corner of the stage, pointed toward it, but Megan could relax for now, as they were clearly not running.

A bell rang, cameramen appeared at their instruments, and the last of the guests rushed to their seats. Intro music that might have been the beginning of an epic movie began to play, the cameras turned on and swept the crowd, and a voiceover said, "Ladies and gentlemen, welcome to the twenty-fifth annual Ravello Awards! Please welcome Board President John Egan and Contest Chair Didi Ravello!"

"Oop," Megan said to herself. A woman in her midfifties, with long black hair worn over a stunning red strapless gown, glided onto the stage, helped by a nondescript man with heavy jowls and a tight tux.

"What is oop?" Alessandro whispered while they kept on clapping.

"That's Kane's ex-girlfriend," she whispered back. "She's the reason he got famous."

Alessandro looked at her. "Is it awkward?"

"No. She has no idea who I am. I just hadn't made the connection with the award name."

"Thank you, thank you!" Didi was saying, raising her hands so the applause died down. "I cannot believe that twenty-five years have gone by since my father told me his germ of an idea for this award. Thanks to his work and the creativity and drive of every single person in this room, in this town, in this industry"—she paused for cheering and more applause—"Dad's foundation has now been able to give more than two hundred million dollars to emerging movie makers throughout the world. Thanks, Dad!" She raised a glass that sat on a table behind her to the ceiling. "To Salvatore Ravello."

The audience obediently repeated her words, then were invited to sit. As people Megan had only seen on big screens began to parade in front of her, announcing finalists and winners of each category, her favorite parts—apart from seeing what everyone was wearing—were the clips they showed from each movie. With fewer awards than other ceremonies to hand out, each clip was longer, giving a good feel for what the movie had been trying to say. Even Megan, a complete newbie, had to admire the craftsmanship in each film.

When Anupam Kher read out Mohammed's name as Best Director and then Didi herself announced that his movie had won for best film, Megan yelled herself hoarse, despite knowing the man for less than two hours. Mohammed leaped, literally, onto the stage, forgoing the stairs for a hip-cracking parkour move three feet from the floor. His producers followed more sedately, and together they hugged and whooped.

Back at their table, Megan again saw that ecstatic side of Alessandro, this time in his hollering after Mohammed. If the cameras caught him, his reputation as a moody hottie was shot. He didn't look like he cared.

Didi closed the ceremony while Mohammed was still on the

stage. Megan wondered if the TV broadcast had caught his final shout of joy. The crowd laughed, and everyone began to find their way out at the back of the room. Alessandro instead took Megan's hand and went forward to the stairs on the stage's right-hand side.

Several people milled about there, assistants and crew and the like, Megan supposed, and no one came down the stairs right away. And when they did, it wasn't Mohammed but Didi. And the first person her eyes landed on was Megan.

"By God," she said, pointing at her. "I wouldn't have believed it until I saw you with my own eyes. Megan Fielding, all grown up!"

Megan had been almost grown up when Didi had met Kane. Also, they had never met. "Did you know what I looked like when I wasn't grown up?" she asked, smiling.

"Of course! Your brother went on and on and on about all of you." Didi circled her hand, laughing. "And in any case, you've got the Fielding looks. I would have known any one of you anywhere. It's nice to meet you in person."

Megan gave her outstretched hand the requisite gentle squeeze. Close up, Didi was just as beautiful as she was in front of the lights. She carried her small crow's-feet and laugh lines with the same insouciance as the diamonds on her fingers. "It's a pleasure to meet you at last, Didi."

"Bro!" Mohammed yelled, almost knocking Didi off the top step as he tackled Alessandro, forcing him to step away from Megan to take Mohammed's weight and save the women from getting trampled. In his absence, Megan became aware that she and Didi were the center of attention. Cameras began flashing. Automatically, Megan smiled her biggest five-hundred-watt Fielding smile.

"There it is," Didi said approvingly. "Phew. You know how many dental sessions I had to do to get a smile like your brother has naturally? And you inherited the same damn thing. It's not fair. It really isn't." She pouted.

Megan had to laugh at her difference in tone from a few minutes ago, when she'd controlled the entire room. "If my brother was a fool enough to let you go, then I think you won."

"You're so sweet." Didi patted her arm. "And now another Fielding has come to Hollywood. Will you stay this time? Not going to run back to Bahston and find a spouse?"

The cameras flashed like crazy. Was Megan blushing? Maybe the flashes would bleach it out. "Um, no. No spouse in my plans. Not—no."

Where the hell was Alessandro?

"Oh, but I forgot your young man! Where is he? *Dov'è, Signor Rosselli? Dov'è, amore?*"

"*Sono qui*," Alessandro replied, emerging from a crowd and looking a lot more rumpled than when he'd gone into it. "*Onore, Signora.*" Didi offered one cheek and then the other for Alessandro to kiss.

"I've been wanting to meet you," she said in English. "Why haven't you done an Italian language movie? I can't find any work you did before *All the Things!*"

"That is because there is nothing to find," he said. "I only began acting when I got to America. Believe me," he went on with a self-deprecating smile. "That is better for everyone."

"But where did you go to school? You didn't even do a play?"

Megan felt the stillness of his body, knew that he was searching for an answer that would satisfy Didi but not reveal his past. She surreptitiously eased next to him, hoping the pressure of her shoulder on his would give him support.

"I was a late bloomer," he said, then looked at Megan. "That is right?"

Had he just exaggerated his accent? Would he really pretend

his English was worse than it was to deflect questions? "Yes, that's right," she said reassuringly.

"I guess that explains it," Didi said, though she didn't sound pleased. "Well, get on it. Next time you go back, tell me. I have a director I want you to meet."

Alessandro bowed. "That is very kind of you."

"Over here, please?" a voice asked, and Didi said, "Yes, we have to preserve this moment!" and they turned, a camera flashed, and Megan prayed she and Alessandro looked normal. Then Didi was waving her fingers at them and saying, "I'll see you around, Megan. Say hi to your delicious brother from me," and, thankfully, she left, because Megan wondered if her champagne might come back up.

"I do *not* want to think of her and Kane in–in–" she spluttered. But quietly.

Alessandro laughed, a relieved sound, and his shoulders relaxed. "I understand. Let's go home before Mohammed drags us out all night."

◆

Chapter 21

Yasmin's office building was the ugliest thing Megan had ever seen. Brutalism schmootalism. It shouldn't have been allowed in this city. But Megan had to get through a security guard to get into Yasmin's office suite.

Yasmin's office itself was the opposite of the building: modern, clean, shot through with gold and blue accents, showing her success while at the same time reassuring her clients she didn't spend all their hard-earned money on tchotchkes.

"So, what can I do for you?" Yasmin asked, pulling out a chair for Megan. "Coffee?"

"Not right now," Megan said. She was mollified by the industrial coffee machine in the corner. The woman wasn't above making her clients coffee, at least. "We have to talk about this clothing issue."

Yasmin sighed and sat behind her desk, steepling her fingers and looking past them at Megan. "Yes. We do."

Megan knew what that meant. "Look, I know what you're going to say. You know this town. You know this business. I haven't done red carpet events of this scale. You have a narrative to uphold about Alessandro and me, and I need to dress for that narrative. East Coast, West Coast. Blueblood versus immigrant."

Yasmin inclined her head. "Just so."

"Right." Megan reached for the tips of her hair and tossed them over her shoulder. "I will do all that. I will make Alessandro look as good as I possibly can while staying quiet and out of the limelight." Yasmin opened her mouth, but Megan barreled on.

"But I will *not* wear clothes I haven't chosen myself. It would be counterproductive to your job, Alessandro's, and mine. I would be uncomfortable, awkward, and self-conscious. The team that came to his house yesterday were professionals, and they did everything right. Except ask me what I wanted to wear. I'm not going to be in that position again. You know this business, but I know fashion. I know what looks good on me, and that is what I'm going to wear."

Yasmin looked at her for a long moment. Megan, the adrenaline pumping her heart faster and faster, lifted her chin. She was not going to apologize for this, not make herself smaller to fit into someone else's vision.

"Have you ever thought about writing a book?" Yasmin said.

"I—what?"

"A book. You know, pages. Pictures. I think you have a book in you."

The adrenaline began to send heat into her cheeks. "What on earth would I write a book about?" Yasmin must have mistaken her for another client.

"Fashion. Advice for young kids on staying true to themselves. Not following the pack."

Megan's determined chin dropped. "I thought you liked the pack."

"Oh, honey." Yasmin shook her head. "We really need to have lunch. I know you got kinda thrown into this. We didn't have time to set up a decent brand launch for you and 'Sandro. We would have gone through all this. Everything just happened too fast."

Megan coughed at the idea of being a "brand." Especially of her and Alessandro's relationship being one. But what had she done with Kane's image for the last two years? What had she seen him do all throughout his career? Branding.

She let out the breath she'd taken in to blast Yasmin with. "That is true. You don't know me. And I don't know you. And you took me on as a client anyway."

"That was an easy decision. Not just because I could tell you have something to share with the world as soon as I saw your Instagram, but because of what happened with your brother and the girl he dated."

"Married. He married her."

"Yeah. But if he'd had a manager, they wouldn't have gone through half the problems they did."

"So you took me on to... protect me?"

Yasmin raised one eyebrow. "Has it worked?"

Megan thought back over the last two weeks. Ever since the fundraiser, she'd felt out of control. But the plan from Yasmin's office had not included having Alessandro stay overnight. When she'd deviated from that plan, things had gone sideways.

She couldn't blame Yasmin for her fight with Cat. And she sure the hell wasn't going to feel guilty for taking Alessandro to her bed. Even the words in her head made her thighs clench a bit. So, she'd had to take the consequences of her actions. And when Alessandro had gotten nominated and brought Megan along, hadn't Yasmin pivoted with style and laid out a plan that got both of them to LA and into a house filled with food and soft beds and safety?

Did Yasmin see Megan's shoulders lower? Megan could certainly feel the tension leave her body. "Okay," she said. "So, let me start again with a thank-you. I appreciate that you've tried to mitigate the problems my brother and sister-in-law went through. That was very thoughtful of you."

"You're welcome," Yasmin smiled. "Don't paint me out to be

too selfless, though. I wouldn't have taken you on if I didn't think you have a career here. A career I will earn money from."

"Understood." Megan still didn't see how she was going to make any money for the woman. "But no one's going to listen to me when I just arrived in town and I'm here to look pretty next to your A-list actor."

Yasmin wagged a finger at her. "You and I both know that's not what you see yourself as."

"I'm trying to be realistic. Isn't that what you want?"

"I want a power couple. That's how *I* see you two. How do you feel about that?"

Megan sat back in surprise. Before she could formulate an answer, Yasmin went on. "If you make it, of course. But yeah. I can see you two producing movies, launching clothing lines."

Megan couldn't speak. What kind of future was this?

"Helping more than one small community center in Boston," Yasmin added. "What charities are you involved with?"

"I..." Kane's was the only one that came to mind. And that was his. Like she'd taken on his company, his apartment, his goddamn car. "I'm figuring that out," she hedged.

"Well, do that. Doesn't matter which coast. Just make it relevant." Yasmin's finger was still pointing at her. "Clothes. Fashion. Self-esteem. That's what I see for you."

"Most advocates will tell you fashion and self-esteem don't go together."

"So change their minds."

◆

Alessandro met Megan at the Greenerie, a hot new restaurant that allowed them to be photographed but not to be overheard, after her appointment with Yasmin. He could tell by the way she floated in that it had gone well.

He stood and kissed her cheek before the maître d' pulled her chair out for her. She looked ravishing, as always, now in a fluttery-sleeved peach and blue summer dress that made her look tan when she obviously couldn't be. He looked forward to all the weeks ahead, when he'd get to see her in summer clothes rather than the thick coats and heavy tweeds of Boston. Her hair was half up, showing a pair of mother-of-pearl chandelier earrings and the sweep of her jawline that he had to struggle to keep from kissing.

"Yasmin told you that you were right and she was wrong," he stated after the waiter had taken her drink order.

"Not exactly." She smiled. "We realized that we were both right and we had both been wrong." She took a sip of water. "You still have time to go shopping with me this afternoon?"

"It is all I wish to do," he replied. "She will stop sending you clothes?"

"Yes. And I will stop thinking she is an unfeeling machine."

"That is good." Between Yasmin and Megan, he'd back Megan any day, but he did like and admire Yasmin and would have hated to lose her.

Outside the restaurant, after a lunch spent making plans and dreaming dreams, a camera was pushed in front of them. Alessandro felt Megan pose next to him—very casual, very natural, just a step back and a slight turn to the side, with her hand flat on his arm—and he felt a surge of pride at how well she knew the business already.

"Megan," the voice behind the camera said. "How are you enjoying LA?"

The same question as yesterday. "I love it," she said as though she'd never heard it before. "What's not to love?" And she moved a hair closer to Alessandro. He laughed and looked at her. She raised her eyebrows at him while grinning. She knew how to play this game. He moved his hand more securely around her waist.

"You guys in love?" the voice asked.

Alessandro's heart somersaulted. The question was bound to come sooner or later, but he'd wanted later. Much later. When he could organize his own feelings for her and convince himself that he didn't love her more than he loved his own career and he might have to let her leave him one day and—

"Uh-uh-uh," Megan said, wagging her finger at the pap. Yasmin had done that to him many a time. "Not gonna answer that one. Got your pictures?"

"Okay, okay," the pap said, while Alessandro marveled at the ease with which she'd stopped the train of conversation. Now he really loved her. "Instead, you got any fashion advice for your fans?"

Megan laughed, a bark of surprise. "Sure. Be comfortable. Be yourself. And be fabulous. And say hi to Yasmin for me."

And Megan, who'd been in LA for all of forty-eight hours, steered Alessandro out of the line of fire and into the car that waited for them.

◆

Alessandro put his Corona on the teak poolside table and squinted at his partner on the chaise longue next to him. Megan, finally, had a moment to breathe. At least, she had a moment to breathe while he was around. Donna and Yasmin seemed to think that if Alessandro and Megan were going to spend any time together, they should be working. And in the last three weeks, they'd done just that. Almost every evening had been a new event, which was quite the achievement, considering the nominees weren't allowed to attend parties hosted by studios or other producers.

Megan was lying back, her vintage style navy-and-white bikini showing off all her curves, an enormous pair of sunglasses holding her wet hair off her face. Her eyes were closed, so Alessandro could look at her without her knowing.

"I can feel you watching me," she said through almost-closed lips.

Oh. So much for stealth. "Admiring you, *cara*."

"Admire me another beer, would you?"

"*Certo*." He stood and got a wolf whistle for his efforts as he passed her chair. Well, if he was going to be in the gym for five hours a day, he had the right to wear smaller swimming trunks than Americans were used to, didn't he?

They had come to Cassidy Garfield's house for the day. Cassidy, who'd been famous longer than Alessandro had been alive, was married to Colson Brewer, the stuntman who'd helped Alessandro through his first action movie. She was fifty-seven; he was thirty-five. The age gap between them had been fodder for all the gossip sites three years ago, but the truth was simple: they loved each other.

Cassidy owned a palace in Malibu, complete with high walls, guest lodges, security cameras, and guards, as well as a team of gardeners who kept everything inside those walls pristine. Her pool was more of a resort, with three diving boards, a separate plunge pool, and a splash and play section for her first grandchild. The pool house contained a full kitchen, three grills, and a chef to make sure everyone was fed and no one had to lift a finger. After the last three weeks of nonstop interviews, photo sessions, and parties, Alessandro understood why Cassidy needed the luxury. He was, as Megan would say, pooped, and while Megan had taken the attention like a champ, he knew she was tired, too.

Thank God Cassidy had taken to Megan as soon as she met her. She'd introduced her to everyone she possibly could, including all the Chrises and both Ryans and their other halves. And those other halves had immediately invited Megan to their houses when Alessandro had been off doing interviews. So in between their own private moments in his backyard, they had a smorgasbord of pools to relax at and people Alessandro was proud to call his friends to impress Megan with.

"Cass," Megan was saying as he returned to the chaises. "I've been looking for something else to do here."

Cassidy was sitting on Megan's other side. Her beverage of choice was a white wine sangria. Between the two women sat a plate of precisely chopped up fruits and vegetables with a spicy fruit salsa.

"I recommend turning onto your front," Cassidy said in a tone like a cat's stretch. "Get that East Coast pallor off you."

Megan laughed and thanked Alessandro for the drink he handed her. He sat on his chaise and faced the two of them. When he hadn't been able to take Megan with him to events, she'd been working via email and Zoom with the Studio and several other charities in Boston, improving their social media presence. When he was very lucky, he got to sit on the couch and listen while she talked to her clients. He loved how much she loved this.

Then there was her own social media profile. Her quote from lunch that day had gone viral, along with every outfit she'd ever worn in front of a camera. Megan was always ready. She and Alessandro could only be walking down the street with a cup of coffee, but she treated the photographers with respect, allowed the scrutiny, talked about her designers, and gave more matter-of-fact truths about feeling good and looking good.

This couldn't last. Even someone as comfortable with her style as Megan was going to get sick of the interruptions one of these days. And wasn't she supposed to go back to Fielding Paper? Alessandro hadn't dared to broach either subject or plan for the future. They often talked late into the night, but their conversations were more about their childhoods. By eavesdropping on this conversation, he might get a better clue of what would make her happy.

"Okay, but after that," she answered Cassidy. "When 'Sandro is off interviewing and lunching, I've been touching base with some of the groups who asked me for help with their websites after the Studio fundraiser. I can do that stuff in my sleep. I think there's more I can do."

Cassidy turned onto her side and put her hand under her cheek. "I've been wondering when you were going to ask me. All that 'fashion advice' you've been handing out every time you get interviewed."

Megan's cheeks went pink. "Not just fashion advice," Alessandro protested. "She is turning the conversation around on self-esteem and actresses."

"Yeah"—Megan laughed—"because I showed half an inch of fat under my blouse at the Ravello Awards."

"No, no, no," Cassidy said before Alessandro could. "Well, yes. But you already know that was part of your thing, right? Comfort, being natural, and what was the other one?"

Megan was blushing hard now. "I mean it, though."

"I know you do. What has your manager said?"

Megan outlined the changes she'd made to her social media accounts. "She's pretty happy."

"You're up to five hundred thousand followers and a million views on your last video," Cassidy said, holding up her phone. "She'd better be happy. You're doing her job. Raising your brand without her."

"Then I'm doing it wrong," Megan said stubbornly. "I want to help other people, not myself. Make them the spotlight."

"In this business," Cassidy said, "you don't get to do one without the other. It's okay." She reached out to shake Megan's leg. "You're doing everything right. I'd hire you in a second to figure out my wardrobe, for a start."

"That's kind of you to say so," Megan said.

"Ha! Don't say it until you see the state it's in. Rooms of crap I haven't worn for a decade."

"Donated by fashion houses?"

"Yep. Or bought by me and stupidly not worn."

"Aren't there places you can donate clothes like that?"

"You can, but last time I looked, they didn't want my donations. You're talking about the practical clothes, the ones women coming out of homelessness and jail need. A size-two Hollywood maven doesn't have the right clothes for them."

Megan's fingers were tapping on her thigh. Alessandro could feel the plans rolling around in her mind. "So they need someone to donate the clothes and someone to help the women wear them. Right?"

"I guess so." Cassidy leaned back in her chaise and assumed the sunbathing position again. "Sounds like you should call someone about that."

Megan turned to Alessandro. "You think that would work?"

Turning to him for advice? Could she see him swell with pride? "I think if you start it, it will one hundred percent work."

Megan took her phone from the table next to her and walked over to the shade. Alessandro watched her type and scroll furiously for a minute or two before he dragged his eyes away.

"Do not," Cassidy said, her eyes still closed, "let that woman become bored."

A shot of fear ran through him. What could an upstart actor like him offer a woman like Megan? How would he keep her interested when he had to leave for months at a time to film movies?

He wouldn't even be able to ply her with coffee.

♦

Chapter 22

Yasmin didn't call them anymore. They had scheduled Zoom calls, and she and Megan had finally had that lunch, but otherwise, she had silently approved Megan and Alessandro to keep on doing what they did without micromanagement from their management.

So when Alessandro's phone rang one morning two weeks before the Oscars, he met Megan's eyes with surprise. "What did we do?" Megan asked at once.

He laughed, but he had the same question. Megan's outreach to designers and shelters was moving along exactly as she wanted—in a few more days, she was going to rent warehouse space to store the promised donations. They'd only been photographed at scheduled events or "candid" shopping trips. Alessandro had changed his social media to let his fans in on his—carefully curated—private life, talking about the Studio and local stores and restaurants he loved. And of course, he'd included photos of himself and Megan, every one of which immediately flew around the world. He surprised himself by how natural he looked in them, how easy it was to ignore the cameras and smile at Megan, to show his affections with a quick kiss to the shoulder or smoothing her hair out of her eyes. The gossip sites sighed and cooed, and while some questioned their connection after Nikki, for the rest—for Alessandro himself—their love story was out there for all the world to see. And the world was seeing it.

"Only one way to find out," he said. "*Buongiorno, Yasmin.*"

"Buongiorno yourself. Lily Liebowitz wants to interview you. Tomorrow."

"*Tomorrow?*"

"Yes. Don't worry, not at your house," Yasmin said as Megan's eyebrows went up. "We've booked you into The Rosette's presidential suite."

"I—" This was impossible. "They can't mean tomorrow." *Lily Liebowitz* was the number one Sunday night talk show in the country. People stopped watching *Game of Thrones* to see what she could get out of her guests. And get something she always did. As much as Alessandro knew no one was going into these interviews blind, he had to wonder at the shock on celebrities' faces when she went into some subject they had apparently kept off-limits until now.

And shit, did Alessandro have off-limits subjects. Several of them, now, he thought, mouthing "Lily Liebowitz" and watching Megan choke on her coffee.

"We'll handle it," Yasmin said. "They get a list of questions, same as everyone."

"Does she stick to the list?" he asked.

"I was planning this for after your next movie came out," Yasmin said, not answering the question. "But with the buzz around you and Megan at the SAG Awards, her team figures strike while the actor is hot."

Though Alessandro hadn't been nominated for the SAGs, his movie had been in several categories, and many guests had told him he'd been robbed. Megan had accompanied him, dressed in a dramatic blood-red dress with an enormous and intricately pleated design going diagonally from shoulder to hem. She'd made several best-dressed columns the next day, and no one could stop talking about her boyfriend and the shot-through-the-heart looks he'd been giving her all night.

"This isn't just any interview," Alessandro protested. "This is Lily Liebowitz. You know who her sister is."

Megan whispered, "Who?" and Alessandro took the phone away from his mouth and said, "Didi Ravello."

Megan's eyes widened, and a cowl of doom settled over him. Whatever he did, this would go wrong. The same way he'd known since he was fourteen that he couldn't stay in his family. The same way he'd known when that last designer had run his hand over Alessandro's butt while he was supposed to be checking the fit on a loose pair of pants. He knew this was the end of something. He would have to do the interview and risk the Ravello family finding his family in Italy or not do the interview and disappoint everyone whose livelihoods depended on him playing the game.

"I do not have a choice, do I?" he said, his eyes not leaving Megan's.

"No, but 'Sandro, we will handle her," Yasmin said. "She has the questions. You don't have to be like the others. If you don't want to answer anything she asks, just don't do it. What was that moody actor persona for if not for moments like this? Just glare at her like you're probably doing me right now."

Inevitable. His life was full of endings. He could only remind himself that he'd had beginnings, too, and he was now doing a job he loved.

"All right. What time?"

"Makeup at three. Max will pick you up at one thirty. Megan can come, too, by the way. Just not into the interview itself, of course."

"Okay," he said and hung up.

"Sweetheart," Megan said, "you look like she just told you the date of your funeral."

"You have watched Lily's interviews?"

"Yes, but—"

"She has already found out about my family. And my previous job. I know it. Didi has dug around in my history, she has found out, and she has told her sister, and that is why she wants to interview me." He took his phone, which was still in his hand, and googled his parents' names. He showed her the screen. "My father is conducting the San Francisco Philharmonic on Sunday night."

"Oh, Jesus. He's in town? Well, in the state?"

Alessandro shrugged.

"And he didn't even tell you?"

"*Cara*, I thought you understood. They are not my family."

"God." She unfolded herself from her club chair at the end of the bed they'd shared for a blissful month and sat in his lap. She brushed his hair from his temples and kissed them. "I'm so sorry."

"I am not. It is better this way."

"Not to be around your family? How is that better?"

He looked away from her and frowned. "You are away from your family. You have given them up."

"Not forever." She sounded shocked at the very idea. Did she judge him for staying away from his parents and brothers? Of course she would. She saw her siblings as good people.

"No. Not forever. But for me, it is better if it is forever."

Of course, if she wasn't going to fight with her sister forever, that meant she would eventually leave him and go back to Boston. His hands twitched on her hips as the shot punched through his heart again. And all because Megan's brother had caught Didi Ravello's eye more than ten years ago.

"I have another idea," Megan said. She was still stroking his hair off his forehead, and Alessandro couldn't resist leaning into her, breathing in her lemony scent. While he could.

"What is that?" he asked.

"What if you tell Lily all about it?"

He jerked his head away from her soothing hand and looked up at her. "I cannot—"

"I don't mean your parents. But we've been working to control the narrative, and this is an extension of that. Surprise Lily by telling her about your modeling career and why it ended."

"*Cara,*" he said, his entire being shying away from saying the words out loud to anyone other than her.

"I know, I know." She kissed his hair. "I'm asking you to reveal a very secret thing. And if you can't, I get it. But this can be a weapon for the interview. At this point, you're not going to make a dent in your career. People already take you seriously."

He didn't move, and she tipped his chin up so he had to look at her. "You know that, right? You've been nominated for an Oscar, remember? And the SAG Awards. Those people admire your acting skills. You think they'll change their minds because you walked catwalks ten years ago?"

Was this what death by a thousand cuts felt like? Megan couldn't know she was flaying him and sewing him back together at the same time. He would end up bleeding out. He knew it. When he'd opened himself up to his parents, they had rejected him. After that, losing acting roles barely touched him. Now he was supposed to open up to a complete stranger? To the entire world?

"No one will care," Megan repeated. "They will admire your journey. And you'll still be hiding the deepest part of you. If she mentions your parents, you can deflect. Or just stare at her, like Yasmin said."

His hands twitched again. "You are asking too much," he whispered. "You are the only one who has the deepest part of me."

Megan's eyes darkened.

"All I've done is cause you trouble," she said.

"I am not complaining."

"But I still don't know where this will go. I still don't know how to bring you and my sister both into my life."

And then Alessandro knew. She was the most important person in his life. But he wasn't the most important person in hers. She would go back to her siblings one day. As she should. She had chosen him once, but she wouldn't do it twice. And he would never be able to recapture the contentment she'd given him.

The contentment bled away from him even as he kissed her. So why shouldn't he tell the world his secrets? He could no longer tell her.

"What will I say to Lily?" he asked.

◆

The episode aired on Sunday night. Advertising had been wall-to-wall over the TV and internet, so the network got a fifty share even over the premiere of a fantasy series on a streaming service.

Megan and Alessandro dimmed the front windows, poured themselves large glasses of wine, and curled up on the couch to watch.

She had never told anyone apart from her family that she loved them. She hadn't had to. No one had captured her heart the way Alessandro had. From his ambition to his compassion to his stillness—and don't forget his body; there was always the red-hot shot of desire that went through her when she thought of that—Megan couldn't begin to imagine a life without him.

But was that love? Or infatuation? She'd watched her siblings fall in love, one after the other, but it wasn't as though she'd been in the room when it had happened. Half the time they and their other halves had been at each other's throats, and the next thing she knew, they were getting married. She and Alessandro hadn't once argued. Did that mean this wasn't love?

And he'd said she had the deepest part of him. Did that mean he loved her? She wished she had the guts to ask him outright. But maybe that was just some romantic Italian phrase that just meant he liked being around her.

Because he hadn't said anything else of the kind since that day, she remained a coward, getting as close physically to him as she could, while her heart swooped and fell with every word, every soft look he gave her.

Lily Liebowitz's first questions were easy pitches: "How did your role in *The Drummer* come about? What was it like working with so-and-so?" Then Lily moved further back. "Tell me about your relationship with Mohammed Bittar."

He went into their first job together and his pleasure at working with his friend. "I begged Mohammed to take me on in his first movie. I've never been so excited than when he won the Ravello. And we have so much history in common."

Lily laughed, looking to catch him out, to send him off-balance, ready to move in for the kill later. "You can't tell me you have anything in common with a Lebanese immigrant whose father was killed before he was born!"

"Not that, no," Alessandro said calmly. "I'm talking about a deeper feeling. A bone-deep knowledge that we had found a brotherhood in each other. We're both immigrants; we both love movies. We both had to fight to get where we are."

Lily's eyes lit up. He'd opened the door. But she only stuck a toe in this time. "Tell me about that. Your early years of acting. When did you know you wanted to be an actor?"

Alessandro gave her a cleaned-up version of his history, leaving out the arguments he had with his parents and his brothers' sneers and attacks. "But first," he said, "I needed lessons. And that required money. So I began modeling instead."

Lily looked up from her papers. Her eyes widened, then narrowed. He'd flipped the narrative on her, just as Megan and Alessandro had planned.

"Thank you, *cara*," Alessandro said now, curled up next to him on the couch. "I almost laughed at her."

"Well, she'd laughed at you," Megan complained. "She deserved it."

"This is new information," Lily said, though Megan could tell from her tone that it wasn't. Not to her. She'd wanted to pull it out of her hat, but he'd done it first.

"I had a different name then," he said. "I was lucky to get chosen and to find steady work. I made money and took acting lessons when I could. But..."

Megan grabbed his hand and held it very tightly while he outlined to Lily the changes that had come about, that had forced him to leave the career before he was ready. "I grew out of the sample sizes for young men's clothes." He shrugged. "And I was going to move into adult clothing, perhaps even swimsuits–"

Here, he looked right at Lily and gave her a self-deprecating but knowing smile. Her lips tightened.

"Fan-flipping-tastic," Megan murmured.

When he added the creepy designers and photographers and the one who finally made him flee to America, the entire audience was lapping up his trauma. And it was Lily who leaned forward and all but patted his knee. "I'm so sorry." But then she leaned back. "Why didn't you tell anyone about this before?"

"For the same reason others don't. I felt ashamed. Especially as a man. I should have punched that guy. But he held the purse strings. And he was only the latest in a line of them–men and women–in that business. Power is their kink. They would have been happy to blackball me from every catwalk in the industry. I had to make sure I left first."

"But you could have helped others."

"Yes." Megan had helped him get ready for this, too. "I regret that. I will be a lot louder about this in the future. I loved the people I met in my modeling career, but there were not enough gatekeepers, chaperones to keep everyone safe. My story is not the worst I've heard. And I'm going to start a fund to help anyone who's been hurt in that world. Lawyer fees, relocation costs. Whatever they need."

Megan knew what he was going to say and she still felt tears behind her eyes. Perhaps because she knew how much he meant it.

Alessandro had thrown Lily for a second, but there was still half the interview to go. "Take me to that moment, then," she said. "When you got off the plane in America. Why Boston? Why not New York?"

He explained his connection to someone who had a spare room and how he'd loved the old city, its history, and its connections to Italy. He did his terrible Boston accent. The audience could even hear the crew laughing at him. He smiled through his lashes at Lily, and she glared at him. He was winning.

But she still had her ace. "What about your family?" she said.

"Yes, I have made wonderful friends here. On both coasts. I—"

"That's nice, but that's not what I meant. What about your parents?"

The Alessandro on the TV leaned back and gave her an enigmatic smile. The Alessandro on the couch squeezed Megan's hand. She covered it with both hers and kissed his fingers.

"They are not in my life," he said, keeping the smile on his face.

"That's pretty hard on you, don't you think?"

Alessandro let the beat stretch out between them before replying in the same tone, "Not anymore."

"Our sources say you didn't just leave home. You were thrown out. Is that true?"

"No."

Lily wasn't going to be distracted. "That your father is actually Leonardo Russo. The world-famous conductor."

Alessandro shrugged.

"And your mother is Marilena Russo, who just took over from Yo-Yo Ma with the top-selling cello album sales in the world."

"Good for her," Alessandro said evenly.

"They're at the top of their fields, and you're at the top of yours. Why aren't they in your life? Why did they throw you out?"

"You'll have to ask them."

"I'm asking you."

"Yes, you are. And I am not answering you."

Lily had lost all her supposed empathy. She leaned forward, hungry now. "And your brothers? Did they cut you off as well?"

Alessandro paused again, long enough for the camera to pull in on his face, which showed absolutely no strain, no care of any kind. "You will have to ask them," he repeated.

"We did reach out to the Russos," Lily said to the camera as it switched to her, "but they didn't return our calls."

The other camera caught a tight hint of a smile on Alessandro's face.

"Well," Lily said, "perhaps they'll see this and have a change of heart."

"That is very optimistic of you," Alessandro said.

"It happens all the time." Lily waved her pen in the air. "At least you have a new person in your life. Does Megan support you?"

In all the weeks she'd known Alessandro, this was the first

time she'd heard her own name come out of the television. The feeling was bizarre.

"Of course."

"Tell me how you two met. It was right after you broke up with Nicola Kulik, if I'm not mistaken."

"Megan and I have been friends since before my first movie. We–"

"So she's not a rebound? How does she feel about Nikki?"

"Like nothing at all, Lily. We are permitted to have previous relationships."

"Sure, sure," she said. "But she isn't used to the celebrity life, is she? Are you facing any tensions with this spotlight aimed right at her? Was it fair to her to bring her into a new relationship this close to the Oscars?"

"You will have to ask Megan, Lily."

He said it slowly and with his now-trademark smile, but Lily's impertinent questions had been properly quelled.

"Now, tell me about *The Drummer*. Perhaps the defining role of last year. What preparation did you do to get into the role?"

The rest of the interview went as scripted, though Megan said, "She knows she's lost you. She didn't get what she wanted." Yasmin was texting thumbs-up emoji to Alessandro before the end credits rolled.

Alessandro stretched and Megan felt the tension leave him. "I think maybe in the future, I will be like DeNiro and never do interviews."

"He gave that up eventually. And you've shown you can control the story."

Alessandro buried his face in her hair. "The story is still out there. Now people know who my parents are. They will want to know more."

Megan put her arms around him. "And we'll figure out a way to make it work for you."

She couldn't see his face, just feel his breath on her neck. "We?" he said.

"Of course we. Unless you don't want me to help."

His hands tightened around her. "I will always want you to help."

"Okay, then." Megan pulled him with her as she lay down on the couch. Helping wasn't loving, she thought, but she shut it out and focused on the length of his body, his lean, strong legs, and his arms crushing her close.

♦

Chapter 23

The designers Megan liked had been sending racks of clothes for weeks, and another was expected today, so when the doorbell to the house rang a couple days later, Megan said, "I'll get it!" and checked the camera.

But there wasn't a sleekly dressed stylist with a van waiting at the door. It was two men, about Megan's age or a little older. One of them stared into the video camera. "'Ello?" he said.

The cameras were top-of-the-line. She saw at once that this man had Alessandro's gray eyes.

Megan opened the door before she knew it. But she couldn't speak. Both men were Alessandro's height and carried his slim build. One had black hair, longer than Alessandro's, pulled off his face. The other's hair was short but styled so it stood at the perfect angle, above eyebrows that were just like Alessandro's.

Megan opened her mouth. But she didn't even know their names.

"You are Megan?" the one with long hair asked in heavily accented English.

"Yes." Oh good. Something had come out of her mouth. And it wasn't vomit. What was Alessandro going to do? "You're his brothers."

"Si. I am Leo, and this is Massimo." The short-haired one lifted a hand in a half wave.

"Right. Hi." Megan hugged the door to her. She wasn't sure who she was protecting from whom, but she had to do it anyway. "Um, what are you doing here?"

Duh, Megan. They're here to check the drains. "We would like to talk to Alessio—Alessandro," Leo said.

"Yeah. I figured." God. Where were all her words? Nothing in her database of human interactions had prepared her for this. "How did you find his house?"

"We talked to Lily Liebowitz," Massimo said. "She called us. We were in Germany. We flew over as fast as we could."

Of course Lily, through Didi, who knew everything about everybody, would know Alessandro's address. Megan quickly looked behind them to the street, expecting a camera crew at least. The street was empty, but Lily must be playing the long game. She'd probably told Alessandro's brothers that they were next on her interview list. After Alessandro's hints and roadblocks the other day, she was going to punish him.

"You can't... you can't just show up," she said, opening her eyes wide.

"We had no other way to contact him," Massimo said.

"You should have called through his manager." And Megan realized the full advantage of having someone to protect you.

"He would not have seen us."

"He's not going to see you now." Megan's mind ping-ponged with scenarios. He was going to kill them. He was going to kill *her*. He was going to leave through the garage and none of them would ever see him again.

And then Leo did the worst thing he could do. "Please," he said. "Please, will you help us?"

"Oh no." She shook her head so hard, her hair fell around her face. Old Megan reached out to him, to be helpful. No matter what it cost her.

"We have to talk to Alessio," he went on. "We have to ask for our apologies. Please, will you ask him to listen to us?"

"*Cara?*" Alessandro's voice came down the stairs behind her.

Megan spun around. Through the open staircase, she saw

Alessandro's bare feet descending the stairs. His brothers were still on the front step. "Hold on," she said and slammed the door in their faces.

Alessandro, looking delicious in gray pajama pants and nothing else, stopped at the bottom of the stairs and looked around. "Where are the clothes?"

Megan drew a breath from deep in her chest. "Come here, hon." She pulled him to the kitchen stools, which faced away from the window and front door.

"Cos'è?" he asked, frowning. "Why are you so pale?"

"Listen." She held his hands in front of him with one of hers. "Your brothers have come here."

Her hands were useless at keeping him calm. He backed up, scraping the chair on the floor, making a noise that set her teeth on edge. He held on to the counter. "That is impossible," he said.

His voice was raw and low, even his vocal cords denying the truth. Megan hated hearing him like this. "They want to talk," she said. "They've come to apologize."

Alessandro looked at her. "And you want me to talk to them."

"I…"

"Yes. You want me to talk to them. You are helping them."

His silver eyes were like ice. Like he didn't know her.

Then he looked at the door, where his brothers' figures could be seen through the glass. With quick, angry strides, he reached the door and pulled it open.

Megan stayed on her kitchen stool, her hands over her mouth. The brothers backed up a step when they saw Alessandro. She wasn't the only one who found him frightening.

"E?" he snapped. *And?*

Leo began speaking in Italian, low and hesitating, but Alessandro interrupted him. "We are in America now. And I have a guest." Megan's eyes filled at how he spat the word out. From lover to guest. And to take their native language away from them. He wanted them at a disadvantage.

"You are here to ask for money," he said.

"Alessio, I know you will think that," Leo said. "But we are here to say we are sorry."

"Oh, well. That is all right then." He looked back at Megan. "They are sorry, *cara*."

He might have seen the tears in her eyes because he froze before turning determinedly away from her.

"Alessio, *ascolta*," Massimo broke in. "We did not know what they–"

"My name is Alessandro."

"We were children too!" Massimo exclaimed, ignoring him. "We were at the Conservatory. We didn't know you left until we got back for the holidays."

"We told them to tell us where you were, but they wouldn't," Leo said. "They told us you'd assaulted them. They told us they would have called the police if you hadn't left."

Alessandro didn't look at them. "No. I did not assault them," he said quietly, coldly. "I had had enough of being beaten by my brothers. I would not do it to others."

Leo and Massimo looked at each other. Megan saw the pain and guilt in their eyes and was glad of it. The tears fell down her cheeks. Alessandro was so polite, so gentle. And he'd put up with this for his entire childhood?

And Megan had told him to let his torturers into the house.

"We admit it," Leo said. "*Eravamo stronzi.* They told us competition was the only way to succeed. And you did not compete. They told us we were... making you tough."

Megan gulped back the tears and tried to make herself disappear.

"Sure, sure." Alessandro was nodding, but Megan hated the

sarcasm in his voice. "You were innocent in the whole thing. You never made me feel small for wanting what I wanted."

The brothers looked at each other. "We know," Massimo said. "We were... not good brothers."

"There is another word for it," Alessandro said. "*Prepontenti.* Bullies."

"Si. We know." Leo looked at the doorframe. "Can we come inside? We would not like to talk about this outside."

"What do you think, Megan?" Alessandro asked, looking back at her and just as quickly looking away. "I think that my security training would tell me not to let two strangers into the house. Don't you?"

"Just hear them out," Megan said, but her voice was shaky and small and did no good at all.

"I..." He made a show of thinking. "I think I have a ceremony to get ready for. I think you should go back wherever you came from and be with the people who want you in their lives."

He looked at Megan when he said it.

And he went to close the door. "Wait!" she cried. There it was. Her voice, strong and echoing through the room. She impatiently wiped her cheeks and walked toward him.

Megan always went for the easy way out, the path that led to peace. Even at her own expense. All she ever wanted was for everyone to get along. Most especially, she wanted her and Alessandro to get along. She should just put her arms around him, tell him she understood, let him close the door on his brothers. Go back to the way things were.

But she couldn't let him shut them out. She just couldn't. "'Sandro, please. Let them at least say what they came to say."

He gave her that icy stare. He thought she was betraying him. She should be backing him up, letting him dismiss this painful part of his life. Letting him move into the future, never resolving this conflict.

But Megan knew that history never just went away. When a wound cut as deep as his had, it festered until it was dealt with. The broody Alessandro, the loving Alessandro, the hardworking Alessandro—all were in danger if he didn't face these men.

So, yes, she betrayed him. He would never trust her again. She opened the door wider and said, "Come in."

The brothers did so. Alessandro turned his back and went into the kitchen, opening the refrigerator to pull out a bottle of orange juice. Leo and Massimo looked at Megan with wide, nervous eyes. Yeah, Alessandro was terrifying, even when all he was doing was drinking juice straight from the bottle. Maybe that darkness was what made him such a good actor.

They moved a few feet into the room. "Okay, talk," Megan said, swallowing the tears that wanted to burst out of her at her beautiful, damaged man.

"We do not have excuses for—" Leo began. But Megan shook her head.

"Christ's sake, speak Italian. Or you'll never be done."

She walked to the back of the house and out the patio door. With her pajamas still on, she jumped into the plunge pool and stayed down until her lungs burned and the tears had washed from her cheeks.

When she broke back through the surface, she heard Alessandro shouting, so she dunked again. But the tears came back and she couldn't stay down for long, so she hauled herself out and grabbed a towel to hide her sobs, until the sounds inside the house ended.

She didn't hear the door close, but the silence indicated that Alessandro's brothers had left. Perhaps Alessandro had as well. No. He'd been in pajamas. Megan stayed on the chaise, wiping her eyes with the towel, and waited.

The patio door opened, and Alessandro came out to sit next

to her. She couldn't look at him. If she saw that same indifference he'd shown inside, she'd break into pieces.

He didn't relax on the chaise, sitting sideways instead, facing her. About when she thought she was going to burst if he didn't say something, he did.

"You think that my family is like yours."

"I don't. But they—"

"I had told you who they were. I shared with you what my brothers did. And you let them into the house anyway."

Megan had thought she was all done crying. Nope. The coolness of his voice stabbed her. "It's been years. Your parents poisoned them. They know that now. And when they found out, they flew over as soon as they could."

His face a block of granite, he shook his head.

"But, Alessandro, they are *sorry.*"

He rubbed at one palm with his thumb, as though there was a very important piece of dirt on it he had to erase. "This is why you and I are too different. Your siblings are perfect to you."

"They are not!"

"You love them. You have already forgiven your sister. You will go home and you have years of good memories to keep you with them. You will go back to being the Megan they want you to be. I was always myself around my brothers, and I was punished for it. But you will accept being their Megan, and I will not accept being my brothers' Alessio."

"'Sandro," she cried. "Just because I love my family doesn't mean I don't see their flaws."

"That is the difference between us. I do not love mine."

"I'm not asking you to," she said. Hiding the tears was hopeless. He wasn't looking at her anyway. "I'm just asking you to let them in a little. Like you did me."

"Yes, I did that." Now he was looking at her, and she wished he would stop. She bit her lip at the calmness in his eyes. Like in the interview. He had closed off from her. She had betrayed him, and so she'd lost him. "I will not do that again."

"Alessandro," she said one last time.

"I will call Jacqui to help you pack," he said, and he left her on the patio, the mellow burble of the pond at odds with the agony taking over her body.

◆

Chapter 24

Alessandro sat on his couch three hours after Megan left, looking out the front windows at the view. The trees and roofs and the distant skyscrapers. He'd forgotten how beautiful they all were before Megan had come into his house. He'd seen so much beauty because of her.

And then he'd watched her cry. And done nothing.

Ugh. He stood and paced up and down the room before falling, helplessly, back onto the couch.

They were too far apart. She was too enmeshed in her family to see that he could not be with his. Americans and their persistent optimism. She still believed his brothers were redeemable.

He'd told her about them. Hadn't he? Maybe not all the details. Honestly, their physical bullying hadn't been as bad as the emotional kind he'd received from his parents. Who sure hadn't shown up on his doorstep this morning. Any attempts to get a word out of them from the media were met with "no comment" from a spokesperson.

He watched social media to see if Lily had arranged the interview with his brothers, but their names were nowhere. Neither was Alessio Russo's. Pictures of his model years hadn't popped up on every website. Commentators weren't laughing at his presumption to be an actor when he was "only" a model. His Oscar nomination hadn't been withdrawn.

The silence was deafening.

Until six p.m. when his name pinged, associated with a photo of Megan landing at Boston airport, large dark glasses over her eyes, an overnight case dragging behind her.

She'd gone home. Where he'd told her to go.

He looked back at his house. Everything of her had gone, except her scent and two racks of clothes he'd pushed into the guest bedroom and slammed the door on. Every dress on them was so exactly Megan that it burst his heart to look at them.

He stood up with a groan. His body felt like it had just gone through boot camp. Every muscle ached. Then he realized he had been holding in tears for hours, and that picture was forcing them out of him.

He couldn't miss her. He had made the right decision.

He let out a string of Italian curses, shouting them at the house that wouldn't let him let go of her. He strode to the patio doors in the back and pulled them open with desperate violence.

But the yard provided no respite. Just looking at the pool made his fingers itch for her smooth, wet skin, for the lines of her bikini that he could slip under and make her head fall back. He growled and turned his back on it. On the whole place.

She was gone. He had chosen himself over her. He was going to have to live with that.

So why was the pain in his chest so much worse?

◆

Megan took a cab from Logan. No more black cars. No more Nelson and Terry. She was about to become old news.

Until she rebuilt something new. Something on her own terms.

The cab took her through the familiar streets as the sun set. As she pulled up to the Fielding family home, she saw the porch light click on. Pulling her suitcase out of the trunk, she squared her shoulders and walked into the house.

"Who—" Cat said as she came out of the kitchen, wiping her hands on a well-worn tea towel. Then she dropped the towel. "What?" she said instead.

Megan let go of her suitcase and walked directly into her sister's arms.

Cat took half a second to react to Megan's arms around her, but then she was hugging her back, and Megan let the sobs she'd held in since LAX go free.

"I'm gonna fucking kill him," Cat said.

Megan laughed despite herself. "Get in line," she said.

Cat squeezed her more tightly. "God, I missed you."

"Me too, you," Megan admitted, crying again. "I'm sorry I said—"

"I'm sorry too." Megan felt dampness on her shoulder and realized Cat was also crying. "I didn't know you were so stressed out. Honey, if we'd known..."

"I didn't even know it myself until..." But she couldn't say Alessandro's name.

"Thank you for coming here," Cat said. "Thanks for coming home."

They held each other in the front hall for a little while longer, then pulled away and laughed at the tears on each other's cheeks. "We're pathetic," Cat said.

"We're allowed a cry once in a while."

Cat blinked at her. "Wait till you're a mother. You'll see. Come on. We need wine."

In the kitchen, Cat turned off the stove, where she'd been cooking dinner, and pulled out the bottle of wine Megan knew would be ready and waiting. She shooed Megan into the family room where they could both sit on the squashed couch, sharing a blanket, drinking their wine, and rubbing bare feet on the back of Bofur, who'd happily greeted Megan as though this were just another Sunday.

"Luckily, Antonio's picking up the boys from practice tonight," Cat said. "We have the house to ourselves. So you want to tell me about it?"

"Some of it. But do you think the others would come over? I'd rather tell you all at once."

Cat immediately sent a message to the group chat: *Megan is home. Get over here now.* Sam sent a question mark, and Cat conceded that from New Mexico it would be hard to *get over here now.* So Sam dialed in on video chat.

"Imma fucking kill him," she said as soon as they answered.

"Get in line," Cat and Megan both said.

"Christ, and Kane's really going to kill him," Cat said. "Remember how he was with Liam?"

"It doesn't matter," Megan said, causing Sam to choke with laughter. "I mean, he doesn't need killing. He was just... protecting himself. And I..."

Nope. Couldn't talk about it. She shook her head, and Sam tsked.

Thea arrived first, as she lived closest, school was out, and she could bring Benji, her younger son. After he'd greeted his auntie with all the lack of enthusiasm of an eight-year-old, Cat sent him upstairs to play in the guest bedroom that used to be Sam's. Ten minutes later, Kane arrived.

Cat's hugs were tight. Kane's were rib-crushing. "I'm going to kill him," he said when he finally let go.

"Get in line," everyone answered.

Megan smiled at them all while rubbing her rib cage. "Thanks. Thanks for coming so quickly, too."

"Of course we would," Thea said. "We're so glad you're back. We hated you and Cat being mad at each other."

Megan glanced at Cat. They still had things to talk about. But right now, she had something more important to say.

"Sundays have been really weird without you," Cat agreed.

"Only because you didn't have your servant to do your bidding," Sam said.

They all looked at Cat's phone, propped up on the coffee table. "Ouch," Cat said.

"That's not what it was," Megan said. "It was more than... Okay, wait." She pressed her fingers into her eye sockets for a second. "I'm starting in the wrong place. Listen."

She took her hands away and looked at them all: Kane, sitting in a huge armchair that he managed to make look normal-sized, dressed in a suit as he'd probably come straight from work; Thea, in sensible pants and a sweater, taking the third seat on the couch next to Megan; Sam, russet hair and tan skin singling her out among them as someone who lived her life outdoors as much as possible; and Cat, older, harder, her hair always in a topknot because she was too busy to do anything with it.

Megan's siblings. God, how she loved them. But six weeks away had given her clarity: they couldn't keep on going as they had been.

Would they listen to her? The youngest, the caboose? The surprise?

But the alternative to speaking was to say nothing. To go back. And Megan couldn't do that. She had somewhere to go now and a career to build that would fulfill her.

Nowhere to go but forward. "Kane," she said. "Hire Cat." Cat gave a very catlike squeak next to her. "You know you're the one who should be running Fielding Paper with him," Megan said to her. "You two fight about it every weekend. You could run it with your eyes closed. And you're bored as hell being a stay-at-home mom."

Cat's mouth dropped open, as did Kane's. "I am *not* bored!" she protested. "I'm raising my kids."

"I know." Megan put a hand on her knee. "And you've been raising all of us at the same time. I can tell it's driving you crazy. The boys are going to start college in the fall. You'll have the time to work. To do more with your skills."

"God," Kane said. "Cat, it's been right in front of my face. I didn't think you wanted to."

"I didn't—I don't—"

"You're an amazing mom," Megan said. "I should know." Cat turned watery eyes to her, and she smiled at her. "You can be that and be an amazing executive. You were born to it."

"She was forced into it, you mean," Sam put in. "If Mom and Dad hadn't died, who knows what Cat might have done?"

"We're all a product of that time," Thea said. "We've all made decisions that might not have been healthy for us because of them." She grimaced, probably thinking about her first husband. "And before you sit there too smug, Sam," she went on, "you know full well you made some questionable choices as well in your time."

Sam had the grace to blush, but she lifted her chin. "I've paid my dues," she said stoutly. "And Cat's paid hers. I think her going to work for Kane is a fantastic idea. They can fight in the privacy of their own offices and not all over us every Sunday."

"You're never here every Sunday!" Cat complained.

"Maybe I would be if you guys would shut up for half a second!"

"All right, all right!" Megan put up her hands. But she had to laugh. Cat and Sam would also always fight. But the heat had been taken out of it. Since getting married, Sam had come to understand Cat a lot better. Maybe she would come to visit more often.

"If Cat's coming to work with me," Kane said, making Megan look at him, "what are you going to do?"

"I'm going to resign. I'm going back to LA."

As she'd known they would, all four of them erupted. "What?" "You just got here!" "I thought you guys broke up!" "You're fucking kidding me."

"Yeah, I know," she replied, leaning forward to rest her elbows on her knees. There. She'd told them something they didn't want to hear. And the world hadn't collapsed around her. "But this has nothing to do with Alessandro."

Oof, there. She'd said his name. And the spike in her heart twisted. But it didn't change her decision. "There's a place for me there."

"With all those cameras pointing—" Cat began, but Thea shushed her.

"Yes, with all those cameras. Turns out, I can help kids with their self-esteem when I post on social media. I can build websites for charities and improve their fundraisers. I can use my contacts in the fashion business to find good clothes for women reentering the workforce." She smiled at Kane. "And I can look really good while I do it."

"You *like* the attention?" Cat said, scandalized.

Megan shrugged. "I kind of do. Think of it as how you feel when the boys' basketball moms rave over your chili. It's what I'm good at. It's what I can do."

"Those things sound great," Kane said. His voice sounded a little rougher than usual. "You know we only want you to be happy, Megs. But—"

She knew there'd be a *but*.

"Can you be happy over there without him?"

Their faces swung over to her in such perfect sync that she had to smile, even though the thought of a life without Alessandro felt like a rainbow without its color. "I had a whole plane flight to think about it," she told them. "Being in LA without Alessandro is still a better place for me than being in Boston without him."

There was a silence. Then Cat said, "I can't believe I'm losing two sisters."

"We're not lost," Sam said before Megan could. "You have my address."

"Things were never going to stay exactly the same," Megan said more gently, scooting over to take Cat's hand. "That's not how life works."

Cat shrugged and a tear fell off the end of her nose. "But that's all I wanted."

"Dammit, Cat," Kane said, launching himself out of his seat to crowd them all on the couch so he could hug her. "If you cry, I will, too, and no one wants to see that."

Cat laughed and sobbed and laughed again.

"We'll figure it out," Kane said, reaching behind him for the box of tissues that was always on the end table. "Maybe Megan'll get you a meeting with Hugh Jackman or whoever it is you like these days."

"Oh, shut up," Cat said, swatting at him and grabbing a tissue. "And it's Josh Brolin, for your information."

"I did meet him, actually," Megan said.

"You are *freaking* kidding me!" Cat said, forgetting her tears.

Thea stood. "Lemme finish up the dinner Cat started out there, and Megan can tell us everything that happened. As much as she wants to, anyway."

"Not fair!" Sam said. "I have to go pick up the kids and make dinner here."

"Sucks to be you," Cat said, reaching for her phone.

"Megan!" Sam begged. "Call me!"

"I will." Megan laughed. Cat clicked off on Sam's protests.

♦

Chapter 25

Alessandro ignored Yasmin's texts and calls and tried to sleep. But for two days, he couldn't. The little house was too empty, too hollow. "Sources" had said that Megan had gone to visit her family for a few days. Gossip leaped on the tiny crack in their happy image. That Alessandro couldn't drag himself to two pre-Oscar parties that week didn't help either.

Finally, he called Colson, his stuntman friend. "Can I come work out at your place today?"

"Sure. Everything okay?"

"Yes. It's fine. I just need to… blow off steam."

"Is Megan coming too?"

"No."

There was a pause on the line, then Colson said, "Well, sure, buddy. Come on over."

Max was ready to pick him up within minutes of his call. The car was too damn big without her in it. Max said nothing. If Alessandro noticed that the man looked in the rearview mirror at him a few times, he ignored it.

The car was ushered through the solid wood and steel gates at the end of Cassidy's driveway and carried Alessandro away from his disaster of a life into comforting arms.

Colson said very little, just brought him to the fully equipped gym in a glass-fronted room at the back of the house and gave him a towel. Alessandro pounded the treadmill for longer than usual, but the pain in his heart wasn't replaced by exhaustion. Then he went to the weights. He needed to extend himself, to punish his body until it submitted and he could stop thinking about her. But when he began to set up for a bench press and kept on loading up the weights, Colson finally spoke.

"Dude. You want help with that?"

Alessandro hadn't been counting. He was in shape, sure, but even he couldn't lift the number of plates he'd added to the bar. And he was on the bench, about to lift the damn thing off the rack and probably cave in his ribs.

His body collapsed, his arms going out to the sides, his back arching, his legs splaying out. Sweat poured off him; he felt shaky. That was when he realized he hadn't had anything but coffee today.

Colson sat on the bench next to him. "Wanna talk about it?"

No, he didn't want to talk about it. Nothing like this had happened to him since he'd left home, and any setbacks he'd had, he'd dealt with himself.

"I will be okay," he said.

"I beg to differ." Cassidy appeared out of nowhere holding a pitcher of water filled with lemon and orange slices and two glass mugs. "Here. Sit up." Alessandro did as he was told, which was when he saw the servant come in behind Cassidy with a tray of bagels with lox, eggs Benedict, and fruit.

Cassidy handed him a glass and poured him a drink, then directed the servant to put the tray down on a third bench. She sat gracefully next to it and began to put cream cheese on a poppy-seed bagel. "You're here without Megan," she said conversationally as she did so, "and even this dumb actress can see that she isn't just hopping over to the East Coast for a family weekend. What did you do?"

He laughed shortly and took another deep draft of the water. "Of course it is something I did."

"If it wasn't, you would have told us by now," Colson said.

Alessandro shook his head at them. "There are some things you cannot joke your way out of, *amico*."

"Can you love your way out of them?" Cassidy asked.

Alessandro couldn't bear to meet her eyes. Could he have done that? Could he have simply loved Megan, listened to her, changed his whole way to be and welcomed in her way?

Not this guy. "Not this time," he said. "I discovered that she doesn't know what"—he gestured to his chest—"what makes me, me. My brothers showed up, and she let them in."

"That monster," Cassidy commented.

"I have not told you about them. And I won't start now. But I hope you believe me when I say I did not need to see them again. Or anyone in my family. I did not need to."

Why had he repeated that?

"And Megan pushed you to?" Cassidy asked.

"Yes."

"Because she and her siblings are famously close, and she wants that for you."

"Yes. She did not understand that I don't need that."

"No. He doesn't need anybody. That's what we've always said, isn't it, Cole?"

Alessandro heard the sarcasm in her voice, and he definitely couldn't miss how it dripped from Colson's reply. "Right. Darn tootin'. No one better help that island of manly broodiness, Alessandro Rosselli."

"Now you are misunderstanding me," he protested.

"You're misunderstanding yourself," Cassidy said. "It sounds like your brothers hurt you a whole lot, and I get that it'll take a while to forgive them, if you ever do. But you shot the messenger. Lemme ask you a question: has anyone ever understood your drive for excellence in your job like Megan has? Or made your professional life better the way she has?"

"That was two questions."

"Two questions, then." Cassidy bit into her bagel.

He thought back to their early morning conversations, to

their strategies, which seemed to come naturally to Megan while never dimming her enthusiasm for the moment. She lit him up. He could do his job better because she'd helped him do so.

"This would not have made my life better," he tried, although his muscles shook with missing her. "Now I would have to always wonder if she would make another decision like this without me."

"Oh God, no," Cassidy said, her perfectly made-up eyes wide. "A woman who thinks for herself. The horror."

Colson laughed, but Alessandro was in agony. "That is not what I meant. I love that she thinks for herself."

"Until it was inconvenient for you."

"Inconvenient!" The fear, anger, betrayal, and rejection that had swamped him when Leo and Massimo had walked through that door was a little more than inconvenient.

"Don't get mad." Cassidy handed him a plate of eggs Benedict. "Eat."

Before his mouth started saying things he'd regret in front of these people he used to think of as his good friends, he filled it with egg. *Gesù*, the damn thing was so good, he could cry.

"I get it, 'Sandro," Cassidy said. "You're frightened. No, don't interrupt. Keep eating. I've never seen a man more in need of a sandwich. I'm gonna guess this is the first time since you left home that you've been in love?" He choked, and his eyes began watering. Colson hit him on the back—kinda hard—but otherwise didn't come to his rescue.

"'Sandro?" Cassidy went on relentlessly. "You love her, right?"

Fuck. He almost dropped the plate. The heat that pulsed through his whole body at the words, heat not only from how completely Megan had taken over his life but from how frightened he was to commit to her, should have sizzled the sweat right off him.

Was he going to ignore that feeling? Was he going to turn his back on the best thing that had ever come into his life, because of one surprise action?

"Si," he said. Now he was exhausted.

After a pause, Colson spoke. "When I met Cass and found myself incapable of looking at her without hearing wedding bells, I took a job in New Zealand to get away from her. Never been so scared in all my life. Could have played Orcs until Doomsday, never have known any of this." He looked around them and then back to Cassidy.

"And you let him go?" Alessandro asked with a painful smile to Cassidy.

"You think I wasn't afraid, too? And for me it was worse because I was worried about my career. What a stupid-ass reason not to be in love."

"That is not why—"

"I know. You have a whole stupid reason of your own."

Alessandro took a sprig of parsley off the side of the plate and chewed on it. The taste was so clean and fresh, and he felt so spent and grimy. "Americans are too truthful," he said.

"Isn't that why you came here today?" Cassidy said. "Besides, aren't you Italian? Home of the loud arguments and waving hands and smashed plates?"

"Not in my family." He looked at Cassidy. She was twenty years older than him, but he realized he'd come to see her as a sister and Colson as his brother. "I have family here, and you two are a big part of that."

"Good. We love you too."

He winced. "Americans say that too much, too." Especially in LA, where terms of endearment were thrown around like confetti.

"Sure, in this business. But you don't believe we can really care for each other and tell each other so?"

"What she means is," Colson said, "when are you going to go find your gal and tell her you love her before her family convinces her to stay in Boston?"

"She will not have me back," he said, wincing at what he had said to her. What he had believed.

"Possibly," Cassidy agreed, making him clench his teeth. "But possibly, you great buffoon, she loves you too."

"What am I to do? Fly to Boston and beg her siblings to give her up?" Her brother would break his arm before Alessandro got out of the airport.

Cassidy circled her finger at him. "I love this for you," she said. "You've had things too easy up till now."

Alessandro spluttered. "Easy?"

"Yep. Time for a real challenge. Go get your gal."

♦

He had Max drive him home so he could pack. The worst part was, he had to call Yasmin.

"Hmph," she said when she picked up.

"I am sorry."

"You have missed two parties where I had told two very promising directors you would be."

"I am sorry, Yasmin. I have not been myself." Or maybe he'd been too much himself. Closing off, thinking he had to do everything alone.

"Well." He imagined her pushing her glasses up her nose. "You're lucky I like you."

"You do," he admitted, "and you know I appreciate you more than I can tell you."

"All right, all right. I assume you called for something, not just to flatter me."

"Yes, though I will remember to do that more often in the future. I need to get through LAX as quickly as possible."

There was a pause. "You're going after her?" she said.

"Yes." He didn't have to ask if Megan had filled her in on what he'd done. "I have many apologies to make."

"Right. Okay, listen. I need you to stop by here first. You won't get a flight that lands before midnight anyway. Take the red-eye tonight. You can do your big grand gesture tomorrow. You've forgotten about your fitting this afternoon."

He had completely forgotten about it. He'd chosen his tux for the Oscars with Megan. They'd spent a perfect afternoon getting gelato at Ponte's before Federica and Megan bonded over the benefits of shawl versus peaked lapels. Then Max had driven them out to a private house in the hills, where a chef had served them and them alone. Late that night, tipsy and giggling and slumped against each other in the back seat, they had come back to the house and fallen asleep on the couch like puppies. Megan had awoken next to him with her hair tangled and her makeup smudged, and he'd never seen anything more beautiful. The perfect day.

Could he still wear that tux if his trip to Boston didn't work?

But he couldn't stretch Yasmin's patience any further. "I will be there. Two o'clock. Yes?"

"Yes."

"The show must go on. Right?"

"Don't feel sorry for yourself, Alessandro. You did this. I'll see you at two."

He hung up, shaking his head with a laugh at Yasmin's bluntness. He deserved it.

He needed a drink before going upstairs to shower. And maybe now he'd sleep for an hour before he had to leave.

He got out a glass and went to the refrigerator to fill it. But the ice shot out of the dispenser so fast, a couple of cubes fell on the floor. When he looked under the kitchen island to pick them up, he found a piece of paper. Pulling it out, he saw it was a phone number on an airport convenience store receipt.

An international phone number.

He straightened and stared at it, his fingers tapping the counter behind him. Even that tiny sound echoed through his empty house.

"Fuck it," he said to no one and dialed the number.

"*Pronto*," the voice on the other end answered.

"It's Alessandro," he said in Italian. "I'm ready to listen. And this time, I will listen better."

◆

Chapter 26

He was really beginning to like that word, *fuck*. It covered so many emotions. All he wanted to say, as he showered and dressed, grabbed a to-go cup of coffee and a banana, and got in the back of Max's car, was *fuckfuckfuckfuckfuck*.

Could he rebuild a relationship with his brothers? They sounded like different people, once he'd calmed down enough to listen. Was he the same as he'd been as a teenager? Of course not. So was it possible that they'd genuinely changed?

Megan would say it was.

He would tell her tomorrow. When he'd finished with this damn fitting and faced the music—that was the phrase she'd taught him—with her siblings. He didn't believe he could walk this back, but at least now he believed he should try.

The value of the tux he was wearing to the Oscars was so high, a representative from Federica's had to accompany it everywhere. So when he walked into Yasmin's offices and got past the receptionist, he went directly to the conference room slash studio that was set up for these fittings.

Jacqui saw him, gulped, and scurried out of sight. He hoped she'd bring more coffee, whatever she thought of him. Opening the door to the conference room, he found Yasmin, Donna, his stylist, the designer's rep, and a tailor. Yasmin introduced everyone, gave him a giant stink eye, and left. Donna handed him a sheaf of questions he needed to have answers for the next day, including where Megan was—a made-up answer—and then she was gone as well. At least she gave his arm a sympathetic pat before she left.

Since the people from Federica's knew nothing, of course, he was able to be somewhat normal, following their instructions, raising and lowering his arms when requested, and discussing shoes. Easy. Could do it in his sleep.

Only he hadn't slept.

Next, a jeweler arrived. The tux didn't make room for much of it, but Alessandro had chosen a starburst ear wrap in sapphires that fought with his eyes, and a two-finger ring for his left hand. Because Megan would have been on his right side, of course, and his arm would have been around her. Embracing her waist. Resting on her hip. Anticipating the end of the night.

The jeweler's rep was serious to the point of rudeness. Which suited Alessandro's mood just fine. He let his helpful smile relax into the moody, standoffish character who'd glared back at him from photographs for years.

Megan had made him smile. That was all. She'd made him smile.

After more than an hour of this emotional torture, he was released. The tux was carefully put away with a promise to deliver it to his house on Oscar day, and the jewelry was hidden in a velvet box with a hint that *if* he was pronounced worthy and the designer didn't change their mind and the wind wasn't blowing the wrong way, he would be permitted to put them on in the car on the way to the ceremony. His car would be followed by the jeweler's, who had several pieces on the red carpet to worry about.

Alessandro tried to sound sincere in his thanks, but when they'd all gone, he stayed in the room, leaning his hands on the table at one end and letting his head slump.

The show must go on.

Fuckfuckfuckfuckfuck.

Voices from outside reminded him that he couldn't stay all day. He took his cup of coffee—which Jacqui had refilled with a pained smile he thought was trying to be neutral—and opened the heavy door to the room.

And ran into Megan.

He could hardly take in the fact that she was here, one foot away, her face showing as much surprise as he felt, before someone pushed his shoulder so hard he staggered back and almost fell into the door. His coffee splashed all over him, soaking his black-and-white floral button-down and burning his chest.

"Are you kidding me?" a woman's voice said, but it wasn't Megan's. She was still staring at him, her eyes huge.

"Megan," he could only say. His hand reached out to her. Was she real?

"Don't touch her," the other woman said. "Not before I've kicked your ass, anyway."

He didn't want to stop gazing at Megan lest she disappear, but the other woman pushed in between them, and Alessandro had to look up at her.

Yes, up, because she was taller than Megan, with wiry copper hair and skin that looked as though she spent most of her time outside. Unlike the chic clothes of everyone around her, she was in a Humboldt Redwoods T-shirt, cargo pants, and walking boots. And she wore no makeup.

This collection of clues came together in his mind. "You are Sam," he said.

"Yeah." She put her hands on her hips. "I am Sam. And you"—she poked him in the shoulder again and, *cazzo*, did she do exercises with her fingers or something? Because that hurt—"are high on my shit list, buddy."

No more than he was on his own shit list. He glanced back at Megan. "Don't leave. Please."

"Why not?" Sam said for her. "Give me one good reason why

she shouldn't be leaving you and everything here after what you did to her?"

Megan's eyes were boring into him. Alessandro waited, and she said, "Yes, Alessandro. Why not?"

The entire office was looking at them. If people had been behind glass walls or in offices, they weren't anymore. Alessandro was in a hallway with no way out. And he couldn't ask her to come into the conference room with him. That would be the coward's way.

But if he was going to speak directly from his heart, he had to use the language he'd grown up with. "*Perché*," he said, guiding Sam out of the way with his hand while the other pulled Megan toward him. "*Perché, cara—*"

Megan's eyes filled with tears.

"Shit, dude. I'm gonna kill you," Sam said.

Megan slumped against the wall behind her, breaking Alessandro's hold on her. Sam elbowed Alessandro out of the way and put her arm around her sister's, pulling her away from him so firmly that Megan stumbled.

♦

Why? Why did he have to find her here? She'd had no time to fortify herself against seeing him again. They were both still Yasmin's clients, so one day she'd known it might happen. But today? When she'd just flown in and Sam had come from New Mexico to help her begin the next chapter of her life? If he hadn't seen the photo of her in the Boston airport, this was proof that he'd been right, that she'd run back to her family as soon as things got hard.

This morning, she and Sam had taken a regular ole cab from the airport hotel into the city to sign the lease on the warehouse Megan would be using for her charity. Sam was the perfect travel companion: nonjudgmental, ready to trash Alessandro as soon as Megan got teary, and enthusiastic about Megan's future without him.

More enthusiastic than Megan was, for sure.

But now Alessandro was here. And he was looking at her, those gray eyes back to the ocean storm she'd always loved. They held no anger, no ice. Nothing of what he'd given her three days ago.

And Megan wasn't ready for it.

Alessandro followed them back to the waiting room, where Sam made for a couch and deposited Megan into it. "You don't have to do this," Sam said to her. "We can come back later."

"No, don't go," Alessandro said—begged. And then he really begged, dropping to his knees in front of her. "Mi dispiace tanto, cara. E colpa mia. Mi dispiace tanto."

Megan looked away from his face in front of hers. She tried not to cry in front of him, because who the hell did he think he was? But she couldn't stop her shoulders from hitching, and she'd forgotten her wet cheeks.

"I am so, so sorry," he went on in English. "You were right, and I didn't want to listen. I have spoken with my brothers. We are going to try to be... family again. And you were right that I am better when I try to heal those wounds rather than ignore them."

Well, she sure the hell wasn't able to stop crying now. He'd talked to his brothers. He'd changed his mind. Because she'd asked him to.

He moved to wipe her tears, but she couldn't have it yet. She could not let him touch her again. Not before he suffered as she had. He could have talked to his brothers days ago, and she wouldn't have had to go through this.

She blocked his hand with hers. "Not the face!" a voice somewhere in the room said. Yasmin. Megan couldn't help tilting her mouth, just a little. Maybe her hand was a little close to his perfect face.

"You can hit me if you like," he said, taking her fist and holding it to his chest. "I chose wrong. I gave you pain, and I will pay for it for the rest of my life. I should have chosen you. I will always choose you. Forgive me, *cara*. I am an idiot, an asshole. A dumbass."

Megan shook her head. But she smiled just a little bit more. Alessandro leaned forward so his torso was against her knees, his knees on the floor on either side of her legs. "*Ti amo, cara. Ti amo tanto.*"

Dammit. Did he have to say it in Italian? It just made the words even more romantic. She gave one brief sob, and Sam growled from above them.

"*Mi dispiace, cara*," he went on. "*Ti amo, ti amo.*"

He kept saying it, his voice low, melting her heart and her hurt and everything except that he knew what he'd done and he was trying to make amends. Megan let out a shaky breath and let him take her into his arms. Her head fell naturally onto his shoulder, and she let her tears soak his coffee-smelling shirt. She probably had coffee on her blouse too.

"*Ti amo anch'io*," she whispered. "You shit."

"I forgot that one," he said into her hair. "I am a shit."

She shook again and laughed. Laughed! How was that possible?

"Are you crying?" another voice said above them. Jacqui.

"Me?" Yasmin said, her voice tight. "Of course not. I never cry." She cleared her throat. "I'm too busy for this. I have to make a phone call. Megan, I'll talk to you later. Remember, eleven a.m. Sunday for makeup." Alessandro didn't move from Megan's hair as she heard Yasmin's heels tap up the hallway.

Megan's heart swooped upward for the first time in two days. Alessandro pulled back, wiped her tears from her face, kissed her wet eyelids, her wet cheeks, her mouth. Megan had never in her life looked so disheveled in public. Her silk blouse was blotched with tears and coffee; her makeup was shot, and her skirt was crumpled from Alessandro leaning on it.

She'd never cared less.

"Well, I haven't forgiven you," Sam said. But she was very far away, and Alessandro and Megan understood each other perfectly.

Max brought the car back around. Megan promised Sam she'd call her later, hugged her tight, and sent her back to the hotel.

Megan and Alessandro got into Max's car. "No hickeys!" Donna yelled. "I'm talking to you, 'Sandro!"

Max closed the door. Megan immediately straddled Alessandro's thighs, her light summer skirt thankfully making it easy. She didn't care what Donna said. She had lost time to make up.

His hands went to her ribs and slipped around to her back while she bent over his mouth and kissed him hard, punishing him one more time.

"My blouse smells like coffee," she said between kisses.

"I am sorry."

"You'd better take it off, then."

He groaned and opened his mouth, so Megan let her tongue play with his for a few more seconds before she broke off and began to pull at his shirt buttons. He shifted to help her, but when he reached for her blouse, she slapped his hand. "I changed my mind." And she crossed her arms and took off her own blouse, loving the way he gazed at her breasts, revealed in their lacy bra, right in front of his face.

"Megan," he moaned. The car was moving, bumping his hips into hers.

"We fought," she said against his ear while his hands covered her breasts and began to stroke her nipples through the lace. "That means we can make up. That means we'll be o-*kay*!"

The last syllable was a gasp as he ducked his head to take one breast in his mouth. "*Si*," he said, bussing her skin with his breath. "*Si, cara.* We will be okay."

The car bumped again, and now Megan had more reason to gasp. Her brain had completely given itself over to her loins, which were crushed against his, the minor difficulty of his pants and her underwear teasing her. She wasn't about to wait for this until they got home.

She reached between them, unzipped his pants, made the arrangements, and lifted herself up and down onto him.

"*Gesù!*" he yelped, his hands fisting against her hips.

"That's right," she growled, rising and lowering again. "You're all mine, now. All... mine."

Alessandro dropped his head back; she saw the tension in his neck while his hands opened on her hips and helped her to raise and lower, raise and lower, and he lifted his own hips and bucked and groaned and brought his mouth back to her breasts and bit her nipple lovingly. Megan burst apart, and Alessandro muffled his cry against her chest.

The car, its partition firmly closed, drove their panting, spent, connected bodies home.

◆

"*Cara*," Alessandro said the next morning after she'd told him everything she'd told her siblings. They were watching the sunrise through the windows of his master bedroom—their master bedroom. "Are you sure? You will really live here, with me?"

"Yes." She stroked his beard with the palm of her hand. She loved that beard. He might have to shave it for his next role or the one after that, but his growing it while they'd gotten to know each other made it feel like something he'd done just for her. "And not just for your sake. I've never been more myself than I have since I came here."

"I am so happy to hear that." He tipped his head so she was cradling it in her hand. "That is all I ever wanted for you."

"And I know that you're going to be on set, maybe for months at a time."

"That's right. Will you not be lonely?"

"I don't know," she said honestly. "But I already have so much to do, so many people to talk to, that I think I'll enjoy the time I'm alone."

"Not too much, I hope," he said, drawing her into his arms. "Because I will always come home to you."

"You'd better."

"I will almost enjoy going away so I can look forward to coming back."

Megan laughed and lay on top of him, touching him from chest to knees, even putting her bare feet over his.

The sun blazed out of the horizon, fading the ocean of pink and orange out of the sky. "No regrets?" Alessandro asked quietly.

She looked up at him and kissed his beautiful, waiting mouth. "*Nessuno. Assolutamente nessuno.*"

♦

Chapter 27

"And the Oscar goes to…

"Alessandro Rosselli, for *The Drummer*."

The packed auditorium leaped to their feet, some in joy, others, perhaps, in surprise, since great performance of the year or not, Alessandro was still comparatively new in the business. But that didn't matter one iota to Megan as she watched her lover's mouth drop open. He let out a yell that turned the audience's shouts into a laugh, then took Megan's face between his hands and kissed her fast before following the usher to the aisle.

They'd been put with other members of the cast and crew of the movie because the movie itself had also been nominated. The director leaped up and hugged Alessandro right there in the aisle.

Alessandro walked onto the stage to the swelling sounds of the music, while Megan clapped her hands raw for him. She'd never seen him so radiantly happy. His smile was infectious; she could see people in rows in front of her grinning indulgently as he hugged everyone on the stage before they could get him to the microphone.

He wore a dark-purple velvet tux that turned him almost vampiric. His beard was longer than at the Ravellos, and the cuff around his ear flashed in the lights. He was her devil again.

"Woohoo!" was the first thing he said. "Thank you! *Dio mio!*" Then he put a hand to his chest as though he couldn't remember how to breathe. "*Son' sopraffatto. Grazie tutti.*"

And then his voice got stronger. "So many to thank. Of course the team, the vision of everyone on *The Drummer*." He reeled off some names and everyone cheered. "And I have to thank those who never get their due. No one makes it to this stage without a family. And I have had a family for the last ten years who have raised me up, who encouraged me when I failed and celebrated with me when I succeeded. To all of you: Etta, Susie, Roman, Grace, Sophia, Jaelyn, Melanie, Mohammed, Cassidy, and Colson." They were in the audience, so the crowd cheered again, because everyone knew who he was talking about. "To Yasmin and Donna and Jacqui and—" He got several more names out before the music started.

He laughed again. "I love you all! Vi *amo, tutti! Ti amo*, Megan!" and he stepped back from the mike.

Everyone heard it, everyone turned to her, and Megan wondered if she was going to float to the ceiling. Even more so when she imagined the shriek that must have come from her siblings in their homes. She'd never been more ready to leap on a plane and take Alessandro to celebrate with them.

With only two awards left to announce, Megan didn't expect to see him again until after the ceremony, but a huge song and dance number and another commercial break meant that he was back by her side, beaming and panting, just in time to hear that *The Drummer* had won for best movie. And if she'd thought the joy was incandescent when he'd won, it was nothing to the eruption that shook the building now. She almost had to stand on her seat to avoid getting crushed in the wall of hugs and backslaps that took over her row. Eventually, they filed out into the aisle, leaving Megan and a few other plus-ones to smile at each other. Alessandro all but leaped onto the stage the way Mohammed had previously.

Megan took a mental snapshot, watching her beautiful, talented Italian bounce on his toes among a crowd at the top of their respective games. The director's speech was played out and no one cared; the host tried to give his goodbye speech and no one cared; the credits began to roll and no one cared.

At last Megan was able to leave the auditorium and go to the room where winners got their statues engraved with their names. Cassidy found her and made the crowds part so that she could join Alessandro waiting with his group.

He whooped when he saw her and squeezed her to him, burying his face in her hair, which she'd worn down tonight, giving a forest goddess vibe to her thickly embroidered, plunging neckline dress. "*Amore*," he said so only she could hear.

"I'm so, so proud of you," she said. "You've earned all of this. I love you."

"I love you," he said back. "I could not be so happy if you were not here with me."

She kissed him and gave him a beaming smile she didn't have to regulate for anyone. Not anymore.

◆

Acknowledgments

Thus we come to the end of the Fieldings' ride (if you want to know how Cat and Antonio met, though, let me know). It's bittersweet to say goodbye to my beloved first fiction family, but thankfully, like Alessandro, I have a huge family of supportive writers and readers who have helped me create and produce this series.

To my editors, Julie Sturgeon and Kimberly Dawn: thank you for making me sound so much smarter than I am. To my critique group crew on this book: Lena Pinto, Victoria Farhat, Noreen Lekhak, Shruti Khare, Renee Ann Miller, and Delores Stewart. You know how many versions of this are out there. Thank you for not screaming at me through the screen while I figured out the right one.

To Tina Rose, encouraging librarian and kickass friend, who patiently listened to me complain on our shifts together and gave me advice (and Cheez-Its) to get me through. Thank you for your patience and your constant support.

To my family, who have not said a thing about the house being a complete shambles while I got this done.

And to you, dear readers, who have written reviews and come to signing events and generally made me believe I had another book in me. And another one... and another one... Thank you all so much.

Kimberley

Book Excerpt

Want to know where it all began? Here are the first two chapters of BREATHE, Kane and Ellen's story.

♦

Chapter 1

Somewhere beyond the lights, someone probably had a camera pointed at him.

On a normal day, Kane wasn't bothered by this; on a normal day, he encouraged it. But not tonight. Not while he stood, alone, watching his second building this week collapse into a pile of charred beams and wet ash. The smell in his nostrils was that of the day his father had died: the smell of grief and fear and helplessness.

The site manager puffed over to him, a short, round man, perspiring despite the winds coming off Lake Michigan. "There's nothing else to see, Mr. Fielding. Let me get you some coffee."

Kane's jacket wasn't thick enough for this October night in Grand Rapids; he could feel the contrast between his freezing back and the heat still coming off the doused building. "You're right, Art," he said. But he didn't look at the man, and he didn't move.

"I am sorry, Mr. Fielding." The site manager shifted his feet. "Is it true that the Chicago fire was arson?"

"Yep." That news would have drawn the cameras here. The press would perk up at the word, look up his company. They'd find out about the explosion thirteen years ago that had killed his father. Swoop down to see what fresh hell Fielding Paper was going through. The presence of the camera-friendly president would help.

He'd been trained to analyze the way he looked when the photographers were around, because Kane, to quote his public relations director, was hot, and that was good for business. His messy dark-brown hair, hardly touched since he'd been woken four hours and a three-hour drive ago, was his trademark. His dark clothes were calculated decisions, worn to emphasize his height. He had deep-set, brooding dark eyes and a chiseled jaw, and all that crap that made his PR man rub his hands with glee—and Kane blush if he caught a description of himself in print.

But he was grateful. These tools had kept Fielding Paper in the news—and the gossip columns—for years. So sure, on the outside it was business as usual. But he hoped to God the camera didn't have a long enough lens to pick up the muscle clenching and unclenching in his jaw.

The site manager looked at him more closely. "At least no one got hurt," Art said encouragingly. "And most of the lumber is saved."

Kane worked to keep his face impassive. He could give a crap right now about the lumber. "Yeah," he said again, and then, because Art seemed to be looking for conversation, "Maybe the security cameras picked up something."

"Uh…" Art shifted again. Kane's own feet were cold, and Art had been out here for hours before him. "Everything shut down when the electric was cut."

"But the backup generator would have—"

"He killed that, too."

"*Shit!*" He spat the word so loudly Art jumped. So much for not looking as if this was getting to him. Kane wondered if he was far enough away from the firefighters to light a cigarette. Then he remembered the cameras and tapped his numb fingers against his thigh instead.

There was a surprisingly delicate *whump*, and another corner of the building collapsed.

"The forest is good, too," Art reminded him. Kane had had the trees to their left planted after his father died. They were still several years from maturity.

That had been one of his first acts as CEO. One of the crazy decisions of a twenty-two-year-old, numb with grief, fresh out of college, desperate to save his family's business. "Buy American," he'd touted to any news channel and TV show that would have him. "Buy Fielding Paper." He'd planted acres in the US and given land back to the villages in Central America. The goodwill had been priceless.

People *liked* him, goddammit! Why was someone setting fire to his mills?

The manager was hovering uncertainly, his breath visible in little puffs. The Fielding family history seemed just as visible.

But he had to get them all back on track. He couldn't let this get worse than it was. "Thanks, Art," he said, rolling his frozen shoulders and smiling down at the man. "I'll take that coffee. And hey." He made an effort to shrug off the fear. "Happy Halloween."

◆

Several hours later, behind the podium at the local town hall hastily commandeered for this small press conference, Kane was more in his element. His quick phone call with Leo Palmer, his PR director, had solidified the story they needed to tell. He was very good at giving the press what they wanted.

He stood with his hands on either side of the podium, looking into the cameras or catching the eye of each reporter there.

"Will you rebuild?" they asked.

"Of course," he reassured them. "We have a commitment to this area that spans decades."

"What do the workers do now?"

"We'll find them shifts at other plants if we can."

"What if you can't?"

He looked appropriately serious. "We take care of our own." Whatever that meant. "I'm just glad no one got hurt."

"Didn't you have security cameras? Can you get any leads?"

"I'll have to leave those questions for the fire chief and the police," he said, sweeping a hand behind him where the men in uniform were standing. "But I want to emphasize that the fire was not the fault of the employees. It's all too easy to set fire to a lumber mill if someone really wants to. We spend a lot of time and energy reducing fire risk, but it can't be eliminated altogether."

"Who do you think did it?"

Kane gave a magnificent, all-encompassing shrug. Fielding Paper were the good guys. He couldn't have any enemies. "Just someone with a fixation for setting fire to things, I guess."

He put one hand in his pocket and slouched to indicate that he was relaxed and confident in everyone's ability to fix this problem. "Our reputation means that people won't settle for less than Fielding Paper," he said, leaning more heavily on his Boston accent, as it was part of his image, part of the centuries-old story of the company. "I'm happy to say that we'll have no problem delivering on our orders." *Don't worry*, his body language said, *I got this*. Never mind that in his head a voice was hammering *what if, what if, what if... What if there's another one... What if I can't fix things this time... What if the next time someone dies?*

Someone with a sly edge to her voice said, "On a different subject, are you dating anyone we know?"

Kane grinned at her and said, "Why? Are you offering?" The crowd laughed. The reporter held his look and grinned back. To Kane, this showed that he'd succeeded; if they'd moved on to his social life, they had stopped worrying about the future of his company. If he could convince them, maybe he could convince himself.

Chapter 2

Ellen really didn't want to be here.

She sat on the hard black leather couch, her skirt pulled determinedly below her knees, and tried not to let the receptionist see that her toe was tapping the air with impatience. She had far too much to do today to spend it on a sales call.

The receptionist was almost exactly what Ellen would have expected of a company run by a man with a reputation like Kane Fielding's. She was beautifully dressed and coiffed, with perfect nails painted a professional pink and lipstick to match. The only surprising thing about her was that she was in her sixties, not a *barely out of college* girl like the ones Fielding was always seen with. This woman had greeted Ellen perfectly politely and asked if she could get her a drink before Ellen had even sat down. Ellen had said no, just as politely, and then glowered at her from the couch, disliking her even more because there was nothing to dislike.

Ellen had to be here, because whatever her opinion of its owner, Fielding Paper was one of the largest companies in Boston, and the Rosette hotel wanted to have exclusive rights to Fielding conferences. So when her friend Lucía Jimenez, the conferences' manager at Fielding, had called to suggest she come in "for a couple of minutes" to leave a brochure, Ellen couldn't say no. But she'd been here for fifteen minutes already; the morning was ticking by, and she had a gala for fifteen hundred people to organize that would influence the rest of her career.

After another five minutes, the receptionist—Gloria, according to her nameplate—apologized to Ellen for the wait. Ellen wondered what would happen if she threw her shoe at the woman.

"That's quite all right," she said instead.

"I just love your accent," said Gloria. "You're English?"

"Yes." The accent was an advantage in her work, one she hadn't had back in London. "But I've been here for about four years now."

"Well, you still sound pure English to me."

Too bloody right. Ellen wasn't about to mess with a good sales tool. She gave Gloria a small smile and tried not to sigh with impatience.

The heavy glass entrance doors opened, and the atmosphere seemed to sharpen. A tall, broad-shouldered man with dark hair that brushed his shirt collar backed into the room, carrying a black overnight bag. He wore a rumpled dark suit and had a wool coat in his other hand. He turned to face the receptionist, his back still to Ellen. Gloria came around her desk to meet him.

"Hi, Gloria," the man said, dropping his coat on the floor and putting out his arm.

"Kane, you poor thing!" the receptionist replied, tucking

herself under the arm for a hug. "You look pooped. When did you get back? You should have gone straight home!"

For a second it looked as though she was holding him up. His shoulders were hunched, and he dropped the bag without looking to see where it fell.

"Just thought I'd check in," he said.

"You smell like a forest," Gloria said, wrinkling her nose.

His laugh was cracked and harsh. "Yeah, after a wildfire." He ran his hand through his hair. "Guess I need a shower. I slept hard in Chicago last night. Had to hustle to make my flight this morning."

"So go *home*," Gloria insisted. She untucked herself and shook the arm that had hugged her. "You drove from Chicago to Grand Rapids and back again in one day? No wonder you overslept."

Ellen couldn't stop staring. This woman was acting like his governess, not his employee. What kind of company was this? And was this really the great, all-powerful, crooks-a-finger-and-gets-any-woman-he-wants Kane Fielding? He looked almost normal, standing there, silently asking for a little sympathy before getting back to real life. He still had his back to Ellen, so she couldn't see the famous smile or the dark deep-set eyes; she only saw the hunched shoulders and heard the exhaustion in his voice.

"I will, I will," he was promising. "I just want to give Leo a debriefing." He hugged Gloria again quickly, let her go, and began to walk to the inner doors.

Ellen watched him turn to face her and freeze. For a second, the dark eyes still held worry and strain. But then that hundred-kilowatt smile spread over his face. "I'm sorry," he said. "I would never have turned my back on you if I'd known you were there. Kane Fielding." He held out his hand.

Heck. She felt the pink begin to creep into her cheeks. Not that she followed the tabloids or anything—okay, she did, but only when she was getting pedicures, so it didn't count—but he was even finer in real life. Ellen had automatically stood when he came over, and even though she was taller than many men she knew, she had to look up to meet his dark-brown eyes. His hair looked just messy enough to be messed up some more. His broad shoulders fit the line of his suit exactly. But what was really undoing her was the way he'd talked to Gloria—the warmth, the fatigue in his voice, and the tension that still lingered around his eyes. Wasn't he invincible? And didn't he treat women like Kleenex? Use once and discard?

She had to be imagining it. He represented everything she hated about men. Her surreptitious perusal of the tabloids proved it. "Ellen Hunter, from the Rosette," she said stiffly and shook his hand.

A ping went up her arm. Her breath caught in her throat. *What was that?* If she didn't know better, she would have said it was arousal. But no, it was probably fear. That was a feeling she knew well. She dropped his hand and gripped her portfolio case more tightly. She'd gotten used to the occasional wash of fear threatening to overtake her whenever a man stood too close or made his interest clear. She was good at swallowing it, ignoring it, telling herself she'd never be afraid again. And she wasn't, until the next time.

"The hotel?" he said. "One of the best in town. Impressive." He was standing a perfectly respectable distance away, and his smile, while wide, was professional. He didn't look anywhere but at her face. But a wicked glint in his eyes showed he wasn't just talking about the hotel.

This was the kind of attention she hated. She knew she was attractive in a standard kind of way—thin, blond, blue-eyed, etcetera—but she couldn't stand it when men noticed her. She tended to dress conservatively for that reason, keeping her hair pulled back, wearing boxy jackets and skirts that her friend

Penny had called "Sister Mary Margaret length." She still got more attention than she wanted, but she couldn't do much about it, other than use the ice-queen role she easily slipped into these days.

"We think so," she answered firmly. "That's what I'm here to talk to your conferences' manager about, anyway."

As if summoned by her title, Lucía appeared, pushing through the inner glass doors in a hurry, her thick dark curls spilling down her back. "I'm so sorry," she was saying before she'd even focused on Ellen. "This conference call–" Then she noticed Fielding. "Kane!" she exclaimed, and Ellen watched, fascinated, as Lucía's harassed frown turned to a sweet smile. "We didn't think you'd come in today."

"Just checking in," he said again.

"Hmm." Lucía unabashedly looked him over. "You must be tired," she said.

"I'm fine," he said. But Lucía didn't look like she believed it any more than Gloria had. What was *wrong* with these women?

Lucía apparently decided to drop it. She moved to hug Ellen. "I *am* sorry to keep you waiting, hon. I know you're busy right now."

"That's all right," Ellen said. "Shall we?" She nodded toward the doors.

She wished Fielding would go away. Why didn't he give his debriefing, or whatever it was? But he just stood there, smiling at the two of them.

"Why don't you use my office?" he said. "You can spread out on the conference table."

Okay, he *had* to know what that had sounded like. Bloody man, couldn't even have a simple conversation without that gleam in his eye. Gorgeous deep-set eyes, x-raying her from under straight brows, with that lock of hair falling over them. Not that she was looking.

Maybe she *had* been reading too many tabloids. He wasn't even that famous, for God's sake. Just another spoiled brat who'd had everything handed to him and who'd happened to catch the eye of an actress a few years ago. He'd been trading on that publicity ever since.

Lucía was already saying, "That's great, thanks, Kane. Better than that hole you call a conference room, anyway," and Fielding was holding out an arm to usher Ellen through the doors, saying to Lucía, "Hey, does or does not your office have a window? Well, then you can't complain when the conference room doesn't," and Ellen had no choice but to follow Lucía through.

The office spaces looked around a hundred years old. The walls were lined with dark wood paneling. The desks were old-fashioned wooden ones. The only signs of the twenty-first century were the large touchscreens on the computers.

The three or four secretaries outside the other offices greeted Fielding with surprise, and more pleasure than Ellen thought appropriate. She couldn't see his face as he replied, but she could just bet he was flashing that come-hither smile at them. His own secretary, a pretty blonde with shoulder-length hair that had a wave in it Ellen envied, was the only one who didn't adjust something as he approached. In fact, she looked quite stern.

"Hi, Anna," he said warmly, and there he was again, being all *nice.*

"What are you doing—?" But then she saw that Lucía and Ellen were with him.

"This is Ms. Hunter," he explained. "She's going to use my office to present..." He frowned and turned to her. "Which hotel was it again?"

"Boy, do you need coffee," said Lucía.

"Boy, do I. Lots and lots of coffee." For a second Ellen saw the exhaustion hit him again. He scrubbed one hand through his hair, and there were gray shadows around his eyes.

Anna tutted but obviously didn't want to say anything else in front of an outsider. "Go on in. I'll get the coffee," she said.

"Thanks," Fielding said and put out his hand to guide Ellen into his office.

She had to pass quite close to him when she got to the door. *Dammit, dammit, dammit.* His height and the dark suit or the smell of him or something... Her legs began to feel odd. This was not good. Unanticipated wobbles about the knees were not permitted; they were, in fact, beginning to send licks of fear into her stomach. *No. I am not going to do this again, feel like this again.*

All it took was one memory of Edward, so contained and collected right up until he wasn't, to bring her back to herself. The barriers once again clanging into place, her cheeks perfectly cool, she was able to move to the conference table at one end of Fielding's corner office and take her book out of her briefcase.

The office looked out over the mix of old and new buildings that made up downtown Boston and was just as old-fashioned as the rest of the building—dark mahogany and leather, with heavy furniture that had no idea mid-century modern was back. Had this all belonged to Fielding's grandfather? *Great*-grandfather?

Fielding pulled out the chair at the head of the table for her and sat on one side, with his back to the window. Lucía sat opposite him. Ellen turned the artist-size binder to face them and began. "Well, as Mr. Fielding said—"

"Kane," he said.

What a ridiculous name. He sounds like a soap opera character. She gave him a tight smile and continued. "The Rosette *is* the best hotel in Boston. We've had our five stars for more than thirty years and not one, but two of our restaurants are Michelin-rated. You won't find a more prestigious location for your conferences in the entire state. I'd go as far as to say the entire East Coast."

She showed them the range of meeting rooms, the added facilities that the Rosette gave their clients, the newspaper articles that showed the cachet that came with the name.

"I don't know," Fielding said slowly, but his eyes lit up. "You guys might be too fancy for us millworkers."

She looked at his custom suit, at the expensive furniture they were sitting on. She thought of the news and videos she'd researched from the last few years, where Fielding's face appeared, relentlessly perfect—apart from the hair, and even that looked premeditated—reminding everyone of the quality that his company could produce because it was all American-made. His family probably hadn't worked in a mill in all the ten generations it had owned this company.

"Mr. Fielding, I don't have to tell you about the value of image." She hoped her intrinsic dislike of his public persona didn't trickle into her voice. "Fielding stationery is known for its quality. You work very hard to keep it that way. We can help with that."

"Yeah," he said, leaning back in his chair and tapping one finger on the table, "you don't have to tell me about image."

What did that mean? He sounded almost irritated, as if he didn't like the constant attention.

No way. No one was that good an actor. She went on. "Your clients will appreciate being put up in the Rosette when they come to town, and we can host anything from an intimate meeting for five to..." She turned to the last page, where a large room with high ceilings and spectacular chandeliers was decorated for a banquet. "A ball fit for a queen."

Fielding stopped tapping the table. His gaze centered on her.

"The Queen's Ball? That's you? I mean..." He waved a hand, seeming to apologize silently for his slowness. "I know, it's the Rosette. But..." He looked at her again as if he'd only just noticed her. "You run it."

The Queen's Ball was the corporate event of the fall season. The Rosette partnered with a local foundation, charged huge prices per plate, and raised thousands for charity. Thousands more were spent on the food and decorations. Every penny was Ellen's responsibility.

Fielding had attended all four years that she had run the ball. Each time he'd had a different hot chick on his arm.

Not that Ellen had paid attention.

"Haven't you seen her there?" Lucía asked him.

"I—" He still held Ellen with those dark eyes. Her barriers shuddered. "I'm surprised I don't remember you," he said.

She wasn't. She'd developed such a dislike of him that she'd made a point of avoiding him as much as possible at the event. The only time he might have seen her was when she welcomed the chairman of the hotel and the charity at the beginning of the night, and she was on a stage dozens of feet away.

"Well," she said, "there are fifteen hundred other people there."

"Still," he said, "I should have remembered you."

Her inner ice castle shook again, and she wasn't sure if it was from fear or... something else. That one speech was the worst part of her whole year. She had to dress to be noticed that night, to show the hotel in its best light, to put on her best Queen's accent, to let man after man look at her, to shake hands and allow those hands to move occasionally to her elbow or her back...

Anna appeared with the coffee tray. Fielding stood up, and even though the corner of the table was between him and Ellen, he suddenly seemed to take up so much space that she instinctively cringed. She tried to recover, to relax, but he had already noticed.

The scene froze. Fielding's smile had finally gone; he was frowning at her. Ellen was trying to look back at him with her usual expression of cold disdain, while holding the arms of her chair in a death grip. Anna and Lucía looked between the two of them, evidently sensing that something had happened.

Fielding moved first, giving a small shake of his head, and took the tray. "Thanks, Anna," he said, again with that more-than-boss-to-secretary burr in his voice. Anna left, closing the door behind her. Ellen wanted to tell her to leave it open, but that would mean admitting she was afraid, which she refused to do. This was just a business meeting, and she was safe. *Safe*, she reminded herself. She was suddenly so grateful for Lucía's presence she gave her a smile, which Lucía returned with a slightly confused one of her own.

Fielding poured coffee for her and Lucía, then made himself a cup which he drank, black, almost in one gulp. He did the same with the second. He had to be burning the crap out of his throat.

Ellen put milk and sugar into her own coffee and drank it, feeling that she was missing something. Why was he so tired? Why was everyone so concerned about him?

With his third cup in hand, Fielding went over to his desk and leaned against it. She couldn't help noticing how long his legs were and how his thighs strained against the fabric of his trousers.

Now she burned her mouth on her own coffee.

"Let's get to the numbers," Lucía said, snapping Ellen out of her catalog of Fielding's body. Ellen pulled out another piece of paper and went over the costs. He stayed by his desk, listening but not coming any closer.

"That's a lot of money to commit to one place," Lucía said when she'd finished.

"To commit to peace of mind? You know we can handle any event you throw at us."

"I know *you* can handle it, but how long before you get transferred out of the country, and poor old Fielding Paper disappears into your rearview mirror?"

This was true. Lucía knew that Ellen's visa was up in four months. To continue on the career path she'd been working on for ten years, she needed to move to other Rosette hotels, other continents.

"You're leaving?" Fielding said. He'd put down his coffee and one hand was playing with a cigarette lighter, while the other tapped out a beat on his thigh. *He's late for his next cigarette.* She was pleased to find that he had at least one fault. But then why had he smelled so damn good when she got close to him?

Focus, Ellen! Her career was all she had to work toward these days, and to move up the ladder, she had to go. The fact that the idea of leaving Boston dropped a lead weight into her stomach whenever she thought of it was irrelevant. "Yes. But our department, and my replacement, will make the transition seamless," she added, mentally crossing her fingers. She didn't know if her boss had begun looking for her replacement yet.

"I'm taking that into account," Lucía said in a warning tone. She stood up. "Anything else?"

Ellen shook her head. "I'll leave you this price list and some brochures you can send around if you'd like," she said and began gathering her papers. Fielding hadn't moved. He had his back to the windows and looked even more hooded and tired in the shadows cast by the weak fall sun.

When she couldn't think of an excuse not to, she went up to him. "Thank you for the opportunity," she said, holding her hand out, bracing herself.

He stood up, putting his weight back on his feet, and shook her hand. This time she didn't pull away—didn't feel she could, with Lucía watching—and the jolt that went up her arm at his proximity, at the way his hair brushed against his shirt collar, sent the heat rushing to her cheeks. He wasn't smiling, for once, but watching her closely.

"It was... interesting to meet you, Ms. Hunter," he said.

"Likewise," she said, trying to keep her voice firm.

She was aware of exactly when his fingers wrapped around hers, and when, after a much longer pause than the first time, they pulled away.

Other Books by Kimberley Ash

The Fieldings:
Breathe (Kane and Ellen)
Hold (Thea and Liam)
Stand (Sam and Ty)
The Van Allen Brothers:
Forgive Me
Forget Me
Free Me
Available now from Tule Publishing.

Connect with Kimberley!

Join my Facebook Group, Read Your Ash Off, sign up for my newsletter, and follow me to get the latest info on my new releases and events. I look forward to meeting you!

Website: www.kimberleyash.com

Bookbub: @KimberleyAsh

Instagram: @KAshAuthor

Pinterest (for pictures of Alessandro and Megan's fabulous clothes!): @KAshAuthor

Goodreads: Kimberley Ash

TikTok: @kimberleyashauthor

Facebook Page: Kimberley Ash Books

Twitter (ok fine, X): @KAshAuthor

About the Author

As a teen, Kimberley Ash would sit in her boarding school dormitory and read Silhouette Romances with her friends. They would have passionate arguments about the kind of American hero they really wanted to see in the books, so to settle things, Kimberley wrote one. While she took great pleasure in deconstructing alpha males and exposing their chiseled but vulnerable underbellies, life and inner demons made her put away her dreams for twenty-five years. She was forty before she realized that what she wanted to be when she grew up was what she'd always wanted to be: a romance writer. So she joined New Jersey Romance Writers, took all the classes she could find, and has never looked back. Her first novel, *Breathe*, was published in 2018. She has since published the Van Allen Brothers series with Tule Publishing (2019) and the Fieldings series (2022-23), which includes sequels to *Breathe*.

Meanwhile, to her great surprise, Kimberley was swept off her feet by her own all-American hero. Now making her home in rural New Jersey (yes, there is a rural New Jersey) with him, two hybrid children and two big furry dogs, she can be found staring into a computer screen, wrestling with plotlines and ignoring the giant dustbunnies.

Kimberley holds a bachelor's degree in French from Queen Mary College (spectacularly useful at PTA meetings) and a master's in English Literature from Drew University (NJ).

Kimberley writes about real life and therefore celebrates and supports diversity in all its forms. You can find her obsessing about tea on Facebook, Instagram, and Twitter.